PASSION FLOWERS

CAROLINE D'ARCY

First published in 1996 by
Marino Books
An imprint of Mercier Press
16 Hume Street Dublin 2

Trade enquiries to Mercier Press
PO Box 5, 5 French Church Street,
Cork

© Caroline D'Arcy 1996

ISBN 1 86023 039 3

10 9 8 7 6 5 4 3 2 1

A CIP record for this title is available
from the British Library

Cover illustration by Eorna Walton
Set by Richard Parfrey
Printed in Ireland by ColourBooks,
Baldoyle Industrial Estate, Dublin 13

For Ben, David, Elizabeth and Evan

ONE

Nora Davis sat in her dressing-room on the set of *Docklands.* She had already had the full treatment in make-up but she took a lipstick brush from her bag and touched up her perfectly shaped lips. Her jet-black hair cascaded over her shoulders in pre-Raphaelite abandon and she brushed back one stray lock that had fallen across her forehead. She looked in the mirror and stared into the startling green depths of her eyes. Then she smiled. She was pleased with what she saw and she relished her part as Debbie, the mistress of Jack Hanley, a womanising Cockney whom viewers of *Docklands* loved to hate.

'Two minutes, Nora.' Sarah, one of the production assistants, poked her head round the door. 'You look like something the cat dragged in!'

Sarah withdrew her head quickly, as Nora fired a cushion at her. It was an ongoing joke between them. Sarah had become a close friend of Nora's since she had got the part on *Docklands* two years ago, and they teased each other mercilessly. Meeting her had helped Nora forget the loneliness she felt on arriving in London fresh from acting school. She had been unable to find work in Dublin and everyone had told her that London was the place to get started. She remembered those early days with a little shudder. The cold bare bed-sits, the failed auditions, the walk-on parts that hardly paid the rent and the aching sense of homesickness. Above all, she had missed her two older sisters, Frances and Aisling. She still missed them of course, but since getting the part in the hugely successful soap, *Docklands*, she had finally settled down in London and had begun to enjoy herself. Tomorrow she would be flying home for her father's wedding to Madge Tierney and would be reunited, for a few hours at least, with Frances and Aisling before flying back to London the next day for the reading of the following week's scripts. Glancing at the gold-leafed wedding invitation on her dressing-table, she reflected ruefully that it was a pity that the series' hectic schedule would not allow her more than a day in the company of her sisters.

She left the dressing-room and went out on to the set. The crew whistled appreciatively as she strode across the street that had been specially built in the studio grounds with housefronts that were as familiar to the viewers of *Docklands* as their own homes. She held her script in her hand, just in case she fluffed, but although she was only twenty-two Nora was already a true pro and rarely forgot her lines. Today the plot was exciting: she would be confronted by Jack's wife, who would at the end of the episode attempt to strangle her with a length of curtain cord.

'Should keep the audiences glued to their sets!' said Veronica Harris, who played the part of April, Jack's long-suffering wife.

'It's a great cliffhanger,' agreed Nora. 'I wonder how she'll get out of it?'

'No doubt Jack will come storming in to the rescue,' said Veronica. 'And even if he doesn't, you'll be able to fight me off. I mean look at the size of me!'

Veronica was indeed a pint-sized actress who would lose in any physical struggle with someone of Nora's physique.

'Yeah, I'll probably have to fend for myself. After all, your Jack spends so much time in the boozer, he's bound to be too drunk to rescue me!'

'Did I hear someone take my name in vain?' They were joined by Ralph Peterson, the swarthily attractive actor who played Jack.

'We're just saying that you'll probably be too pissed to rescue me at the end of the episode,' said Nora.

Ralph ruffled her hair, affectionately.

'And sure can't a fine strapping agricultural lump of a girl like you look after herself?' he joked, with a fair attempt at an Irish accent.

'Please – I'm not agricultural.' Nora put on her best uppercrust accent. 'I come from Dublin 4!'

Laughing, they went into the huge studio where the interior sets of *Docklands* were ready. While they waited for their call, Ralph regaled them with accounts of the many times he had barely escaped from the jaws of death within the series. The writers of *Docklands* had a penchant for cliff-hangers and the most dramatic of these had found him perched in the cab of a lorry that was about to plunge into the freezing waters of the Thames.

'I didn't think I'd get out of that one,' he said, 'because Jack can't swim! It was lucky there just happened to be a couple of handy frogmen around at the time!'

'Quiet, please!' the floor manager called, as Dave Stewart, the series producer, strode on to the set. He greeted Ralph and Veronica but ignored Nora who, only the the previous night, had turned down yet another of his sexual advances. Nora was far from being prudish and since coming to London had had several lovers. But Dave made her flesh crawl with his arrogant assurance that he could have any woman he pleased. He had been trying, unsuccessfully, to bed her since her arrival on the series. Last night he had turned up at her flat at midnight. She had been curled up on a couch with a script when the doorbell rang and she was horrified to hear Dave's voice on the intercom.

'I ran out of petrol. Just let me in and I'll phone a cab.'

'No doubt it was sheer coincidence that it happened to run out in Ealing?' she asked sarcastically, as she looked up a taxi number in her phone book. She was horribly conscious that he was staring at the outline of her body, visible through her thin cotton pyjamas.

'Let me stay the night, Nora,' he pleaded, attempting to take her into his arms.

'If you try anything on, I'll report you to the Director-General.'

The threat had worked before, because Dave was basically a coward, but last night he had been drinking and was coldly vitriolic.

'You think you're something special, don't you?' His blue eyes narrowed. 'Well, let me tell you – you're just a two-bit actress. You'll be sorry for this, you little pricktease!'

She was relieved when he stormed out of the flat, refusing to wait for the cab she had phoned. Seeing him now, she thought what a creep he was. She knew that she wasn't the only actress he had attempted to seduce. Many had given in to him, fearful of losing a part if they didn't. She had thought the casting couch was a thing of the past, but since coming to London had learnt that it was very much alive. The sad thing was that Dave had no respect for those women who gave in to him. More often than not, they never got the parts he promised. As she watched him discussing the scene they were about to play with the director, she was filled with loathing.

'We're doing scene nineteen first,' the floor manager announced.

The first scene on the typed schedule sheet was a much earlier one in which Debbie and Jack discussed the fact that his wife had discovered their affair.

'Why have you changed the running order?' Nora asked Pete Swan, who was directing the episode.

'Dave says we're to shoot the last scene first.' Pete didn't look up from the camera script he was studying and she felt guilty for interrupting him. 'Probably because it's the most difficult.'

Satisfied with the explanation, Nora and

Veronica took up their places on the set of Debbie's living-room. As the cameras rolled, the butterflies that invariably fluttered in Nora's stomach before each take settled down and she relaxed into the performance. Veronica fluffed a few lines and they had to do several takes, but eventually they got it right.

'That's a wrap!' declared Pete, and the scene ended with Nora lying across the table as Veronica pulled the curtain cord tighter and tighter around her neck.

'Get out of that one!' joked Ralph, as she came off the set.

'I'll have to – I'm scheduled to appear next week!' she replied, heading to the canteen for a cup of coffee before her next scene. The coffee always tasted vaguely of polystyrene from the cups in which it was served, but (as her father would have said) it was warm and wet. Her thoughts drifted with pleasurable anticipation to the prospect of seeing Frances and Aisling tomorrow. Her reverie was interrupted by an Irish accent.

'Can I borrow the milk?'

She looked up and saw a tall man with sleek brown hair. He was smiling at her, and she instantly liked his open expression and his laughing eyes.

'You're Irish,' she said, wishing she could think of a more original line.

'Tim Mulcahy.' He held out his hand and she shook it

'Nora Davis. I work on *Docklands*.'

'Yes, I know. I've seen you.'

She was delighted by the look of frank admiration in his hazel eyes.

'I'm a director. I'm just in England to . . . '

But she never heard what he was here for because suddenly they were joined by Sarah.

'Sorry to interrupt,' she said, glancing briefly at Tim, 'but I'm afraid I've got bad news.'

'I'll just take this, if I may?' Tim lifted the milk-jug from the table and was gone.

It wasn't like Sarah to panic and from her strained expression, Nora immediately knew that something was badly wrong. Sarah sat down opposite her.

'What is it?' asked Nora, in alarm. Sarah's face had paled and as she lit a cigarette, her hand was shaking.

'They've written you out. They're going to kill you off. Pete just told me.'

She recalled Dave's threat of the night before and suddenly everything fell into place. The bastard was taking his revenge!

'You were meant to survive the murder attempt,' Sarah said but Nora was hardly listening, as the awful reality sank in. 'As you know, you're scheduled to appear in next week's episodes but Dave has told the writers to alter them.'

'I can't believe he's doing this!' She crushed the empty polystyrene cup. 'After two years on the series!'

'He wanted to get the last scene shot first, before you got wind of it.'

'Pete said it was because it was difficult!' She

gave a bitter laugh. 'Mind you, he didn't actually look me in the eye. Now I can see why!' She had a sudden thought. 'What about the earlier scene? The one where Jack tells me that April has found out about the affair?'

'They're dropping that. It's not essential to the plot.'

'Nor am I!' said Nora, bitterly.

'Oh, Nora – I'm so sorry.' Sarah put her arm around her, and Nora burst into tears. There was no need to explain to Sarah why it had happened. She was well aware of Dave's attempts to seduce her and of his vindictive personality.

'What will you do?' Sarah asked, when Nora had calmed down a little.

'I don't know. Try my luck in Ireland, maybe. I'm going back tomorrow, anyway.'

She hated the thought of having to tell everyone that she had been dropped from the series. Being chosen to play in *Docklands*, which was hugely popular in Ireland as well as in Britain, had been a feather in her cap and her first part of any significance since finishing in acting school. Now she was back to square one – resting with no immediate prospect of employment. She recalled her father warning her that acting was a notoriously insecure career, but from her childhood it was what she had wanted to do. It was still the only career she was interested in, despite this setback.

She stood up, suddenly certain of what she would do.

'Where are you going?'

'Back to Ireland,' she said, 'but first, I have to

say my goodbyes to the cast.'

She had forgotten all about Tim, but he saw her as she left the canteen and, noting her tearstained face, wondered what had happened to make her cry. He had been smitten by her ever since he had first seen her on *Docklands* and although he wondered whether her acting range extended to anything more demanding than was called for by a soap, he thought her absolutely gorgeous. And she was even more beautiful in the flesh than she was on screen. Whereas her *Docklands* accent was pure Northside 'Dub', in reality she spoke with the softer lilt of Dublin's south suburbs, which, as a Limerick man himself, he found most attractive. He had come to London to audition a television actress for his latest theatrical production. It was a shame that he would be here for only a few hours and would have no chance of chatting to Nora again.

Followed closely by Sarah, Nora marched back to the set, her head held high. She was aware that her eyes were swollen from crying and that her mascara had run but she didn't care. She was in a temper now, and as Sarah knew only too well, when Nora lost her temper she did so in a dramatic way. She stormed on to the Crown and Anchor set, where several of the cast where preparing to do a take. They watched in astonishment as she went in behind the bar and poured a glass of beer from one of the kegs. Unlike the spirits, which were merely coloured water, the beer used on set was the genuine article, since substitutes looked fake.

'You may not know it,' she announced, 'but I'm leaving the series and I'd like you all to have a drink on the house!'

There was a general hubbub as the actors took this in.

'You can't do that!' warned Dave, as she poured glass after glass of beer. Several of the actors had approached the bar now, delighted at this sudden interruption to their hectic schedule.

'Can't I?' said Nora, pouring yet another glass, her green eyes flashing dangerously. 'If you can write me out because I won't sleep with you, I don't see why I can't say goodbye to my friends.'

'He's written you out!' Veronica was incredulous. 'You can't do this, Dave!'

She grabbed him by the arm but Dave shook her off impatiently.

'I'm warning you, Nora,' he said. 'Stop this at once.'

'Why? Are you going to send me the bill?'

Ralph was standing beside Dave now, and was attempting to reason with him.

'You can't write her out, mate. The audience loves her character and you'll be losing one of our best storylines.'

'Don't you tell me what I can or can't do,' Dave warned, 'or you'll be the next to go.'

Ralph gave him a dirty look but said nothing more. Nora was aware that he had a wife and three children to support, so she could understand his hesitancy. She noted with glee that several of the actors were drinking the beer and Dave was growing more and more furious.

'Clear the set at once!' he shouted but nobody paid any attention. Some of the actors approached Nora to offer her their sympathies. The camera crew and sound men were also queuing up to say goodbye. With the beer and the condolences, it was like an Irish wake, she thought.

Cold with rage, Dave leant across the bar and grabbed Nora's hand as she was pulling a pint.

'I said, "Stop it!"'

With her free hand, Nora took one of the glasses she had already filled and threw it over Dave's face. The crew and cast looked on in startled silence. They admired Nora's pluck but wondered whether she had gone too far. Dave pulled a handkerchief from his pocket and wiped the foamy beer from his face. Without another word, he walked off the set.

'He'll bring in security,' Ralph warned. 'If I were you, love, I'd scarper.'

Nora could see the wisdom of this advice. She had no desire to be escorted off the set by the station's burly security officers. She raised her glass, and addressed the cast.

'Till we meet again!'

'Till we meet again!' they replied in unison, full of admiration for this tempestuous Irishwoman. With the sound of their voices still ringing in her ears, Nora left the set with a smile and a wave.

Back in her flat, her exuberance faded as she thought about the future. Her good friend Fintan Doyle, an actor like herself, had told her that work was hard to come by in Dublin. The recession had bit hard into the theatrical profession and the number of actors far outweighed the available parts. On the plus side, she had two years' television experience under her belt now and might just manage to get a part in an Irish soap. Moreover, her sister Aisling worked as a journalist for the commercial station Channel 3 and would probably have some useful contacts. Her first thought was to call Frances and Aisling and tell them what had happened but she decided to wait until she got home. It would be better to tell them face to face.

That night, Sarah called round for supper. They ate a delicious Marks and Spencer curry washed down by a chilled Chardonnay as Sarah filled her in on what had happened after her dramatic departure. Dave had, indeed, brought security men on to the set and had been nonplussed to find that Nora had gone.

'He was all set for a battle,' she told Nora, 'but by the time he got back, the cameras were rolling and he couldn't say a word!'

'I won't ever work in this town again!' Nora laughed. 'Ah, well!'

At about midnight, it occurred to Nora that she ought to start packing and she and Sarah spent a hectic hour stuffing her possessions into boxes and plastic bags. They formed a large pile in the centre of the living-room. How had she managed to accumulate so many things in such a small flat?

'I won't be able to take all this on the plane. Do you think you could send the rest on?'

'Why not?' laughed Sarah. 'I've been picking up

after you on set for the past two years. No reason to stop now!'

'I'll miss you!' Nora hugged Sarah tightly and felt tears welling in her eyes. Sarah had been a good friend to her and despite her sometimes feckless nature, Nora valued friendship.

'Me too,' said Sarah. 'In fact, I'm going to go right now, before I burst into tears.'

When Sarah had gone, Nora sat for a while in the living-room, staring at the empty shelves and cupboards. The flat no longer seemed like hers now. It was just as cold and anonymous as it had been when she first moved in. It brought home to her the fact that one significant part of her life had ended. She was sad to bid it farewell but she couldn't help feeling a little thrill of excitement at the thought of what the future would bring.

TWO

'Here she comes,' Frances nudged Aisling as Nora, laden down with plastic bags and boxes, walked through the glass doors of the customs hall at Dublin airport.

'What does she look like?' Aisling laughed. 'A very elegant refugee?'

Nora rushed up to her sisters and, dropping her paraphernalia, tried to hug them both at the same time.

'Terrific! I didn't think for a minute you'd be here, I thought you'd be holding Dad's hand. Is the wedding cancelled?' she asked hopefully.

'Nora, you're incorrigible!' Frances laughed. 'Dad is fine, cool as a cucumber, drinking cups of tea and trying to decide whether to wear grey or black socks.' She stood back and looked at Nora. 'You look great, almost as beautiful as on telly. If I were April, I'd finish you off for good!'

'Are you psychic?'

Before Frances could answer, Aisling began organising the trio. 'Let's get moving.'

She picked up some of the bags and stuffed the rest of them in the her sisters' arms. 'Did the customs men steal your suitcase, Nora? No, don't tell me, we haven't time. You can give us all the news in the car.'

'The traffic's as bad as ever, I see.' Nora settled down in the back seat as Aisling's soft-topped Golf edged its way on to the motorway. 'I think I'll resurrect my old bike. Best way of getting around.'

Frances laughed. 'Not much point in that. Aren't you going back tomorrow?'

Nora took a deep breath. 'I'm home for good, girls. I've lost my job in *Docklands*.' She blurted out the whole story. Her voice began to break; she was more upset than she had realised.

'Don't worry, love.' Frances turned around and took her hand. 'You're better off out of that place.' She tried not to show that she was seething with rage that anyone would take advantage of Nora, whom she still saw as the baby of the family.

'The rest of the cast were great. I'm delighted I gave them drinks on the house. And,' she began to giggle, 'I'm even more delighted I threw a pint at that pig, Dave!'

'You'll get some kind of work here, Nora,' Aisling reassured her, 'even if you don't get what you want immediately. In any case, it will be great to have you home. It would have been lousy if you had to rush off in the morning and miss the bitching about Madge's wedding dress!'

Their father's bride-to-be had rather flamboyant taste in clothes and had hinted to Frances and Aisling that her wedding regalia would be memorable. She had worked for years in a small boutique specialising in wedding dresses and had been constantly advising others on what to wear on the big day. Now, at forty-one, she was getting married for the first time and was determined to have all the trimmings, including bridesmaids and a flower girl.

'We shouldn't be so mean,' Frances protested. 'She's entitled to wear whatever she likes today.'

The next couple of hours went in a whirlwind of activity. Nora barely had time to hug her father, who, when she arrived at the family home in Donnybrook, was sipping a large Jameson with his best man, Pat Fagan, a partner in his national chain of turf accountants.

'That'll sort him out.' Pat winked at the girls. 'He might have time for another before he has to put the monkey suit on.'

'Ah now, Pat,' Mr Davis protested, 'Let's not lose the run of ourselves.'

By a quarter to three, the sisters were ready to go to the church. Nora was the most striking of the three. In a flimsy lime-green silk trousers and top, she looked dressed for a summer beach party in California rather than an Irish wedding in March. A keyhole cut out at the back revealed her creamy smooth back.

'You'll freeze to death,' said Frances looking at her in admiration, 'but you look fantastic.'

Frances could never have worn such an exotic outfit. Although, like Nora, she was tall, she was not slender and at times she looked a little older than her twenty-eight years. But she had the fine classical bone structure that big women some-times have and her face stopped just short of being beautiful. Her hair, a soft brown, was cut into a pageboy and she was dressed in an attractive apricot silk dress by Paul Costello.

'Ready to go?' Aisling, elegant in an impeccably tailored blue suit, her smooth blonde hair pulled back into a French pleat, impatiently jangled her car keys. 'Dad left ages ago.'

The church was filling up when they arrived and the organist was playing softly in the background. They walked up the aisle, admiring glances following them, and sat in the seat which had been reserved for them.

Frances stole a glance at her father, who was sitting in front of them and fidgeting with his top hat. Perhaps he should have had the second Jameson. She could tell he was nervous. After fourteen years of widowhood and with his sixtieth birthday on the horizon, it had been a brave – or foolish – decision to take a chance on happiness with Madge. Thinking about her future stepmother (how ridiculous 'stepmother' sounded!), Frances felt a familiar apprehension gather in the pit of her stomach. She straightened her back. No matter what she felt about the woman, she was her father's choice and that was that. She would learn to accept her.

Aisling looked at her watch. Madge was overdoing the bashful bride. It was twenty past three. 'I hope she's not going to do a bunk,' she whispered to Frances. 'People are getting anxious.'

Frances agreed. The level of noise in the church was certainly rising. In the pew behind her she could hear Seamus O'Connor ask his wife, Una, to tell him once again what time it was. Frances turned to smile at Una and nodded at Seamus, who was not one of her favourite people, although both he and Una had been very good to all of them when her mother had died. In fact, at one time, she had been their babysitter and had been very close to the O'Connor family.

At that moment the organ began the Wedding March. A collective sigh of relief could be heard as the congregation stood up and turned to look at the bridal procession.

Clutching the arm of her brother, who was giving her away, Madge was dressed in a traditional cream silk wedding dress. At least, Frances reflected, it was well cut and slimmed down her voluptuous figure. Behind Madge trailed a voluminous tulle veil, embroidered with small daisies. She carried a huge bouquet of waxy white lilies. What was visible of her bright blonde hair underneath the impressive veiling was lacquered and curled. She looked lovely if a little vulgar. Two bridesmaids, old school friends, wore pink organza dresses. Kiley Matthews, one of Madge's grandnieces, had been chosen as flower-girl and wore a junior version of the bridesmaids' attire. The excited four-year-old followed the others up the aisle, hopping from one foot to the other, and every so often clasping the front of her dress in the manner of a child who is very anxious to visit the toilet.

'Talk about over the top!' whispered Nora, stifling a giggle.

'Come on, Nora; it's their wedding day,' Frances admonished.

John Davis turned to look at Madge as she reached the altar and his face lit up with pleasure.

Noticing his joy, the three daughters felt a sense of gratitude to Madge for giving him happiness again after so many years on his own. Frances, in particular, who had been fourteen when her mother died from cancer, remembered her father's terrible loneliness.

Everything went off very well in church. The only hitch was that little Kiley had to be taken out just before the exchange of vows. The hopping and clutching had reached a crisis, and a perceptive mother on the bride's side of the church had hustled the child down the aisle and out to the nearest secluded green patch.

After the photo session and the usual kissing and cooing, the wedding party gratefully escaped from the March wind and headed for the reception in Killiney. The three sisters were asked to take Aunt Cathy with them in the Golf. On the way to the hotel, she quizzed them about their father's whirlwind romance.

'He only met her last summer? Tell me truthfully, girls, what do you really think?'

Aunt Cathy had a reputation as a gossip monger and, with barely a glance among them, the three girls united in a show of discretion.

'We're delighted.'

'It's great for Dad.'

'He's been very lonely.'

The voices echoed each other.

'And,' Aisling added, 'Frances can really get on with her life now. And not have to worry about anyone but herself.'

'And how are things, Frances?' simpered Aunt

Cathy. 'Still working at the childminding?'

In fact her job had come to an end last week. Frances, who had trained as a nanny, had lived with the O'Reilly family for the past five years. But now the youngest child was going to school and the parents didn't need fulltime nursery care. It was going to be a wrench for Frances to leave all that behind her and look for somewhere new. She must find a job pretty quickly, because her father had made it plain to her that he didn't want her to hang around at home, under the new Mrs Davis's feet.

'Fine,' Frances lied. She didn't want to talk about her problems to Aunt Cathy.

' . . . and I just want to finish by saying that no man ever had such wonderful daughters. Great girls they are, all three of them,' the father's eyes were misty with brandy and emotion. 'And I'm sure Madge will agree with that.'

Madge nodded her head. Privately, she thought that Aisling was rather too cool a customer; she hadn't seen much of Nora but she had the feeling that she could be a bit of handful; as for Frances, no matter how nice she seemed, Madge had no intention of sharing her family home simply because Frances was out of work. She had made it clear to John that Frances was welcome to stay in the house until the honeymoon was over but she had emphasised that she did not want to find her there on her return. 'I'm sure you understand, dear,' she had said, 'a woman must be mistress in her own home.' Lovestruck as he was, John Davis had agreed with her.

The band struck up 'True Love' and Madge and John were the first to take the floor.

'There's going to be no crack here,' Nora complained to her sisters in the Ladies. 'Aisling, let's all go off to Leeson Street.'

'We can't leave at this stage.' Frances was adamant. 'Not until Dad and Madge go.'

'There's nothing but nerds here – country cousins and Madge's awful relations.' Nora looked pleadingly at Aisling. 'Please, you're the one with the car.'

'I'm sorry, pet. I know you'd love to go out on the town but we've got to stay.' She sat down on a gilt chair in front of a dressing table and carefully touched up the moss green eye-shadow that complemented her hazel eyes. 'Anyway, now that you're home for good, you'll have lots of time to check out the nightlife.'

'I hope some work turns up soon or I'll have no money to check out anything! Oh well,' Nora applied scarlet lipstick with confident strokes, 'I'm not going to worry about it tonight. Am I right, Jean?'

She looked across the mirror at Jean Maher, Frances's best friend from childhood. Jean was now an air hostess travelling the transatlantic route. They didn't see her as much as they would have liked and were thrilled that she was able to come to the wedding.

'Nora, honey,' Jean put down the tissue she was using to remove a wine stain from her white linen jacket, 'looking the way you do today, you'll have no trouble getting a job.'

'I hope you're right, Jean.' Nora beamed at her. 'Well, I'm going out to knock them all dead! Coming?'

Aisling followed Nora to the door.

'I'll have another go at trying to get rid of this wine.' Jean turned to Frances. 'Do you think I should put salt on it?'

'Give me a look.' Frances took the jacket from her. 'We'll be out in a minute, girls. You two go on.'

When Aisling and Nora were gone, Frances filled one of the basins with cold water and carefully submerged the stained part of the jacket.

Jean watched her with affection. They had been friends since their first day together at nursery school and Jean had been part of all the joys and sorrows of the Davis family.

'That's Nora and me out of work.' Frances gave Jean a wry look. 'Thank God, Aisling has a great job.'

'Aisling was lucky to be able to go to college and get a good degree and,' Jean emphasised, 'that was thanks to you.'

'Come on, Jean, Aisling has more brains than Nora and I put together.'

'Rubbish,' Jean shook her dark head in exasperation. 'If you hadn't had all that responsibility when your Mum died, you'd have easily got to college. You were just unlucky.'

'Maybe,' Frances demurred. 'Anyway, I love looking after children, so I'm not complaining.'

'That's great, Fran, but don't do yourself down.'

She had a quick look in the basin. 'That jacket's had it. God, I'm a terrible messer!'

'How did you ever get to be an air-hostess?' Frances laughed, remembering all the other occasions when clumsy, left-handed Jean had come to grief. 'Do you spill wine on your passengers, as well?'

'You won't believe this but up in the air, I'm a different being. Graceful and elegant. I must have been a bird in a previous existence.'

'Oh, yeah?'

'Come on, you,' Jean gave her an affectionate thump, 'let's go and suss out the talent!'

The dancefloor was crowded with an energetic older generation. Frances and Jean sat down at the table where Aisling and Nora were sitting with some relatives. With an impatient gesture, Nora shifted her chair so that Frances wasn't blocking her view. She had just caught sight of a striking dark-haired man at the bar.

'Who is that hunk?' She grabbed Frances by the arm.

'You haven't changed, Nora!' Peter, a cousin from Cork with a pronounced cauliflower ear, raised his eyebrows in mock horror. 'Still doing the *femme fatale*?'

'Where?' Frances ignored Peter.

'Over there, talking to Frank O'Neill. You can't miss him. He's the only attractive man in the hotel.' Nora was looking at the man with open admiration. He turned towards them and she deliberately held his eyes.

Frances followed Nora's stare and saw a tall, angular man with slightly long hair and a beard. He had a beautiful face – the kind of face you see in Renaissance paintings. She felt a strange sensation of *déjà vu*, a shock of recognition. At that moment he made an excuse to his companion and began to walk towards their table.

'I gather you're John's daughters.' He stood over them, smiling. He had a wonderful smile that took away a slight air of melancholy that shadowed his features in repose. He pulled out a chair and sat down next to Aisling. 'May I?'

'You already have!' Nora leaned towards him, her lips slightly parted and her eyes glistening.

'Well, so I have!' He seemed amused by her unashamed seductiveness.

Frances watched them, her mind confused by her feelings. She knew nothing about the man who sat opposite her, flirting with her little sister, but she felt a strong attraction to him.

'I'm Patrick Comerford.' He held out his hand to each of them in turn.

'Frances, Aisling, Nora,' they recited. 'Jean Maher, and Peter Johnson and his wife, Pauline.' Aisling indicated the cousins at the end of the table.

'Are you a friend of the bride?' asked Peter.

'No,' he turned to Frances. 'I'm a friend of your father's. We met when I was doing a painting of a horse at Ballycross Stables.'

'That's it!' Aisling exclaimed. 'I knew the name rang a bell. You're *the* Patrick Comerford.'

'You're famous?' Nora was even more intrigued.

'I'm a painter. Not famous at all.'

'Don't be modest,' Aisling insisted. 'Having exhibitions in London, Paris and New York sounds pretty famous to me.'

Frances was quiet. She had never heard of him but she wasn't in the swing of things like Aisling. She was pleased he was a painter. It seemed appropriate that, with such a sensitive face, he was not a bank clerk or accountant.

Aisling and Patrick were discussing the pomposity of certain television arts programmes. Nora became restless, beating her fingers ostentatiously to the hip hop rhythm.

'Some decent music at last.' She looked at Patrick, a question in her eyes.

'I'd love to stay and dance, but, unfortunately, I must get back to the kids.'

'Your wife is here?' Frances hid her disappointment.

'I'm a widower. My wife died last year.'

There was an awkward silence.

'I'm sorry . . . ' Frances stammered.

'It's OK. I've managed reasonably well, thanks to the nanny I had for the children for years. But,' he said with a shrug 'she left to get married last month and I'm having terrible trouble finding a replacement. My children are still young – four and two.'

'That's quite a coincidence!' Jean was quick to seize an opportunity for her friend. 'Frances is a qualified nanny and is looking for somewhere.' She looked expectantly at Frances who nodded, overwhelmed by the speed of events.

'It's certainly worth having a chat about.' He took out his wallet and scribbled an address and phone number on a piece of paper. 'Maybe you could ring me and we'll arrange to meet and talk about it.' Frances nodded mutely, unable to believe her good fortune.

'Please don't leave it too long,' he gave a wry grin. 'I don't think I can take much more twenty-four-hour bonding with my children!' He stood up. 'I really must go. It was great meeting you all.' His eyes lingered on Nora's disappointed face and he turned to leave. Looking back, he called over his shoulder, 'See you soon, I hope, Frances.'

She watched him as he negotiated his way through the crowds on the dance floor.

'I never heard of him.' Peter was unimpressed.

'Just because you haven't heard of him . . . ' Aisling dismissed him with a wave of her elegant hand. Peter was a close enough cousin to be treated with contempt.

'Peter's not interested in anything but rugby. I don't know how you stand it,' Nora sympathised with the long-suffering Pauline, who laughed and threw back her fifth gin and tonic.

'Well, at least, I'll give you a dance, Nora. Come on.' Eye-catching in her brilliant green, Nora followed Peter on to the dance floor.

Very shortly the rest of the table accepted invitations to dance. Aisling did her best to be charming to an old trainer who had known her father for years. Jean was dragged to her feet and bounced around the floor like a sack of potatoes by an over-enthusiastic country cousin. Every so often she threw expressive glances from her mischievous dark eyes at Frances, who was reluctantly dancing with Seamus O'Connor and trying to keep as far away as she could from his enveloping arms. Frances was thinking about Patrick Comerford and beginning to believe that, perhaps, a whole new life was about to open up for her.

THREE

'OK on camera two?' From the producer's box, Frank Martin addressed the cameraman, whose initial head and shoulders shot of Carmel Rafferty would open *Ireland Today*. It was three days since the wedding and Aisling was engrossed in watching the live production of the twice weekly programme. Wearing a set of headphones, she was able to listen in as Brian, the floor manager, instructed Carmel to sit just a little more to one side so that the camera could pick up her best angle.

'Ready to go, Frank,' Carmel gave them the thumbs up sign as the credits rolled. Her opening was crisp and to the point. *Ireland Today* was Channel 3's most prestigious current affairs production and Carmel had been presenting it for so long that when audiences thought of the programme, they thought of her. She had perfected the art of interviewing politicians, who had learned to respect the mixture of mild flirtatiousness and savagely incisive questioning that was her stock in trade. But lately, she had begun to make the occasional slip – forgetting small but pertinent facts, or failing to find the salient word or phrase with which to disarm her subjects.

Carmel was fifty-five, older than many of the

male political presenters and Aisling believed that, sooner or later, management would decide to move her off the show. Longevity was more acceptable in a political presenter than it was in a quiz show hostess, who had to be young as well as glamorous, but, even so, the management tended to move presenters, especially the female ones, to off-peak programmes when they grew older. Aisling knew it was unfair, but it was undeniably a fact of life. What was more, Carmel was rumoured to be developing a drink problem following the break-up of a longstanding romance with a well-known newspaper editor. On a couple of occasions lately she had slurred her words at the afternoon briefing sessions and Aisling guessed that lunch, for Carmel, was a liquid event. She always managed to sober up before going on air but it was probably only a matter of time before she disgraced herself in a major way. Aisling felt sorry that the woman who had been such a true pro now seemed to be sliding into alcoholism, but she couldn't control the little *frisson* of excitement that bubbled inside her at the thought that she would be a candidate for Carmel's job.

At twenty-six, Aisling had two years experience in working on *Ireland Today*. Her speciality was location reports but she had presented a children's news programme when she first came to work in Channel 3 and Frank Martin had assured her that she possessed all the qualities necessary to get to the top. She knew that Frank's encouragement wasn't completely disinterested. He had 'dis covered' Carmel some twenty years earlier when they had both been working for RTE. When Channel 3 had started up the station managers had headhunted Frank who had insisted on bringing Carmel with him. His career in the station had blossomed with hers. Now he had his eye on the position of Head of Current Affairs. It would help him if he had a number of his own trusted people to front the various programmes for which he would be responsible, and he had let Aisling know that she was one of what he called his 'team'.

Despite this, Aisling was by no means certain that if Carmel were moved from *Ireland Today* she would step into her shoes. She was still considered a relative junior and she had one major rival in Fred Kennedy, a news reporter with considerable experience. But Frank favoured her, and assuming he realised his ambition she would almost certainly rise with him. She hated herself for thinking in this calculated way, but it seemed that that was how you got on within Channel 3.

'She's going good,' Frank said as Carmel interviewed her first live guest, the Minister for Social Welfare. Aisling watched, with a mixture of admiration and envy, as Carmel tore into the government's welfare policy in relation to the unemployed, the disabled and prisoners' wives.

'He seems to be able for her,' she commented. The minister, who had only recently taken over the portfolio following the unexpected death of his predecessor, was answering Carmel's questions in a calm and even humorous way. He had laughing blue eyes and dark blond hair and while he was not conventionally handsome, he seemed to exude a kind of witty intelligence that Aisling found very appealing. 'What's his biog?' asked Stephanie, the young personal assistant.

'He was a junior minister in Justice,' Aisling replied promptly. She had been watching Michael Whelan's political progress with some interest and hoped to get to meet him in the hospitality suite after the programme, if Carmel didn't try to dominate his attention.

'Here's your piece now,' said Frank as Carmel turned away from the minister and introduced an item on women who travelled to England for abortions.

'Our reporter, Aisling Davis, went with one of these young women, a twenty-year-old who wishes only to be identified as 'Laura'. We followed them on their journey.'

Aisling's report, flashed up on the monitor, took the viewer on a trip to the Liverpool abortion clinic, where Laura, whose face was never shown, had had her abortion. As well as giving hard facts on the number of Irish women leaving the country for abortions each year, Aisling presented Laura's case in an interesting and compassionate way. Laura had come from Mullingar to Dublin, where she had met the man she hoped to marry. On learning that she was pregnant, he had abandoned her and, because she was working in a badly paid job as a waitress, she had felt she had no other option but to abort her baby. After the operation, she confided to Aisling her contradictory feelings of loss and relief and an almost overwhelming fear of being prosecuted if she were found out. Aisling had felt a mixture of pity and anger on her behalf.

'Is the government turning its back on women like Laura?' she asked, in a final piece-to-camera. 'Is giving women information about abortion abroad a sufficiently honest way of dealing with the problem, or are we, as some would allege, simply continuing to sweep our dirt under an English carpet?'

'Well done!' cried Frank, as Carmel introduced a final short item. Aisling allowed herself a moment's self-congratulation before going to the ladies' room to freshen up. She removed her shoulder-length hair from the French pleat she had been wearing and combed it out. The plaiting made her normally straight hair ripple attractively. She smoothed on lipstick and eye-shadow then went to the hospitality suite where Carmel and Frank were already ensconced at a table near the bar. The room was crowded with production staff and various hangers-on. Aisling glanced around for Michael Whelan but she couldn't see him. She felt a moment's disappointment; then rebuked herself for feeling like a teenager.

Geraldine Ryan, a vivacious redhead and the programme's chief researcher, was ordering a glass of wine from the bar.

'You look great, Aisling!' she said. 'What's all the glamour in aid of?'

'Nothing.' Aisling felt herself blush. She wasn't going to admit that she had made a special effort with her appearance because she had hoped to meet Michael Whelan.

'What'll you have?' Geraldine asked.

'A white wine, please.'

As Geraldine ordered the wine, Aisling could hear Carmel talking loudly about the programme's continued rise in the ratings.

'Who's she trying to impress?' Geraldine laughed. 'The catering staff?'

Aisling said nothing. She thought it was sad that someone like Carmel should need her ego boosted. As she watched, Carmel lowered half a glass of gin and tonic in one go.

'I need a drink after that ghastly man!' She gulped down the remainder of the gin and demanded another from a waitress.

'Does she mean Michael Whelan?' Aisling turned to Geraldine. 'I thought he was quite nice.'

'But she couldn't get a straight answer out of him,' said Geraldine. 'She's definitely losing her touch.'

'Where is he now?' Aisling asked, in a way that she hoped sounded casual.

'He had one quick drink and then went straight to the Dáil,' said Geraldine, 'For a late-night vote. At least, that's his story.'

Aisling felt her face drop. If she hadn't spent so long dolling herself up in the ladies, she would have met him!

'Are you disappointed?' There was a twinkle in Geraldine's eye as she watched Aisling's reaction.

'I wouldn't have minded meeting him,' Aisling tried to sound matter-of-fact, but Geraldine saw right through her.

'Watch out, kid – married men are trouble. I should know!'

Geraldine lived with Billy Moore, a married journalist whom she'd been seeing for years. During the course of their stormy on-off relationship she had frequently confided in Aisling, and the two were now firm friends. There was no point in trying to hide anything from Geraldine – she knew Aisling far too well.

'Oh, well – another time, another place!'

'He liked your piece,' Geraldine said. 'He watched it on the monitor. Wanted to know all about you.'

To her surprise, Aisling experienced a thrill of pleasure. In spite of his married status, she couldn't help finding Michael Whelan attractive. She hadn't had much of a love life since she had finished college five years before. In university, she had enrolled in several student societies and had met many boyfriends as a result but since then she had been busy pursuing her career, first as a freelance journalist and then in Channel 3. In those five years she had had only one serious relationship, with John Flynn, a cameraman. Initially, theirs had been an idyllic romance, with candlelit dinners and cosy evenings in her flat but as she became more successful, John's passion for her had changed to resentment. He constantly belittled her in front of their friends and she finally ended the relationship when she learnt that he was two-timing her with one of the secretaries on *Ireland Today*.

'He didn't look very far, did he?' she had asked Geraldine at the time.

'He *wanted* you to find out,' Geraldine had

insisted. 'Men always do, when they dirty their own doorstep.'

After that, she had dated only irregularly. The men she attracted never appealed to her and the few she met who interested her seemed overawed when they heard about her job, or perhaps they were simply not ready for a long-term relationship with a woman whose career would always come first.

'Typical!' she said, taking a sip of wine. 'The first man I fancy who might just be interested and he has to be married.'

'They always are!' said Geraldine. 'But take it from me, Aisling. Michael Whelan's one to avoid. They say that if it moves, he screws it.'

'I only wanted to *meet* him, not make love with him!' laughed Aisling, but a small voice inside her told her that she was lying.

FOUR

Frances checked the address on the slip of paper
Patrick Comerford had given her. It was written
in purple ink in a large scrawling hand.

She stopped in front of an imposing Georgian
house in Monkstown Terrace. It had a discreet
stone coloured façade and a bright red door which
looked as though it had been recently painted.
Patrick Comerford might not be sufficiently
organised to have printed name cards but as an
artist he was obviously conscious of style.

Given the formal exterior of the house, Frances
was expecting an interior of Aubusson rugs and
mahogany tables and was somewhat startled by
the bright Mexican druggets on the stripped
floorboards and the stark white walls that were
covered in modern paintings by artists whose
names she didn't recognise.

'Sit down a minute, love,' the woman who had
opened the door spoke in a broad Dublin accent.
A house coat was stretched to bursting point over
her ample bosom and she smelt of Brasso. Frances
guessed she was the housekeeper.

Sitting down tentatively on a thin, wrought-iron
chair which looked as though it might collapse
under her weight, Frances looked around her. She
decided she liked the décor. It was quite unlike

the faded elegance of her father's home but the effect was warm and welcoming.

'He'll see you in the studio,' the woman called from the back of the hall. Frances followed her through a kitchen, which, in contrast to the hall, was decidedly traditional. She took in an Aga cooker in front of which a large tabby cat was sleeping, an old-fashioned larder and a dark oak kitchen table covered in copper pots which the housekeeper had evidently been cleaning before Frances's arrival had interrupted her.

They walked through a narrow and somewhat overgrown garden to the converted mews which was Patrick's studio. He stood at the open door, waiting for her. She saw that he was wearing an artist's smock which, with his long black hair and beard, made her think, once again, of a figure from a Renaissance painting.

'Thanks, Mary,' Patrick said to the housekeeper, who returned to the house. He smiled at Frances and she felt her heart beat faster.

Patrick extended a hand in greeting.

'Great to see you, Frances.' He was about to grasp her hand when he saw that his own was covered in paint. He laughingly withdrew it, wiping it on his smock.

'Come on in,' he said and they entered a large room that was flooded with light from the huge windows which Patrick had put in when the mews was converted into a studio. Brightly coloured canvases in both modern and traditional styles lined the walls. They competed for space with plants which hung from the exposed rafters of

the studio, creating an almost tropical environment which reminded Frances of the greenhouses
in the Botanical Gardens. She felt suddenly
uplifted and her self-consciousness of a few
moments before seemed to dissolve.

'You like it?' Patrick had noted her approval
and it was more a statement than a question.

'It's lovely! So full of joy and light.'

'That's how life should be, don't you think?'
He rubbed a speck of paint from his black beard.
'I want my children to grow up in the sunlight,' he
laughed, 'metaphorically speaking, since we're
living in grey old Ireland.'

The photo of a serious-looking, fair-haired boy
stood on a wooden crate in which Patrick kept his
oil paints.

'That's Mark,' he said proudly. 'As you can see,
he's not like me at all. He inherited Deirdre's
looks.'

Patrick fell silent, obviously saddened by the
memory of his wife's death.

'He's lovely,' Frances said, filling the silence.
'What age would he be? About four?'

'Spot on,' Patrick smiled at her. 'He'll be five
next birthday and the baby – Aoife – is two. Mark
goes to school in September but at the moment
he's attending a playschool down the road.' He
glanced at his watch. 'Mary'll be going to collect
him in a minute. So you can meet him and the
baby when they come back.'

'Sounds like you're very well organised. You
hardly need me,' Frances joked, surprised at how
easy and relaxed she felt in this man's company.

'Oh, but we do! Mark is a sensitive child, he was badly affected by his mother's death. You see, he was in the car with her when it happened. A drunk driver ploughed straight into them. It's a miracle Mark wasn't injured but as you can imagine, he was deeply affected just the same.'

'It must have been awful for him.'

'Mary's a kind woman, but she can't give him the sort of attention he needs. He's intelligent, needs stimulation but he's vulnerable too. I'll warn you, he can be quite a handful. Aoife's uncomplicated – bright and happy.'

'I'm sure we'll all get on fine,' said Frances, 'that's if . . . ' She paused, conscious that she had already assumed that the job was hers. 'I have references,' she said, rooting in her handbag to find them.

Patrick gestured at her to put them away.

'Anyone can produce a reference. I tend to go by instinct.'

He gazed at her seriously for a moment, his brown eyes looking into her grey ones as though he were trying to read her mind. She felt strangely embarrassed, as if he was seeing all her past, and she was relieved when he turned his gaze to the easel at which he had been working.

'What do you think it is?' he asked suddenly.

Surprised at being asked, Frances gazed at a whorl of colours – blues, reds, greens and purples – which filled the canvas. At first, it seemed like a hopeless, meaningless confusion, but then she discerned the shadow of a building and what seemed to be an arm that was releasing the brightly coloured shapes into the blue sky.

'I don't really understand modern art,' she said hesitantly, ' but this painting makes me feel happy. As though someone had sent a thousand balloons into the sky.'

'That's just what it is!' he said, delighted. 'Have a look around at the other paintings.' He gestured to several canvasses leaning against the wall. 'I'll go and get us a cup of coffee. I'm sure Mary won't be long.'

As Frances took the Italian pottery mug from Patrick the studio door opened and Mary came in, ushering two small children ahead of her.

'Dada, dada.' A little dark-haired girl ran to Patrick, holding open her arms. The boy stayed close to Mary at the door, his eyes fixed on Frances.

'Come over and meet Frances.' Still holding Aoife, Patrick beckoned to Mark.

'Hello, Mark.' Frances bent down to reach the child's level.

'How do you do?' he said, solemnly holding out his hand. Her heart melted.

'Frances is going to come every day and help Mary to look after you and Aoife. Won't that be great?'

'Gweat, gweat,' Aoife struggled in Patrick's arms. 'Want din-din now.'

Laughing, Patrick put her down and she ran to the housekeeper. Mark said nothing but as he left the room with his sister and Mary, he turned and shyly smiled at Frances.

'They're absolute pets, Patrick.' Frances looked at him questioningly. 'Did all that mean I've got the job?'

'Yes,' he smiled at her. 'Will tomorrow be too soon to start?'

'No – that's fine. What time should I come?'

'Mark goes to school at nine, so let's say eight?'

'Fine.'

'Most nights I put them to bed myself, so you'll be free when they've had their tea at about six, but I might ask you to stay over the odd night, when I'm away. Of course, I'll pay you for it.'

'But I thought . . . ' She paused. 'Most positions of this kind are live-in.'

'I don't want another woman in the house,' Patrick said, and she saw in his eyes the huge loss his wife's death had created. 'Not just yet.'

'I understand.' She smiled at him, reassuringly.

Frances left, her joy at having got the job somewhat diminished by the fact that she wouldn't be living in. Still, the salary that Patrick had proposed was very generous and, although she would have only the fortnight of her father's honeymoon in which to find a flat, at least Nora was in the same boat. Perhaps they might even rent a place together. All the same, she couldn't help thinking how nice it would have been to have shared a home with Patrick Comerford. Though she did not admit it to herself, she was already half in love with him.

FIVE

While Frances was drinking coffee with Patrick, Nora was sitting on top of a 46A bus on her way into the city. She intended to wander around and, with a bit of luck, bump into some mates from the past who'd fill her in on the job scene. She wasn't optimistic about the chance of work in the theatre because she'd been out of Ireland for so long and had lost contacts. All her problems would be solved if she could get a part in *Southsiders*, a new and already very popular soap opera on Channel 3. She knew that Aisling would do her best to help by introducing her to a few of the right people but after that, it would be up to her.

Nora got off at D'Olier Street and walked past the Bank of Ireland towards Temple Bar. People turned to look at the tall, raven-headed girl, dressed in deep purple leggings and a matching swing coat. Some gave involuntary smiles of recognition at the face they had seen so often on the television. Nora noticed their swivelling heads and felt a bit more optimistic about beating off the competition for a role in *Southsiders*.

Dublin was looking great in the spring sunshine. It was quite warm, very different from the freezing Saturday of last week when they'd shivered outside the church, waiting for Madge to stop posing for the photographer. Although Nora was pleased that her father had found a companion, she was determined to be out of the house by the time her stepmother returned as lady of the manor.

Skateboarders on the piazza in front of the Central Bank whistled and catcalled as she passed. Ignoring them, she went on into Crown Alley. She loved this part of Dublin – the labyrinth of cobbled streets, the music from the classical record shops, the exotic smells from the Greek, Portuguese and Italian restaurants. Stopping to look in a shop window, she was instantly attracted by a pair of long black suede boots. Nora did a fast assessment of her finances. The money she'd brought back from London wouldn't last long if she didn't get a job soon. Could she afford them? No, but to hell! – she'd have them. It was vital to look stunning when she finally got past the gates of Channel 3's studios in Clonskeagh. The boots had seventies-style platform heels that would show off her legs to perfection. Her mind made up, she opened the shop door.

Ten minutes later, she came out wearing the new boots, her old ones in the shoe box. It was typical of Nora to have put them on straight away. 'I want – *now*!' she used to wail as a toddler. In the end someone always gave in, and she would instantly stop howling and trot off happily with the ice-cream, the packet of Jellytots or the cuddly toy.

It was now nearly twelve o'clock and she hadn't met anyone she knew. Turning the corner into

Eustace Street, she remembered that there was a coffee shop and wine bar in the Irish Film Centre. There might be some of the old gang in there.

She walked into the light-filled atrium and looked around.

'Nora!' a voice bellowed from above. Looking up, she saw Fintan leaning over the balcony. He appeared to be alone. 'I didn't know you were due back. Come up here and give us a hug, love.'

Enveloped in his arms, Nora felt really home. Fintan was her closest friend. Being a man, he'd never been in competition with her for the same part, so there was no professional rivalry between them. And because he was gay there had been no problems about his wanting to get into her bed.

'I was hoping I'd bump into someone, especially you.' She released herself from his bear hug.

'You came to the right place; all us 'resting' actors come here now to suck up to the rich and famous. It's desperate at the moment. There's nothing doing at all. You're so lucky to have a "permanent, pensionable job" in a soap. I love your character – I never miss an episode.'

'Thanks, Fintan.' Nora gave him another hug and decided to tell him her bad news over a cup of coffee. 'How are things with you?'

'I've a walk-on part in the Gate for the next couple of weeks,' he grimaced, 'and I'm glad of it.' He pulled out an elegant tubular chair. 'Sit down and tell us what's been happening. Coffee?'

She watched him as he went down the stairs to fetch the coffee and thought, not for the first time, what a waste it was that such a good-looking man was homosexual. He was twenty-seven, tall with a lean and svelte body. His most outstanding feature was his green Slavonic eyes. Unwitting females were constantly having to be warned against falling under the spell of those eyes.

'Great coffee here.' He put the cup in front of her.

'Is it really as bad as that? I mean the work scene?' Nora put some sugar in her cup and stirred. 'It's not an academic question. I'm going to be doing the rounds here myself.' She took a gulp of coffee and blurted out the story of her dismissal from *Docklands*. As she gave a graphic description of the scene in the Crown and Anchor and the expression on Dave's face when she flung the pint at him, she began to laugh. 'It was almost worth losing my job to show that prick what I really thought of him!'

'I wish I'd been a fly on the wall; I'm pissed off with casting couch blackmail.' He gave her a reassuring grin. 'Don't worry! With your looks, you'll pick up something – modelling, kissograms. You'll get by and then... ' he struck a dramatic pose, ' ... one day a big-time director will look at you and say: "That's the one!"'

'Nice thought, Fintan, but in the meantime I need to do more than get by. I'll have to find the money for rent. I can't stay at home now. It wouldn't be fair to Dad and Madge. Anyway, I'd go crazy. She's OK but... '

'The wicked stepmother? Are they married yet?'

'Yeah, last week. That's when I came back. I

was too fed up with everything to get in touch with you. Thanks.' Nora wasn't really a smoker but she occasionally accepted a cigarette when it was offered. 'Anyway, I'd like to be out before they get back next week.'

'If I'd space . . . ' Fintan began apologetically as he lit her cigarette.

'I know you would, Fintan, but it wouldn't be a good idea.' Nora knew that Phil, Fintan's possess-ive boyfriend, would not be very happy about her arrival. 'Anyway, I might be sharing with Frances if she doesn't get a live-in job soon. She's being interviewed for one at moment – with this gorgeous man who was at the wedding. I nearly had an orgasm just looking at him!'

'Still as raunchy as ever, I see!'

'That'll never change. I see someone I want, I want him now!' She took a drag of her cigarette and laughed. 'Do you remember that party in Leeson Street last Christmas, Fintan?'

'You mean the time I spent the entire night in the basement having oil massaged into all my little private places by a six-foot-six Jamaican reggae star? Phil still throws that in my face. He was furious.'

'What an ego! I wasn't thinking about you.' Nora smacked Fintan playfully. 'I was thinking about me in the airing cupboard with Jean-Paul whisper-ing sweet nothings in my ear as we worked our way through the *Kama Sutra*. Well, I think it was my ear,' she added reflectively.

'And Phil found you when he opened the door, thinking he was going into the can! He was upset about that too! He can suddenly go all moralistic, my Phil.'

'Things going well?'

'Fine, except for the odd tantrum because of his jealousy. But he's a great lover. That's what we all need so I'm hanging on in there!'

'You're dead right. I haven't had sex for ages. I'm feeling really frustrated, so I definitely can't stay at home. I can't see Madge welcoming any overnight visitors!'

'If you need quick cash for rent, check out the kissogram scene. I've done it myself. You can work as much or as little as you like and when a part turns up, you just pack it in.'

'I know. I did it in London for a while.'

Fintan pulled out a battered address book. 'I've got a number here. Go and ring. The phone's downstairs.'

Nora hesitated. She'd had her fill of being a Naughty Nurse and a Checky Cavewoman. But the work didn't tie you down like a nine-to-five job. She'd have time to concentrate on pushing for that part in *Southsiders*.

'Right.' She stood up. 'I'll ring them and see if I can go over straight away.'

She came back upstairs beaming.

'Seems like I'm in business. I'm going to see them now. You're a pal.' She dropped a kiss on the top of his head.

Fintan stood up. 'I'll walk over with you.'

The Too Hot To Handle Company was just off Wicklow Street. They cut through Brown Thomas's department store, Nora pausing at the perfume counter to spray herself lavishly with Obsession from a tester phial.

She strode into the kissogram office in her long black boots. Bowled over by her appearance and extrovert personality, the young manager offered her as much work as she felt she could manage, starting on Friday evening as a Sexy Schoolgirl at a birthday party in a stockbroker's office.

Fintan was waiting for her in a nearby pub.

'Great,' he said when he heard the details. 'If you work about twenty hours a week, you'll make a clear £150 and you can escape the Wicked Stepmother!'

'What a relief!' Nora signalled the barman. 'Let me buy you a drink, Fintan.'

Several drinks later, they kissed goodbye at the bus stop.

'Give me a buzz.' She jumped on the bus. 'We'll get together with the gang.'

When Nora arrived back at Marlborough Road she heard the familiar sounds of Frances preparing supper in the kitchen. She couldn't wait to find out if she'd got the job. 'Lucky Frances,' she thought. 'I wouldn't mind sleeping under the same roof as Patrick!'

'Something smells great.' Nora sniffed appreciatively as she opened the kitchen door. 'What's cooking?'

'Lasagne.' Frances was rubbing a large wooden salad bowl with a clove of garlic. She looked pleased with herself and Nora noticed that a bottle of red wine was open on the table.

'You got the job!' It wasn't a question. She knew

the answer from Frances's happy face. She put down her parcel and beamed at her elder sister.

Frances poured out a glass of wine and handed it to her.

'I start tomorrow. There're two children – a little boy of four and a baby girl. They're absolute pets.' She babbled on, full of excitement.

'Fran, that's great, I'm really pleased for you.' Nora gave her sister a hug. 'And I've got a job too. It's just in a singing telegram place, but it'll give me enough money to pay for a bedsit, while I'm looking for real work.'

She took a gulp of wine and gave a sigh of satisfaction. 'And you'll be OK because you'll be living in.'

Frances sat down at the table. 'That's the only problem. He doesn't want anyone in the place at night. He still misses his wife a lot.' Her face clouded over in sympathy. 'She was killed in a car accident.

Nora looked at her sister affectionately. Frances always got upset by other people's troubles. 'The poor man. That must have been terrible. If he wants consolation, send him in my direction.' Putting a leg up on the chair, she went into model pose, 'Like my boots?'

'They're beautiful, but . . . ' Frances put up a hand in protest, ' . . . don't tell me how much they cost.'

'Never mind, I have a job, you have a job and, most importantly, we can get out of here and find somewhere to share.' Nora grabbed her bag. 'While you open another bottle of wine, I'll nip down and get an *Evening Herald*. We want to be well clear of this place when Madge comes swinging in on her broomstick!'

The front door banged behind her. Frances stood in the kitchen smiling to herself. There was a good chance they'd have found a flat before the honeymooners returned. And it would be great to live with Nora again. Of course, she was madly chaotic and untidy, but life was never boring when she was around.

The oven timer chimed and Frances took out a golden lasagne and placed it carefully on an Italian straw mat on the table. She lit a couple of celebratory yellow candles. Things were looking up. Tomorrow was going to be a great day.

SIX

Aisling, Frank and Carmel were sitting in Ashtons pub for a lunchtime briefing before the Thursday night edition of *Ireland Today*. Ashtons was a favourite haunt of Channel 3 personnel and was jokingly known as the 'branch office'. Although Aisling didn't frequent it all that often, she enjoyed the casual atmosphere and and liked seeing so many familiar faces.

Normally, she wasn't invited to these briefings and she saw it as a good sign that Frank had asked her to come and give her views on how Carmel should handle the programme on clerical sex-abuse that they were running tonight. They discussed the thorny issue over sandwiches and coffee.

'I'm going to shoot from the hip,' declared Carmel. 'Celibacy breeds this sort of thing and I'm going to make that point.'

'That's not really valid,' Aisling pointed out. 'There are many abusers who aren't celibate. Don't you think you should be concentrating on what the church should be doing for the victims?'

'Aisling's right,' Frank said. 'Take it from that angle and don't get emotional.'

'Who's emotional?' Carmel's eyes hardened.

'You are, these days. You're letting things get

to you and that makes you less effective.'

Carmel shot Frank a look of pure hatred. 'I'm going to the loo.' She got up and marched off.

'We know what that means,' said Frank, as Carmel left the table. 'She's off for a tipple. Probably has a bottle of gin in her handbag. Did you notice the way her hands were shaking at lunch? She's really got a problem.'

This was the first time that Frank had raised the matter of Carmel's drinking with her and Aisling felt reluctant to discuss it. 'Maybe she's just nervous about tonight. After all, she'll be interviewing the archbishop.'

Frank guffawed. 'It would take more than a bishop to frighten Carmel! No, she's on the slippery slope. Get ready to step into her shoes.'

Aisling sighed. She wanted more than anything to present *Ireland Today* but she didn't approve of Frank's attitude towards Carmel. After all, he had profited from her success, and now, when she was sick and clearly needed help, he was preparing to shaft her. His attitude struck her as ruthless and uncaring.

'If you're sure she's drinking, don't you think you should say something? Perhaps if she joined an AA programme . . . '

'Are you kidding?' Frank was dismissive. 'She'll never admit she's got a problem. She'd chew me up if I suggested it.'

'I still think you should try.'

'What's the matter?' Frank's tone was suddenly as sharp as the creases in his tailored trousers. 'Scared you can't do the job? Maybe we should offer it to Fred Kennedy.' Annoyed, Aisling terminated the conversation by picking up her copy of *The Irish Times*. She turned to the classified section.

'Very polite!' said Frank.

'Maybe she's just trying to keep herself informed,' said Carmel, who had returned to the table. Aisling guessed that Carmel didn't approve of her presence at the briefing and probably perceived it as a threat.

'Actually, I'm looking for a flat,' she said, truthfully.

'You can come and stay with me any time,' Frank joked.

'I'm sure your wife would love that!' Aisling retorted, relieved that the moment of tension between them had subsided.

'What's wrong with where you're living?' asked Carmel, without much interest.

'My flatmate's brought in her boyfriend. Grainne and Diarmuid. But they bear no relation to the mythical couple!'

'The humping getting you down, love?' Frank asked.

'I could stand that! It's his smelly feet and his habit of picking his nose at the table that really gets to me.'

'Then Uncle Frank can help you. As it happens, I've a dinky townhouse in Sandycove that would be just right for you.'

'Are you serious?'

Frank had never mentioned owning property before, and Aisling was surprised. 'It's the wife's, actually. She bought it as an investment when her parents died. The last tenants have just left.'

'Maybe it's worth a look.'

'We could go now. I can pick up the key on the way.'

'But we've got to get back to the office,' objected Aisling.

Frank laughed. 'She's a real workaholic, isn't she Carmel? But I guess that's better than some other addictions.'

Carmel ignored the snide remark. 'We'll be back within the hour,' Frank assured Aisling. 'I'm sure that Carmel can hold the fort till then.'

They drove out to Sandycove in Aisling's Golf. The townhouse was larger than she had expected, with three bedrooms as well as a large lounge-cum-living-room and a fully fitted oak-fronted kitchen.

'I'm impressed,' Aisling told Frank. 'But it's way too big for me. It's bound to cost too much, as well.'

'A snip at six hundred a month,' he told her.

'Six hundred on my salary? You must be joking!'

'Come outside for a minute.' Frank pulled back the French window to reveal a beautifully laid out patio, complete with barbecue, garden furniture and an array of pot plants. 'You can hear the sea from here. It's only a short walk away.'

'It is lovely,' she conceded. 'But it's way too dear.'

'You could always share the rent,' Frank suggested, as they stepped back into the living-room. 'And we'd rather have a tenant we know. You're not likely to wreck the place.'

'My sisters are looking for a flat,' Aisling admitted.

'Well there you are then!' Frank was triumphant.

'But I really do want my own place. I like to be independent.'

'Don't want your sisters to know what you're getting up to?'

'It's not that!' she assured him.

Much as she loved Frances and Nora, she wasn't certain that, at the age of twenty-six, she wanted to live with them. It would be like being a little girl again. She thought about Frances's set ways and Nora's fiery temper. Could she really cope with these shortcomings? She rebuked herself, remembering that she too had failings that probably irritated them. And, she reminded herself, living with her sisters couldn't be half as bad as living with Grainne had been. Even before Diarmuid's arrival, Grainne's sloppy habits had got on her nerves.

On the drive back to Clonskeagh, Frank kept up a running commentary on the joys that living in Sandycove would afford her. She had to hand it to him, he was some salesman. He was still talking when she drew up outside the studio building to let him out before going to park the car. 'Why don't you take the key?' he said, pulling it from his pocket before opening the door. 'Show your sisters the house. See if they like it.'

'I might,' she agreed, as he slammed the door.

He leaned in the open window.

'Don't take too long about deciding,' he warned. 'I've got several people interested in it.'

'I believe you, Frank!'

'It's the truth!' he shouted, as he walked off.

Aisling was too busy for the rest of the day to give the house much thought. There was a huge response to the item on clerical abuse and the editorial team stayed in the office until almost midnight, analysing and dissecting the programme. When she finally arrived home, exhausted, Grainne and Diarmuid were out but their clothes were scattered all over the living-room floor and they had left grease-covered dishes on the kitchen table. Aisling came to a quick decision. She picked up the phone and dialled her father's number. Frances answered it. 'Aisling,' Frances's voice was sleepy. 'What's wrong?'

'Nothing,' Aisling assured her. 'And I'm sorry if I woke you. But I just had to tell you. I've found the perfect place for the three of us!'

Aisling drove to Marlborough Road early the next morning to take Frances and Nora out to Sandycove to see the house. The two sisters were in the kitchen, finishing breakfast.

'Sorry for giving you a fright last night – ringing so late.' Aisling poured herself a cup of coffee.

'Don't worry,' Frances assured her. 'It was great to hear about the house – but I thought you wanted a place of your own?'

Aisling still had some reservations about sharing with her sisters but she hastened to reassure them.

'We'll get on fine. I know we fight a bit,' she added with a grin, looking at Nora, 'but we always sort things out in the end. What do you think?'

'I think it's wicked!' Nora was dancing about in delight. 'Sandycove! I've always wanted to live there. So romantic – you can hear the sea all night! I can't wait.'

'And it's on the DART,' Frances added. 'That'll be really handy, Nora, when you're working in town.'

'So you're a bit interested?' Aisling teased.

'Interested! Let's go now and take it.' Nora headed for the door.

'Slow down,' Aisling laughed. 'Let me finish my coffee. Six hundred a month's not cheap but it's a great house and, between three, I think it's manageable.'

'And dear Frank's organising it?' Frances asked Aisling, teasingly. 'You'd better watch out, Ash. He might start getting ideas.'

'I doubt it! Frank's far too cute to get involved with one of his own staff.'

'Are you nearly finished?' asked Nora, impatiently. 'I can't wait to see it.'

'Right, right,' said Aisling, putting down her cup. 'We'll go now.'

Like Aisling, the other sisters fell in love with the house as soon as they crossed the threshold. They came to an instant decision to take it.

They moved in the following week, a few days before their father was due back from his honeymoon. Aisling made several trips to Sandycove in the Golf, which was filled to bursting point with clothes, books and knick-knacks. Nora's possessions had arrived back from England and Aisling noted wryly that she seemed to have twice as much gear as herself and Frances.

Thanks to an early start, they had made the final run by mid-morning.

'I bags this room,' said Nora, darting upstairs and throwing open the door of the largest bedroom, which overlooked the patio and had a sea view.

'Typical!' Aisling was more amused than irritated. 'Frances or I might like it.'

Frances shrugged. 'Let Nora have it if she wants. I don't mind.'

'Tell you what,' said Nora, plonking down a hold-all that was stuffed to the brim with her many pairs of shoes, 'why don't we two draw lots? Frances can think of a number . . . '

Frances nodded.

'Write it down,' Aisling insisted. 'This must be strictly by the rules. '

'It's a number between one and five,' said Frances, jotting down a figure on a notepad she had taken from her handbag.

'Five!' said Nora immediately and was triumphant when Frances indicated that she had drawn lucky.

Resigning herself to the second of the two smaller bedrooms at the front of the house, Aisling reflected ruefully that Nora seemed to have been born lucky. She had fallen into acting when no other career was available and despite returning broke from England, she had landed on her feet again, finding a kissogram job almost immediately. But perhaps she was being unfair. After all, the life of an actor was tough at the best of times and a job as a kissogram was hardly a career move. Though Aisling loved Nora, she knew she was a little envious of her looks and of the place she had always enjoyed in their father's affections, while she, despite her good exam results and the fact that she had worked hard to make the most of her appearance, had never got the same sort of attention.

After they had sorted out their belongings, the sisters came downstairs and opened a bottle of wine in the kitchen.

'It's quite classy, this,' said Nora, indicating the oak-fronted units. 'Beats the dives I was used to in London.'

As Frances poured the wine, Aisling took out her chequebook. She had already given Frank a deposit of two hundred pounds and now he was looking for the remainder of the rent.

'I've to pay him today,' she warned the others. 'I'll have to ask you for two hundred each.'

'He wants it already!' exclaimed Nora. 'Surely we don't pay him until the end of the month?'

'Come on, Nora,' Aisling objected. 'A month in advance is standard practice when you rent a place. It must have been the same in London.'

Nora shrugged her slim shoulders.

'Yeah, well I haven't got it,' she said. 'I've only made a hundred so far at the kissograms, and I blew some of that on these,' she indicated the new shocking-pink leggings she was wearing.

'You really are the end!' Aisling gave her sister a playful smack. Then she grabbed the jacket of her pin-striped trouser suit from the back of the chair. She had taken the morning off work but had promised to be in by noon for an editorial meeting.

'I'll lend it to you, Nora.' Frances took her own chequebook from her bag. Unlike Nora, she wasn't a big spender and in the years she had worked as a nanny had managed to put by some money for a rainy day. She could see there might be a few of them on the horizon with Nora around.

Impulsively, Nora leapt up and kissed Frances. 'You're a pal!' she said, her green eyes sparkling.

'That's how she gets round everyone,' said Aisling with a shrug. 'If you're not careful, Frances, you'll be her mealticket.'

'Oh no,' Nora giggled. 'I intend to find a hunky sugar daddy, just as soon as I can!' She stood up suddenly. 'Can you give me a lift, Ash?'

'Sure, but I'm only going to the studio.'

'That's where I'm going too,' Nora declared, hastily combing out her splendid hair.

'What for?' Aisling was puzzled.

'I'd love to get a part in *Southsiders*, and you know what they say – there's no time like the present.'

'But don't you need your agent to handle all that for you?' asked Aisling. 'I mean, won't you have to audition . . . ?'

Nora waved these objections aside.

'My agent never me got me anything,' she said.

'There's nothing like just showing up yourself in person. That's how I got the job in *Docklands*. And didn't you say you know the executive producer?'

Aisling said nothing. She was concerned that Nora would be disappointed if she thought she could just walk into an acting role because her sister happened to work in Channel 3 – and not even in the Drama Department. She half wished she hadn't mentioned in passing to Nora that she had once worked with Jane McGrath, now the executive producer of *Southsiders*.

'If you were to put in a word for me . . .' pleaded Nora, wearing her most beguiling look. 'She should, shouldn't she?' Nora appealed to Frances.

'Don't involve me in this one!' Frances was drying the glasses and putting them back in the press. She was in a hurry herself. Patrick had given her a few hours off to move in but she had promised to be back as soon as she could.

'Look, love,' Aisling warned. 'She's not going to cast you just because you're my sister. Of course I'll introduce you, but don't build up your hopes . . .'

'An introduction's all I want,' Nora interrupted with a confident wave of her hand. 'Leave the rest to me!'

When Aisling had finished her meeting, she went straight to the canteen, where Nora was tucking into a large plate of fish and chips.

'I was starving!' she said, as Aisling slipped into the seat opposite her. 'I couldn't survive on that rabbit food you eat!' She indicated the salad that

Aisling had ordered for her lunch.

The chat-show host Joe Moore passed by and Nora waved at him as though he were an old friend. Joe Moore smiled back at her.

'I'm going to love working here,' said Nora, with enthusiasm. 'All these celebrities. Isn't that Mary Black over there? She must be in for a recording.'

Aisling glanced round. 'Yes, it is, but Nora . . .'

'And the *Southside* cast are at the window table,' Nora continued. 'Who knows? I might be sitting with them soon.'

'Slow down, Nora,' Aisling advised. 'I don't like to throw cold water, but you haven't actually got a part yet.'

'But you did speak to Jane?'

Aisling nodded.

'She'll be here in minute. She's just finishing some . . .'

Aisling broke off. Over Nora's shoulder, she had spotted Michael Whelan enter the canteen. To her surprise, she felt her heart beat faster and rebuked herself for feeling like a teenager. Nonetheless, she couldn't keep her eyes off him as he carried a tray to a nearby table.

'She's finishing what?' Nora demanded.

'Some editing,' said Aisling, watching as Michael Whelan was joined by another man, whom she recognised as Noel Kelly, a floor manager who worked occasionally on *Ireland Today*.

'It would be so great to get work on *Southsiders*,' Nora was saying, 'because it will be something permanent. Like I thought *Docklands* was going to be.'

'Well just don't count your chickens,' Aisling tore her eyes away from Michael Whelan and looked directly at Nora. She felt very protective towards her sister, who suddenly seemed like a hopeless innocent in a world inhabited by sharks. 'All Jane said was that she'd talk to you. She knows you from *Docklands*, but if there is a part going, you'll still have to do an audition.'

Nora nodded. 'Of course. I'd expect that.'

'Here she is now,' said Aisling, noticing Jane McGrath's imposing figure approaching the table. Jane was a tall, glamorous blonde who resembled, Aisling thought, a somewhat ageing supermodel. She was wearing a dusty pink trouser suit and her hair hung in perfect curls around her carefully made-up face. She looked as though she'd just stepped from the pages of a glossy magazine. But anyone foolish enough to equate her appearance with a lack of intelligence was quickly put in their place. Jane was a shrewd operator, as any woman would need to be who had risen through the ranks to the position of executive producer of the station's most popular soap.

'Pleased to meet you, Nora.' Jane gripped Nora's thin hand in hers. Aisling observed that Nora looked a little intimidated, and felt sorry for her.

'I'll leave you two to it,' she said, getting up from the table. 'I'll see you back home later, Nora. Good luck.'

Aisling gave her sister an affectionate pat on the back as she left.

''Bye.' Nora gave an absent-minded wave as

Aisling grabbed her jacket from the back of the chair and made her way across the canteen to the table where Noel was sitting with Michael Whelan.

'Long time no see, Noel!' Aisling smiled at the floor manager, who was pleased at being approached by Aisling, whom he greatly admired.

'Hi, Aisling. This is Michael Whelan.'

Aisling turned to Michael. He was smiling at her, and she noted his sensuous lips and his calm blue eyes. She reflected that you did not expect a politician's eyes to be calm.

'I saw you on the programme last week.' She wished she could have thought of something more original to say.

'Yes, and I saw your abortion report. I was very impressed.'

'Thank you.' Aisling blushed, thrilled by the compliment. 'So how come you know Noel?'

'We were at school together,' Noel replied. 'We're old buddies.'

'We're sneaking off this afternoon to enjoy a game of golf,' put in Michael.

'Really, Minister!' Aisling chided, 'And you with such a demanding brief! I'm surprised you can find the time!'

'Oh, we politicians are all the same. Once we get elected, we start living the high life!'

Noel stood up from the table. 'Don't mind him, Aisling. He works harder than anyone I know.'

'It's my first game of golf this year,' Michael admitted. 'This guy will wipe me off the course.'

'Excuse me a minute, will you?' said Noel. 'Nature calls.'

Left on her own with Michael, Aisling was suddenly nervous.

'Well, I'd better be off . . .' she put out her hand. His handshake was cool but firm.

'Perhaps we could have a drink together some time?' he asked. 'I'd like to hear your views on women's topics generally.'

'I'd love to, but surely women aren't your primary concern? I mean, there is a minister in charge of women's affairs!'

'Damn! You've caught me out! And there was I thinking it was the perfect chat-up line.'

They smiled at each other, an electrical charge of animal attraction flowing between them. Aisling hastily reminded herself that the minister was a married man. Nonetheless, she took a card from her wallet and gave it to him.

'You'll hear from me,' he promised, and she knew that she would.

SEVEN

Frances stood in Patrick Comerford's kitchen with Aoife in her arms, looking out the long Georgian window. The morning spring sunshine was warm on her face. Little Mark stood beside her, holding her hand. Outside in the untidy garden Patrick, on his way to his studio to start the day's work, looked up and waved at the children and their nanny. Frances glowed with pleasure.

She watched Patrick until the door to the studio closed behind him. If she were lucky, he might come up to the house at lunchtime. She knew that if he hadn't appeared by two o'clock, Mary would bring him soup and sandwiches. One of these days Frances was going to insist that she save the housekeeper the trouble and take them out to him herself. But she would wait until the time seemed right.

Frances had been working for Patrick for the past two weeks. She had never been so happy. Every morning she arrived earlier than necessary for work – usually at about seven forty-five. Letting herself into the still sleeping house, she put on coffee for breakfast and, going upstairs to the nursery, fetched the placid, smiling baby, who held out chubby arms to be picked up. Mark was usually awake too, sitting up in bed looking at his picture books. He was such a quiet child. Last week, she had been dismayed to find him quietly weeping as he lay in bed. On his pillow, beside his wet cheeks, was the small photograph of his mother that was usually on his bedside table. Frances had knelt by the side of the bed and had gently put her hand in his. For some time they had stayed like that and then, suddenly, Mark had flung his arms about her and sobbed uncontrollably. She had said nothing – just held him tight and let him cry. At one point Patrick had opened the door. They had exchanged glances and Patrick left quietly. Later, over breakfast, when Mark had gone to fetch his schoolbag, he whispered to her, 'I was relieved to see Mark cry like that. He bottles things up too much.'

Since then Mark and she had grown closer and closer. Frances knew she could never take the place of his mother but she was really glad that he seemed to be so fond of her.

Now she got down on her hunkers and smiled into his solemn little face.

'Time we fetched Tigger and took him to school.'

Tigger was Mark's cuddly toy that went everywhere with him. Sometimes he announced that Tigger did not want to go to school because he had a pain in his tummy. Frances always knew how to persuade Tigger (and, more importantly, Mark) that school would be exciting and that she would be there waiting for Tigger, and for Mark, before the classroom door opened at one o'clock.

Happily, Mark took her hand and they went upstairs.

'Tigger wants this and this and this.' Mark was putting wooden farm animals and a tractor in his bag. Frances didn't worry. Mark's teacher was very understanding.

'Leave room for your lunch, Mark!'

'And for a chocolate bikkie for Tigger . . . please.'

Frances laughed. 'Just this once.' She preferred to keep biscuits and sweets for treats but she was in such good humour today that she couldn't say no to anything. Patrick had asked her to stay overnight to babysit. He had received an unexpected invitation to dinner with an American art dealer who happened to be in town. He had explained this on the phone last night when he rang her at home. 'I hope it'll be OK. I know it's short notice. And I'd like you to stay overnight. I might be late so it would be better . . . '

When Frances had gone back into the kitchen Nora, looking saucy in her French Maid's outfit, had immediately noticed her pleased expression. 'Who was that on the phone, Miss Cheshire Cat?'

Frances tried to sound casual. 'Just Patrick – he wants me to babysit tomorrow.' She picked up the coffee pot. 'I'll be staying the night.'

'Lucky you! Want a loan of something sexy?' Nora lifted her tiny skirt, displaying black suspenders. 'Would these turn a smouldering artist on?'

Frances laughed. There was never a dull moment with Nora around.

'Shut up, Nora.' Aisling looked up from a typed piece-to-camera she was attempting to memorise.

'I'm trying to get the gist of this.'

There was a ring at the doorbell. Grabbing her coat from where she had thrown it on the chair, Nora flung it over her shoulders.

'That's the taxi. I'm off. Have a great time tomorrow, Frances, and give him one from me!'

Nora winked at Frances. When the front door slammed after her, Aisling looked up again.

'How Nora thinks she'll pay you back for the rent, I don't know. She spends a fortune on taxis. If she doesn't get a part on *Southsiders*, she's going to be badly in debt. We should talk to her. What do you think, Fran?'

'Mmmm,' said Frances, but she was hardly listening. She was too busy thinking about the next day.

When she had left Mark at the playschool, Frances walked back slowly along the seafront. The tide was full and sunshine glistened on the white-tipped waves. She stood for a few moments watching the gulls swooping for fish. She didn't have to rush because the baby was safe with Mary who adored her. Anyone would adore Aoife. She was such a sunny-natured child. But Mark was the interesting one. With his blond hair and perfect features, he looked like the photo of his young mother but Frances believed his sensitive nature was a reflection of his father's artistic temperament. She felt a strong bond with Mark.

The day passed slowly. Patrick did not appear at lunchtime. It was early evening before she saw him again.

He came into the kitchen, dressed more formally than usual in a pale linen jacket and trousers. He carried a bow-tie in his hand and looked at her ruefully.

'Are you any good with these things?' He made a helpless gesture. 'I feel I'd better wear it, since we're going to Patrick Guilbaud's.'

'Come to the mirror,' she said lightly, although she felt her voice tremble. 'I can do it for you.'

Standing behind him, she struggled with the tie. She felt the hair of his dark beard against her skin and experienced a pang of desire. 'That's fine.' He looked at the result in the mirror. 'Thanks a million.' He turned towards her and his dark eyes were soft. 'What would we do without you?'

'Daddy . . . ' Mark was at the table, with his crayons and colouring books. ' . . . look at my painting.' He pointed to a group of colourful green and yellow penguins on a bright pink ice floe.

Patrick moved across and sat down to examine his son's work. That was one of the things Frances loved about him. He took children seriously and did not talk down to them.

'Very good, Mark.' He patted his shoulder. 'Tomorrow you can draw in something of your own in the corner – maybe a polar bear.' He winked at Frances. It was past Mark's bedtime.

When he had gone, Frances put Mark to bed, checked on the baby and settled down to watch television. She had looked in the paper and was pleased to see that there was a late night film on BBC 2. That meant she could still be up when Patrick got back.

It was two fifteen when she heard his key in the lock. She was lying on the comfortable Mexican sofa trying to stop herself from falling asleep. The film was almost over. She sat up quickly and smoothed her hair.

The door opened and Patrick came in.

'You're still up.' His voice was slightly slurred but he looked happy and relaxed. His bow-tie had been removed and his dark linen shirt was open at the top. She could see the darkness of the hair on his chest. It made her feel uncomfortable and she tried desperately to think of something to say.

'Where's your tie?' She blurted out.

'Voilà!' He pulled it out of his pocket and tossed it across the room.

'Sit down, sit down.' He waved his hand at her, as she went to stand up. 'Have a drink – no, better still, let's open a bottle of champagne.'

Frances looked at him in surprise. He was definitely squiffy. He looked a little abashed, like a small boy. At that moment, she could see Mark in him and her heart melted.

'Don't move.' He pointed a finger at her. 'I've got a bottle in the fridge. Always keep one – just in case.'

'I'll come with you,' she said.

They sat down at the kitchen table, the low lamp overhead casting shadows. Frances had never seen Patrick look so handsome – his face seemed almost Italian in the soft light. He had opened the Dom Perignon expertly and, with a flourish, had overfilled the two flutes that she had fetched from the high shelf of the kitchen press.

Froth fell on to the dark wooden table.

'Leave it, leave it,' he said impatiently as Frances got up to fetch a cloth.

As she sat back in her chair, he raised his glass. 'Here's to American dollars!' He clinked his glass against hers. 'I've just been offered my own show – a retrospective in New York in October.'

Frances lifted her glass. She struggled to hide her disappointment. For one mad moment, when he had suggested champagne, she had thought it was because he was so happy to see her. She smiled at her foolishness. Still, it was terrific news about the exhibition and she felt lucky to be here to share his excitement. 'That's wonderful, Patrick.' She raised her glass. 'To you.'

'October will be lovely in New York. The fall is really special there. I'd love to take Mark with me.' He looked at her, his eyes shining. 'Maybe I will . . . maybe you could come to mind him.' Frances did not dare to think he was serious. Standing up, he moved around to her side of the table and, taking her gently by her hands, drew her to her feet.

'My luck has changed since you arrived. Thank you.' He was standing very close to her. Frances's heart was pounding. He put an arm around her and, leaning forward, planted a gentle kiss upon her forehead. She moved closer and put her arms around him. He paused for a second and then his lips found hers. Almost immediately he began to draw back but Frances tightened her arms about him and kissed him passionately for several moments. Suddenly he pulled away from her. 'We shouldn't do this.'

'It's all right.' She understood his reticence, given his loyalty to his wife. She took his hand. 'Really, don't worry, please.'

Gently he took his hand away.

'I think perhaps we should talk about this some other time.' Patrick was confused and guilty. He didn't know what had come over him and why he had allowed Frances to prolong the kiss. Since she had come to work for him, he had never thought of her in a sexual light. He didn't even find her particularly attractive, although he was certainly growing fond of her. Somewhat abruptly, he guided her towards the door.

They turned off the lights and went up the stairs. Frances was sleeping in the room opposite the master bedroom.

'Goodnight, Frances.' Patrick quickly closed his door after him and Frances, still in a kind of trance, went into the guest room.

She lay down on the single bed, not wanting to break the spell of memory with the routine chores of undressing, washing and brushing teeth. She was suffused with a sexual desire that left no room for caution. Fearful that she might be mad enough to take the few short steps across the corridor to Patrick's bed, she tried to concentrate on something else. She thought with sadness of how David, the serious love of her life, would feel if he knew how she ached for Patrick's body. Suddenly she felt a cold despair as she remembered how she had longed for David to know her fully as a woman, and how every time he tried she had been too fearful to let him take her. Eventually she had seen his bewilderment turn into a calm acceptance that they would not, as they had planned, spend the rest of their lives together. Her mind went back to the April weekend two years ago when their love affair had finally come to an end.

It had been a fine spring evening when they set out from Dublin, in David's secondhand Peugeot, to drive to Marlfield House in Wexford. Frances was feeling apprehensive. She believed that David was hoping that the romantic setting of a country hotel would help her to forget her fears about sex. She knew he hoped that the sexual disasters of the past had been because they had tried to make love in the small bed in his flat, with sounds of boisterous neighbours echoing through thin walls. Frances prayed that he was right. She could not bear to disappoint him yet again.

Daylight had faded by the time they passed through the elaborate iron gates of the hotel and warm lights glowed through the long windows of the eighteenth-century house. With a crunch of gravel, the car came to a halt in front of a curved glass entrance.

'What do you think, love?'

'David, it's fantastic. As you know, I've been dying to come here for years. You're an absolute pet!'

He put his arm around her shoulders and kissed her gently. 'I hope they give us the four-poster bed I asked for!'

There *was* a four-poster bed, draped in pale green and apricot French chintz to match the rest of the decor in the bedroom overlooking the formal rose garden at the back of the house.

'They've thought of everything. Flowers . . . ' Frances pointed out the vase of long peach roses on the walnut chest-of-drawers, ' . . . and fruit and chocolates.' She turned towards him. 'This must be costing the earth.'

'It's worth it, Frances, to see you look so happy.' He put his arms around her and they kissed passionately. He lifted her on to the bed. At that moment Frances wanted nothing more than to give in completely to the desire sweeping through her body. David began to loosen her clothes. Soon they both lay naked, side by side on the bed. He leaned over and kissed her and then moving down her body he gently caressed her nipples with his lips. Feeling no fear, she sighed with pleasure. Encouraged, David lifted himself on top of her.

Now Frances could hear her heart beating. She felt the familiar tightness in her chest. Her breath would not come. She opened her eyes and closed them quickly to shut out the black shadow and then she pushed wildly against the darkness. 'No, don't, don't, please don't!'

David slid off her and held her in his arms.

'It's all right, Frances.' He tried to sound cheerful. 'That was silly of me. We need to relax with a drink. Let's change and go down for dinner.'

The high arches of the mirror-lined dining-room reflected a multitude of candles. The food was wonderful. Frances ate venison for the first time and loved it.

'That was the best meal I've ever had.' She lifted

a last spoonful of chocolate roulade to her mouth and sighed. 'Beautiful!'

'So are you, Frances. No . . . ' David put a finger to her lips to stop her protest. 'You *are* beautiful, especially in that green dress. I haven't seen it before, have I?'

'No, I went a bit mad, I'm afraid. It's a Donna Karen from BT's.'

'That doesn't mean a thing to me, but it looks fantastic.'

Frances glanced in a mirror. The deep jade colour enriched her brown hair and the soft jersey draped her breasts seductively. She was glad that she'd taken Jean's advice and bought the dress and the pure silk ivory nightdress that lay folded across the satin pillow upstairs.

As if reading her mind, David leaned across.

'Will we forget about coffee?' He gave the mischievous grin that Frances found irresistible.

'Coffee keeps me awake,' she grinned back. 'I'd rather you did that.'

The fear came again at the same time. As soon as David's sexual desire became more urgent and it was inevitable that she should take him into her body, Frances was assailed by darkness. She had no choice but to fight it or cease to breathe.

David moved away from her and lay silently in the darkness. After some time Francis heard measured breathing and knew he was asleep. She lay awake for hours but eventually drifted off. She awoke suddenly. A cold morning light was coming through the window. David had drawn back the curtains and was standing looking out over the gardens. She called his name. She wanted to ask him to come back to bed, to hold her and take away this feeling of emptiness but she could not find the words.

When he turned around, she saw that he had been crying.

'Frances,' he crossed the room and sat at the end of the bed. 'Let's just try to enjoy the rest of the weekend. We can talk about things when we get back to Dublin.' She knew then he had given up on her and that the relationship was over. The next day they drove back in almost total silence. As they were approaching the outskirts of Bray, David spoke at last.

'Perhaps I should take that job with *Médecins sans Frontières* – for a while anyway. What do you think?'

'If that's what you want.' Frances could hear the coldness in her voice. 'You've always wanted to go to Africa.'

He dropped her off at Marlborough Road and they arranged to meet for dinner the following night.

Frances rang Jean the next day and, through her tears, told her about the disastrous weekend.

'I'm seeing him tonight. It'll be for the last time. He'll go to Africa and that'll be the end of everything.'

'For God's sake, Frances, tell him not to go. Tell him you love him.'

'He knows I love him. What good is my love, when I can't . . . ' her voice broke off.

As Frances had anticipated, David left for

[83]

Africa as soon as possible. He sent her a couple of postcards from Ethiopia and then there was silence. During the past two years, apart from the occasional date, usually organised by Jean, Frances had had no man in her life.

Now, lying on the bed in the silence of Patrick's house, Frances hardly dared to hope that she could become truly intimate with the man she had kissed with such fervour tonight, and that whatever had been wrong in her past would be made right by the strength of the overwhelming passion that she felt for him.

EIGHT

Nora sat on the set of Snips, the *Southsiders* hair salon where many of the female characters met to exchange their woes. Several other actresses had been auditioned that day and Nora was the last of the bunch. As she sat waiting for Jane McGrath, who was on a teabreak, she studied the set, taking in where each piece of furniture was positioned and deciding what actions would accompany her words. Not that there was much room for manoeuvre – the scene merely called for her to book an appointment at the reception desk, then take a seat in order to wait for the stylist. As always, Nora was determined to be word-perfect and had sat up until midnight with Frances prompting her as she repeated the dialogue. She felt reasonably confident that she wouldn't dry but the fact that she wanted the part so badly was making her nerves jangle and she hoped that they wouldn't affect her performance.

Eventually, Jane strode on to the set. She was accompanied by a young, female production assistant and by Pat Moynihan, the actor who played Gary, the salon owner. He was to read opposite Nora in the scene.

'Nervous?' Jane asked, taking a script from her large, leather tote bag. She was wearing an impeccably tailored suit and Nora suddenly felt underdressed in her black micro mini and long pink jumper.

'A little.' She wasn't sure if she should admit it. 'But I played a part just like this in *Docklands*. *Femmes fatales* are my speciality!'

'I'll bet they are!' quipped Jane and Nora felt a surge of annoyance. She hated being typecast but if nobody offered her more meaty roles, what could she do about it?

'Ready, Mick?' Jane called to one of the two cameramen. The stage directions specified that Nora should appear sexy so she sashayed into the salon, her hips swaying as she approached Gary.

'She's a natural,' whispered Jane to the production assistant, who nodded her agreement.

'I'd like to make an appointment, please,' Nora said, her voice quivering a little as she found her way into the scene. She was playing Denise, a newcomer to the series and was meant to flirt with Gary while ostensibly booking a trim and asking directions to the street where her married lover lived. It was difficult to get across the essence of a personality in what was a brief and rather blandly written scene, but Nora was hopeful that she would manage it. She stood in a sexy pose at the reception desk and spoke in her huskiest voice, leaving meaningful pauses where she thought they were called for. She would have liked a part that demanded something more of her than sexuality but she gave it her best. Midway through the scene, she stole a glimpse at Jane McGrath but the producer's face gave nothing away.

'That'll do,' Jane declared suddenly, when Nora was in the middle of a line. 'Thanks everyone. See you again tomorrow.'

Pat Moynihan gave Nora a sympathetic smile as he walked off the set. She felt tears prick her eyes. Never in all her professional life had she been interrupted in the middle of an audition. She thought it unfair of Jane not to allow her to complete the scene. Seeing how put out she was, Jane laughed.

'Don't worry, Nora. You did fine.' She rested her hand on Nora's shoulder. Nora supposed it was a sympathetic gesture, but somehow, it made her uneasy. She wanted to brush the hand off but she didn't see how she could, without seeming rude.

'Why don't we go for a drink?' Jane suggested, removing her hand and taking a powder compact from her bag.

'I don't mind.'

'You don't mind,' Jane powdered her nose and applied glossy red lipstick with a brush. 'You should be delighted! I don't invite every actor for a drink.'

Something in her tone alarmed Nora. It wasn't simply that Jane was on some sort of power trip, that was obvious; there was a seductiveness about her that Nora found distasteful. Still, she didn't want to jeopardise her chances. She told herself that there would be no harm in having a drink or two in a local pub, and the fact that Jane had asked her seemed like a good sign. Despite the interrupted audition, it might even mean that she was going to give her the part. Nora longed to ask her out straight but she knew that more auditions were scheduled for the next day and that, even if she were going to cast her, Jane would hardly tell her until she had seen everyone.

They walked across the car park to where Jane's Peugeot GTI was parked.

'Tell you what,' said Jane, opening the passenger door to Nora, 'why don't we go back to my place?'

Nora felt the first stirrings of real alarm.

'Can't we just go to Ashtons or the Goat?'

Jane started up the engine. 'I don't like to drink and drive. You can't be too careful. No, you come back to my place and we'll open a bottle of plonk. Then you can get a taxi home.'

Jane lived in Blackrock in a small end-of-terrace house, the façade of which was covered in climbing ivy. Under different circumstances, Nora would have thought it charming. She told herself that she was being ridiculous and that all Jane wanted was drink and a chat but she couldn't silence the warning bells that rang inside her brain.

'I live alone,' Jane said as they entered a tiny hall with crimson walls and ceiling. 'I'm still waiting to find Miss Right.'

Startled, Nora gave an embarrassed laugh but Jane didn't seem to notice. She had marched into the living-room and was opening a bottle of red wine. She took two glasses from a shelf and filled them.

'Here's to *Southsiders*! I hope you'll be joining us soon.'

Nora took the proffered glass and sat down on a low sofa. To her horror, Jane sat down beside her, ignoring the single chair which Nora had assumed she would take.

'So,' Jane turned and smiled at her, 'tell me about yourself.'

'There's not much to tell.' Nora was feeling more and more uneasy but she tried to quell her rising panic. Just because a woman sat on a sofa beside you didn't mean she was planning an assault.

'Where did you train?'

'Here in Dublin – at the Premier School of Acting.'

'It's got a lousy reputation. You must be naturally gifted. Have you an agent?'

Nora nodded. She had had an agent in London but that wasn't much use to her here. Only the week before she had put herself on Eleanor Turner's books. She was reputed to be one of the best Irish agents.

'Good! I'm sure she'll negotiate an excellent deal for you.' Jane's voice was as smooth as velvet. 'That's assuming I give you the part, which I will do, if you play your cards right.'

She smiled and leaned towards her. Nora felt physically ill. She had nothing against lesbians, it was the naked abuse of power she found disgusting. She stood up abruptly.

'If you're going to give me the part, then give it to me on my merits!' Her green eyes blazed with anger. 'Don't insult me by putting me on your casting couch.'

'I like a woman with spirit.' Jane had stood up too, and was standing beside her. 'But you mustn't jump to conclusions, Nora. I'd like to get to know you better, that's all.'

'Well, that's too much for me,' Nora grabbed her bag from beside the sofa. 'You can keep your part, if that's the way I have to get it.'

'You're being very foolish, Nora.' Jane followed her out to the hall door. 'You're throwing away a fantastic role.'

Nora yanked open the door and almost fell down the front steps to the garden path. She turned and looked at Jane, whose elegant figure was silhouetted in the doorway.

'If that's the way you make your advances, then I'm not surprised you haven't found Miss Right.' She'd lost the part now anyway; she might as well say what she wanted. 'You're nothing but a pathetic dyke! A lipstick lesbian!'

She ran down the terrace and on to Blackrock's main street. Suddenly there were tears in her eyes. Why did she constantly meet people who only wanted to get her into bed? She knew of many actors who'd never suffered any kind of sexual harassment. Was she unconsciously giving off signals to attract them? Was it all her fault? She knew she was being unfair on herself and that she wasn't a tease, but it seemed as though whenever she found a suitable part there was someone waiting to seduce her. How would she ever make it as an actress and keep her integrity? If things went on like this, she'd wouldn't get another role until she was old and wrinkled. The injustice of it made her mad. She knew that tomorrow she'd be back out looking for work but for now she needed to walk off her anger. She took the road to the seafront and set off towards Booterstown.

Aisling moaned with pleasure as Michael expertly caressed her, stroking her clitoris and rousing in her feelings she had never thought she would experience. Her lovers in the past had mostly been young and inept, but she could tell at once from Michael that he knew exactly what a woman wanted and had probably had many mistresses.

'You're so sexy,' he said as he pushed himself into her, gently at first, then with greater urgency as they accelerated towards climax. Aisling had never considered herself sexy; as a child, she had thought herself ugly, and had often been hurt by her father's endless lauding of Nora's good looks. Even now, although she knew she made the most of herself, her self-image was somewhat low. But here was Michael, making her feel like the most desirable woman on earth! She wrapped her legs around him writhed sensually in a wordless frenzy of passion. At last, she felt her body bursting, then melting into his as he held her tight.

'Did the earth move?' he asked with a grin.

She nodded, unable to articulate the feelings he had aroused in her.

'Have some wine,' he said, opening a bottle of Chablis he had placed on the bedside locker. In the force of their passion, they hadn't even taken it out of the ice-bucket.

As Michael poured the wine, Aisling looked

about her. The bedroom was anonymously furnished with a large double bed, above which hung a print of Van Gogh's *Starry Night*. There was a television set in one corner, and a desk littered with Michael's paperwork was positioned beneath the window.

Aisling supposed that this was a typical politician's flat, a functional *pied-à-terre* which Michael used while in Dublin. His constituency and his family home were fifty miles from Dublin. He had told her over drinks in Buswell's Hotel that he owned a two-hundred-acre farm that was looked after by a manager. She learnt that he had five children – four sons aged from nine to fourteen, and a four year old daughter, 'our little afterthought', who was, Michael proudly asserted, the apple of his eye. His wife, Cliodna, was a full-time mother, something which he appreciated, even if she did not provide the intellectual stimulus he craved. He managed to make Aisling feel that she could give him this, as he listened with interest to her account of her own job and the various stories she had covered since working on *Ireland Today.* He laughed at her jokes and asked all the right questions, conveying the impression that she was the most interesting woman he had ever met. When he had suggested that they should go on to eat after their drinks, she had hesitated just long enough for him to guess that she wanted to go to bed with him.

He glanced quickly around the bar to make sure that nobody was in earshot; then turned to her, conspiratorially.

'Maybe we could go back to my place? It's only a stone's-throw away.'

She had nodded her affirmation, aware of the decision she was making. For a moment, he had looked into her eyes, a small smile playing on his lips. Then he had called for the bill.

'Goodnight, Mr Whelan,' their waitress had said with a knowing look as Michael paid her. Aisling wondered how many other women had left this hotel with him *en route* to his flat.

Now, naked beside him, she banished such questions, enjoying the wine and their easy conversation. They were interrupted by the bleep of his mobile phone.

'No, Tom, I hadn't forgotten!' Michael assured the caller, getting out of bed as he spoke. 'I'll be there in fifteen minutes.'

'You have to go?'

Aisling glanced at her watch. It was half-past nine. They had been in the flat just thirty minutes and already he was leaving her. It seemed that her worst suspicions were being confirmed. She was simply a political groupie, one of the many he undoubtedly attracted.

'Afraid so, there's a late-night vote in the house,' he told her, pulling on his trousers and hastily buttoning up his shirt.

'Then I'd better go too,' she said, getting out of bed. She felt suddenly conscious of her nakedness and pulled the sheet around her.

'Oh, no you don't!' he said, playfully pushing her back on to the bed. 'We can take up where we left off when I come back.'

'Well, if you say so!' She felt a surge of delight at knowing that he wanted her to stay.

He kissed her cheek, stroking her hair with one hand. 'That was lovely,' he said gently. 'The best ever.'

She wasn't sure that she believed him but it was what she needed to hear. When the door of the flat had closed behind him, she turned on the television and sat back happily in bed to watch *Ireland Today*. Most of her reports were pre-recorded; so, unlike Carmel, she didn't need to be in the studio at transmission time, although she usually made an effort to get there. She told herself that if the relationship with Michael continued, she'd be seeing a lot less of the studio from now on.

It was after midnight when Nora got home. She had walked all the way to Sandymount before her rage subsided. It had rained heavily and she was soaked to the skin. Her wet clothes clung to her body and her hair hung in limp strands. Exhausted, but more at peace with herself, she had caught the last bus home. When she got there, Frances was still up. Since moving in with Aisling and Nora, she had fallen back into the old mothering ways which she had adopted when they were children and now she was ironing their clothes in the kitchen. She was startled to see Nora, who was dripping puddles onto the kitchen floor.

'Are you OK, love? You look like a drowned rat!'

At Frances's kindness, Nora's feelings exploded like a damburst.

'I lost the part,' she sobbed, throwing herself into her sister's arms. As Frances held her, she sobbed out the whole sorry tale.

'Why does it keep happening?' she asked, as Frances boiled up some hot milk for her. 'Is it something I'm doing?'

'It's not you!' Frances was furious on her sister's behalf. She thought Nora looked like a frightened, hurt little animal. 'You did exactly the right thing.'

Nora sipped the mug of hot milk.

'But if I don't sleep with these producers, maybe I'll never get a part.'

'They can't all be sex maniacs,' Frances said with a smile. 'You mustn't give up, Nora.'

In her heart of hearts, Nora knew that Frances was right. Feeling better, she finished off her mug of milk. Then she changed into her bathrobe and sat with Frances in the living-room while she dried her hair. By then, she was ready for bed.

'Don't let them get to you,' Frances advised, kissing Nora lightly on the forehead outside her bedroom door.

'I won't.'

Despite her exhaustion, it took her some time to fall asleep. She felt violated by Jane's approaches and sick with disappointment at having lost yet another role. She told herself that something would turn up the next day. But what if it didn't? Would she be condemned to a career as a singing telegram? Rebuking herself for entertaining such pessimistic thoughts, Nora finally drifted into unconsciousness.

NINE

The room was dark and smoke-filled. A group of young men in shirt sleeves, some sporting scarlet braces, sat around a large table strewn with empty bottles and glasses. They were clapping slowly in unison. Eyes heavy with drink focused with difficulty on a cleared space in the centre of the table where Nora, dressed as Salome, swayed on scarlet stiletto heels. A chiffon veil barely concealed her full breasts and another encircled her bottom. Across her slim shoulders a mass of black curly hair tumbled and a reflection of this darkness glinted between her smooth thighs. A third veil of deep scarlet covered her face.

'Let's see you, girl!'

'Don't be shy; throw them away!'

A small man in glasses reached across and grabbed her leg.

Nora struggled not to fall. 'Fuck off!' she hissed at him. She was beginning to be irritated. This was getting out of hand. When she'd arrived at the pub a half an hour ago, a man called Charlie Ferguson, who was organising the stag night, had got her in a corner before she went into the private function room at the back.

'This is a special night,' he mumbled, stroking her veils affectionately with nicotine-stained fingers; he was half drunk already. 'We want Johnny to remember it for ever. He's a great guy – Johnny.' He pulled two fifty pound notes out of a wallet and leaned over and whispered confidentially in her ear. 'The poor eejit's marrying a right tight-assed bitch. Give him a last thrill! Take the lot off!'

Nora's first thought was to slap his face. But the sight of the fifty pound notes made her draw back. She hated the idea of stripping, but she needed money badly. Jane had sent her a curt note to say that the part of Denise had gone to someone else. Given what had happened after the audition she had not been surprised but she had almost cried with frustration. She still owed Frances seventy pounds and she'd been scrounging lunches off Fintan for the last week.

'What about it, love?' Charlie tickled her chin with the crisp notes.

She hesitated. If Too Hot To Handle found out, she'd be in trouble. The girls were told not to strip completely. Then she remembered that she also owed Aisling thirty pounds rent. There was really no choice.

She whipped the money out of Charlie's hand. 'Right, but I don't want any mauling, OK?'

'I'll look after you,' he promised. 'You're a sport.'

Now slumped in a chair, a bottle of champagne dangling from his arm, it seemed unlikely that Charlie Ferguson could look after anyone. The 'lads' were banging the table as the piano continued to thump out stripper music. Nora made a gesture to the pianist to soften it up. He shifted into something more subtle and the group of men quietened down a little. She began to remove the top veil very slowly. The room was now hushed.

At that moment, the door opened and a man came in. The room was dimly lit and beneath her veil that covered her face, Nora was only dimly aware of a figure standing at the back of the room.

Then the man moved a little closer to the table. The music faded away as Nora slid the veil down over her hips and her perfect body was revealed in all its beauty. The crowd of drunken louts beat a drum roll of approval on the table with their fists.

'One night with you, my pet, and I'd die happy!' the bridegroom shouted. The others echoed their agreement loudly and incoherently. Nora thought briefly of the wives that were probably waiting at home for them. The men would return randy, demanding sex. And those poor innocent women would fondly imagine that they were the objects of their husbands' passion. But at least the deed was done now and she could leave.

She was about to climb down from the table when one of the men jumped up on to it. 'Show us your face.' He grabbed at Nora's scarlet veil and before she could stop him, had ripped it from her face. She heard a small gasp from the man who had come in late. She turned to where he was standing, and gazed into the brown eyes of Patrick Comerford.

It was Friday morning, the day after the stag night. Patrick was sitting at the kitchen table drinking black coffee and trying to waken himself up; he had spent a sleepless night thinking about Nora.

He thought how ironic it was that he hadn't even wanted to go to the stag. He found bachelor nights pretty infantile; which was why he had arrived late. Only a feeling of obligation to Johnny, an old schoolfriend, had induced him to go at all. Johnny had been very good to him after Deirdre's death.

On entering the room, all his worst fears had seemed to be confirmed. The girl on the table, the drunken men, the booze. It all added up to the kind of sleaze he detested. Then he had looked a little closer at the stripper. As an artist, he had been impressed by her beauty. But as a man, he had felt an overwhelming feeling of lust, strangely combined with tenderness. He could not remember ever having felt such a sudden and powerful emotion. In hindsight, something about her had seemed familiar but he had been deeply shocked at finding that it was Nora Davis. After the lout had removed her veil, he had stood gaping at her like an idiot.

'Patrick! Fancy seeing you here!' she had smiled at him flirtatiously, though perhaps she was just putting on a brave face. He had mumbled something in reply and then she was gone, leaving him in a state that he could barely define. A line of a Keats poem sprang to his mind: 'La Belle Dame sans Merci hath thee in thrall.' He knew that he was utterly obsessed by her, by a desire to possess her that was almost overwhelming.

Patrick had always had a possessive nature, perhaps due to his insecure childhood. He had grown up in a charmingly bohemian but constantly changing environment. Unusually for the times, Sylvia, his mother, was a single parent. She was a screen printer, and Patrick's earliest memory was of her back turned to him as she worked on one of the pieces that provided an unsteady income for herself and her child. They moved from flat to flat, often moonlighting when Sylvia was unable to pay the rent. A likeable but somewhat feckless woman, she assured him of her undying love but he was never certain of it.

When he was eight she had fallen in love with a folk singer who toured the country and he had been left with her sister, an aunt whose rigid authoritarianism was in sharp contrast to Sylvia's more easy-going ways. Every night, Patrick had cried into his pillow, praying to the God he then believed in, for his mother's return. Eventually, some two years later, the love affair had petered out and Sylvia had taken him back, but from that day onwards he had never really trusted women.

He had been fortunate in marrying Deirdre, who had understood and tolerated his insecurity, dissipating his jealous tantrums with her good humour. 'Who'd want me?' she'd say when he accused her of having a lover. 'I snore like a pig!'

Her death had devastated him for here, yet again, was a woman who had left him. But he had forced himself to carry on for his children's sake; ignoring the grief with which he had not yet fully come to terms. The children seemed happier now, thanks to Frances, but there was still an aching void inside Patrick. It seemed to him that Nora could fill that void, that longing, if only he could have her. He stirred the coffee and pondered what his next move would be.

'Looks like you had a good night!' Frances came into the kitchen with Aoife in her arms. Mark trotted in behind her carrying Tigger and his schoolbag.

She went to the kitchen press. 'Would you like an Alka-Seltzer?'

Patrick shook his head. 'No thanks, I'm fine.'

'Can't have been much of a stag night if you haven't got a hangover!'

'I wasn't that late.' He had had little interest in staying after Nora had gone.

He wanted to ask Frances why Nora was working as a stripper but decided against it. He supposed it was just a fill-in while she was looking for a part. Frances had mentioned how hard it was for her sister to find anything in the acting world that provided a reliable income. He thought again of the way Nora had smiled at him from under her dark lashes. He knew one thing for certain: he was determined to see her again soon.

'I suppose they did something childish to the groom?' Frances put Aoife into her baby chair and began to organise Mark's breakfast.

'Not really. It was very quiet.'

Patrick drained his cup of coffee. He didn't want to hang around talking about last night. He had no intention of telling Frances that her sister had been the stripper. He wasn't protecting Nora. It was his own confused feelings he wanted to protect. He was determined to keep Nora to himself, for the moment, anyway. He wished he hadn't got carried away by champagne and elation the other night. Kissing Frances had been a big mistake. She might read too much into it. With a sinking heart he remembered the conversation about the art show in New York and his light-hearted suggestion that she could join him with the children. He had better make sure that such a possibility was never mentioned again. If anyone went to New York with him, he was damned sure it was going to be Nora.

'Did you meet many old friends?'

Patrick stood up. 'Johnny's the only one I keep in touch with.' He picked up *The Irish Times*. 'The rest of them can't talk about anything else but stocks and shares and pension funds. Deadly boring.' He kissed the top of Aoife's head and tickled Mark's tummy. 'So long, kids.'

'You're off early.' He thought he caught a hint of disappointment in her voice.

As he went to the door, a thought struck him. Maybe Frances knew that Nora had been doing a job last night and that she had met him. Well, if that were the case, she probably thought he was being tactful in not mentioning it. Anyway, he couldn't get involved in such complications. He had a commissioned portrait to get finished by next week. 'I've an awful lot to do today,' he said curtly. 'See you later.'

'Shift yourself, Nora!' Frances poked her sister in the ribs. 'You're lying on the *RTE Guide*.'

Nora groaned. It was Friday evening and she was exhausted. She hadn't slept well last night after her striptease in the pub. She remembered the lecherous faces staring up at her, their mouths hanging open in desire. She forced herself to laugh at the situation but she was deeply ashamed. It was all right to play the silly roles of a singing telegram but taking off all your clothes was something else. And then seeing Patrick Comerford had really thrown her. She had covered up her embarrassment by being flirtatious. She shook her head, thinking how awful the whole thing had been.

'What's wrong?' Frances didn't wait for an answer but poked her sister again. 'Get up.'

Nora lifted up her bottom so that Frances could pull out the magazine. She flopped back down with a sigh. She should let Frances know that she'd met her boss. There was always the possibility he'd told her himself, although she imagined he would not have gone into details. There was something about Patrick that suggested he was discreet or even secretive. It was part of the mysterious quality about him that she found attractive. She would quite like to have kept the encounter to herself, but she didn't want Frances to find out some other way and feel put out. If she made light of the episode, then everything would be fine.

'It was some night!' She sat up suddenly. 'Hey! Guess who was there?'

'Who?' Frances was half-listening as she leafed

through the *Guide*. 'Do you want to look at the *Late Late Show?*'

'Your gorgeous boss. I nearly died,' Nora fell back on the sofa in a mock faint. 'He came in just when I'd ripped the last veil off.' She blurted this out in a rush and then felt sorry she had said it. She suspected that Frances wouldn't be happy about the idea of her little sister stripping in public. She wasn't exactly happy about it herself.

Frances's voice was cold. 'What are you saying?'

'Patrick was there – artistic, sensitive Patrick gazing at little ol' naked me!'

Frances's face was rigid with anger. 'You took all your clothes off! Nora, how could you?'

'Don't be so uptight!' She hadn't expected approval but she was shocked by this reaction. She knew that Frances was conservative, but now she was behaving like a reverend mother. Nora became defensive. 'What's the big deal about going naked? I only did it for the . . . '

She broke off, as Frances stormed out of the room.

'Hey,' she shouted after her, 'I've got the seventy pounds I owe you.' The only response was the slamming of the sitting-room door and the sound of Frances's footsteps on the stairs.

Nora picked up the remote control and flipped absentmindedly through the channels. She was puzzled and upset. She had seldom seen Frances so emotional. It increased her own shame over what she had done and made her sorry she had mentioned it at all. In future she'd be a little more careful about what she told her older sister.

Upstairs in her small bedroom Frances tried to calm down. She knew she had no right to be angry with Nora, who was an adult now and could make her own decisions. It wasn't so much the striptease that bothered her. She was upset because Nora had met Patrick. She was so happy in his house that she didn't want any other part of her life to intrude on it. Although she loved Aisling and Nora deeply and had always shared everything with them, just this once, she wanted to have something of her own. Even David had not been totally hers because she had not been able to let him take her sexually. She thought again of her feelings the other night when Patrick had kissed her, and an image flashed across her mind of Nora's beautiful body and Patrick standing, watching. Her heart sank. How could he look at Nora and not desire her?

TEN

Patrick rang Nora the next day while Frances was walking with Aoife in the local park. He knew he was being unnecessarily cautious – he was safely ensconced in the studio which Frances rarely visited – but he wasn't taking any chances. As he dialled the number, he prayed that Nora and not Aisling would answer. Frances had told him that Aisling worked for Channel 3 and he hoped she would be there. After what seemed an age he heard Nora's voice on the other end.

'It's Patrick Comerford.' He was aware that his own voice was trembling.

'Patrick!' she sounded surprised but pleased. 'Hang on till I get a towel. I've just stepped out of the shower.'

Patrick glanced at his watch. It was almost noon and she was showering! He had been right in assuming that she didn't surface too early. He closed his eyes as he imagined her standing by the phone, rivulets of water trickling down between breasts.

'Right,' she said. 'I'm back. Sorry for keeping you.'

'I saw you the other evening.' He paused, fearful that he might come across as a dirty old man. 'That's to say, we had a few words and we met at your father's wedding.' He tried to sound casual but his words seemed to rush out in an idiotic babble. He hadn't felt like this since his teenage years. 'I was hoping we might meet for a drink or something . . . ' Patrick's voice trailed off. This wasn't going to be easy. It had been a long time since he'd approached a woman for a date and he was badly out of practice.

'I'd like that,' Nora said but her voice was cautious. She had fancied Patrick the first time she met him; now she was slightly wary of his invitation. She hoped he didn't think she was some sort of slut. 'I only stripped last night because I needed the money.' She gave an embarrassed laugh. 'And I'm not sure it was worth it.'

'You don't have to explain your reasons. When would you like to meet?'

'I'm free this evening. Is that any good?'

'Terrific. Come around for a meal. About eight?'

'Fine.' Nora had heard how lovely his home was from Frances and was pleased that she was going to see it. 'I'll get the address from Fran.'

'No, don't. Let's keep this between ourselves. It's easier.'

He gave her careful directions. He was standing by the window of his studio, a portable phone in his hand. Through the glass he could see Frances with Aoife beside her, picking herbs from a small bed on the sun-soaked side of the garden. It was time to end the phone call.

'See you at eight then,' he said, pleased that things had gone so well.

'Great!'

Nora hung up and went to get dressed. She was intrigued by his request for silence. Perhaps he wanted to separate his public from his private life, something she could well understand. She didn't like lying to her sisters but she too valued her privacy. If Frances heard about their date, she would be sure to adopt a motherly attitude, and would want to know every minute detail. Besides, Nora was still smarting from Frances's violent reaction to her striptease. From now on, she told herself, she would play her cards close to her chest. It suited her very well to keep Patrick's secret and added a rush of excitement to the prospect of the evening ahead.

Nora lay back on the long low sofa in Patrick's living-room. She was wearing a full-length burnt-orange skirt and a cream silk blouse. Around her waist she had draped a patterned chiffon scarf. Despite the fact that she was almost broke, she hadn't been able to resist a visit to the hair-dresser's that afternoon. Her dark hair shone from the salon's most expensive conditioning treatment and was piled on top of her head in a loose knot. Heavy brass earrings finished off her appearance that, by accident, was in perfect harmony with the Mexican decor of the room. She put down her glass of *crème de menthe* next to a black bowl of white lilies on a carved coffee table, and stretched, catlike, with pleasure. Patrick sat on the floor at her feet, fascinated.

'The cannelloni was scrumptious,' she said. 'Where did you learn to cook like that?'

'I spent some time in Tuscany before I got married. It's impossible to live in Italy and not learn to cook.' He made a Latin gesture with his hands. 'It'd be like not making love.'

'Any Italian men I know leave the kitchen to *mama mia*.' She smiled, seductively. 'I like Irishmen better.' Patrick pulled her down from the sofa and kissed her. As he felt her respond he became more excited. She lay back languidly on the carpet and he moved on top of her. He began to unbutton her blouse, but she took his hand gently away.

'I want to make love to you properly, Patrick, really slowly in a great big bed.' She looked up at him beseechingly.

'I'm sorry, darling.' He sat up and for a moment wondered what he should do. Upstairs in the master bedroom there was a Provençal four-poster. He and Deirdre had bought it four years ago when they had moved into this house. He felt guilty at the idea of taking another woman to that bed. Although he had had a few casual sexual encounters since his wife's death, none of them had been planned. They had always occurred at the end of wild drinking parties abroad. When he was in Ireland, reflections of his wife were everywhere and he couldn't even look at another woman. That was until Nora, sexy and vulnerable in her foolish Salome costume, had looked at him from under her heavy-lidded eyes. Since that moment, he had wanted to possess her.

He stood up and held out his hands to her. 'Let's go upstairs.'

Arms around each other, they walked up the wide staircase. He opened the door of his bedroom. At the sight of the familiar room, he hesitated momentarily. He couldn't bring himself to look at the small painting of his wife that hung on the wall beside the armoire. Then he saw Nora's figure reflected in the carved mirror which hung above the fireplace. Her head was tilted slightly to one side as she admired the room; a cascade of curls had slipped from her loosely arranged hair. He turned towards her and took in his arms. The past was forgotten.

Patrick was surprised to find that Nora was so experienced. She was a confident lover, who was willing to take the initiative in a way that delighted him, yet at the same time left him with a lingering resentment of the lovers she must have had before him. They made love for the first time with a desperate hunger that left little time for foreplay.

Exhausted, they lay in each other's arms with their eyes closed. After some time Patrick felt Nora move to the side of the bed. He opened his eyes.

She was sitting up at the end of the bed, twisting her light chiffon scarf around and around her arms.

'Patrick?'

He knew immediately what she wanted.

He moved over on top of her and lightly tied her wrists to the posters at the foot of the bed. The scarf was long enough to do this easily and he wondered wryly if that was why she had worn it. Pretending to struggle, she moaned with pleasure as he moved down her body and parted her legs, so that he could slowly move his tongue towards the tip of her clitoris.

When she could take no more pleasure, he untied her wrists and lay back on the white linen sheets. She sat on top of him and, putting his penis inside her, moved up and down faster and faster until his hardness began to hurt her and she cried out in pain. Moving her gently to the side he took the top position.

'Is that better, darling?' He asked. 'It doesn't hurt now?'

'It does but I don't care.' She whispered. 'Fuck me please now, now.'

He awoke suddenly. Glancing at the clock, he saw that it was six-thirty. He would have time for an hour's rest. Half-awake, Nora stirred in his arms. 'I should go – what's the time?'

'Don't, please.' Patrick held her tightly. 'I want you here close to me.'

Then he remembered that Frances would be arriving at eight or even earlier. Besides, at any moment, Mark might waken and come in to the bedroom. He wrapped a lock of Nora's hair around his finger.

'On second thoughts, maybe you should go soon. Sometimes Mark makes an early appearance. It wouldn't be a good idea . . . ' He didn't quite know how to put it.

Nora could appreciate that he didn't want his son to find him in bed with a strange woman.

'It's OK. I understand.' She tweaked him under the chin. 'Anyway . . . ' She gave a long stretch. 'I'd like to go home and get some proper sleep. I've a job tonight.'

Patrick's face darkened. 'Please give up that work. I hate the idea of you parading about in front of those jerks.'

'But I told you; I don't usually strip.' Nora wished she hadn't brought up the subject.

'Even so – they'll be mentally undressing you,' Patrick insisted. 'I'd rather you didn't do it.'

Nora felt a slight stirring of alarm. She didn't like the job any more than he did, but nor did she welcome being told what to do.

'Patrick, believe me, I don't relish being a singing telegram. I'd give it up tomorrow, if I could get a part.'

She sat up in bed and the sheets fell away from her smooth shoulders and breasts. Patrick felt aroused by her all over again.

'If you're short of money, I can help out,' he said, kissing her neck.

'I couldn't take your money! I'm an actress, not a kept woman!'

'Look on it as a loan.'

'If only I'd got the part on *Southsiders*,' Nora mused. She had told Patrick about her experience with Jane and he had seemed sympathetic.

'There'll be other parts. This will help tide you over.'

'I just can't take money from you, Patrick. I'd feel terrible.' Nonetheless, she was tempted by his offer. It would be a relief to be able to give up those ridiculous singing telegrams and not to have to worry about paying the rent.

'I'll tell you what. You could sit for me and I'll pay you for that.'

'You mean, as a life model?'

Patrick nodded. 'I've wanted for a long time to do more work in that area,' he lied, 'so you'd be helping me out.'

'In that case, I suppose it's OK ... ' Nora was still doubtful. Seeing her weaken, Patrick jumped out of bed and pulled his cheque book and pen from his jacket pocket. Nora looked away as he wrote the cheque. If Frances and Aisling knew what she was doing, they'd say she was selling herself to a man. She looked at Patrick's lean, muscular body as he sat on the bed and tried to convince herself that she wasn't being bought. He handed her the cheque.

'It's not enormous but it'll pay your rent and bits and pieces for the next few months. Look on it as an advance for modelling sessions.'

Nora glanced at the amount.

'A thousand pounds! Patrick, it's too much.'

'I intend to make you work for it. That will cover at least fifteen sittings,' he assured her, embracing her. 'Hey, I think something's stirring,' he joked.

'Wish I could stay, but, as you said, the kids ...'

'Yeah, the kids.'

Patrick released her reluctantly, and she dressed quickly. She was down the stairs and almost out the door before he had collected his thoughts.

'When will I see you?' he called quietly down the stairwell.

'Call me.'

'Don't forget, not a word to Frances.'

'It's our secret!' she assured him.

'How was the party?' Frances was getting ready for work when she arrived home, shortly after seven.

'Fine.'

'How's Fintan?'

'He's great.'

Nora felt guilty about the lie but it had seemed the best excuse at the time.

'You could have told me you were staying over with him. I was a bit worried about you.'

'I don't have to check in like a kid!' retorted Nora, guilt making her defensive.

Frances was immediately apologetic.

'Don't mind me, love. You know how I fuss.'

'It's OK.' Nora felt even more guilty now. 'Don't let me keep you. You'll be late for work.'

'See you later then. Oh – and don't wake Ash. She was in work till after midnight.'

As Frances left the house, Nora mulled over the events of last night. Patrick was a fantastic lover and she was certainly physically attracted to him but there was an intensity about him which made her uneasy. On top of that there was the question of the thousand pounds. Officially, it was advance payment for the sittings she would do but she was not happy about it. She didn't want to be in any way dependent on Patrick, especially when she recalled how insistent he'd been that she should give up the singing telegrams; he had seemed almost angry. She tried to persuade herself it was a sign he cared for her. After all, she had stripped once and no man would want his girlfriend to be a stripper. His girlfriend! Nora gave a little smile of pleasure. She hoped that that was what she would be soon.

ELEVEN

'You have to come at once.' Frank's tone was urgent. 'She's pissed, Aisling. We're trying to sober her up but I don't think we're going to manage.'

'All right, I'll be there.' Aisling put down the phone. Carmel was too drunk to present *Ireland Today* and Frank wanted her to do it. She felt a pang of sympathy for Carmel, who had really screwed up her career this time but it was her own big chance and her heart was pounding with a mixture of fear and elation. She dashed upstairs and changed out of her jeans and into an elegant sage-green linen dress. Taking a pair of pearl earrings from her jewellery box, she put them on hurriedly.

'I have to front the programme,' she told Frances and Nora as she grabbed her coat. 'I'll see you tomorrow.'

'Meeting someone after the show, are we?' Nora joked. 'You're certainly keeping him a secret. Who is he? The director general?'

'Wouldn't you like to know!' Aisling tried to sound casual. The door shut behind her. She had been Michael's mistress for over a month now and her numerous overnight absences from the house had aroused her sisters' suspicions. They had discussed it between themselves and Nora was convinced it was a married man.

'That's the only good reason for keeping quiet,' Nora told Frances. Then her own secrecy about Patrick crossed her mind and she quickly lightened the conversation. 'Unless he's a bishop,' she giggled, 'but I think that's a bit unlikely!'

Frances laughed and then turned serious. 'I think we should keep out of it for the moment. Ash will tell us when she's good and ready.'

When she arrived at the studios, Aisling saw that it was half past eight – just one hour before the programme began. She headed straight for make-up, where Frank was waiting to brief her. As the make-up artist applied panstick, blusher and lipstick, Aisling listened carefully.

'You've to do the intro,' Frank told her. 'Then there's the Bosnian report, followed by your piece on the travellers. The live interview is with the Minister for Finance on the state of the economy.' He handed her a sheet of questions that Carmel had prepared. 'Think you can manage?'

Aisling nodded, not at all certain that she could. Her make-up finished, she dashed to the library and buried herself in the financial pages of the newspapers. A major computer components company was due for closure owing to a dispute between unions and management; the balance of trade was looking good; unemployment was rising; inflation was lower than it had been for decades. Facts and figures danced in her brain. How was she ever going to assimilate enough of them to do this interview? After what seemed like a few minutes but was actually three-quarters of an hour, she left the library and made her way to the studio. Frank was waiting for her at the door.

'How do I look?' she asked, patting her French pleat nervously.

'You look fine,' Frank assured her. 'Carmel's in here,' he said apologetically, as he opened the studio door. 'She says she won't leave until she's seen you.'

Carmel was slumped behind the presenter's desk as they entered. The bun which she normally wore had come apart and locks of her dark hair hung around her face. Her mascara was smeared under her eyes and thin black streaks trailed down her face.

'You bitch!' She jumped up when she saw Aisling. 'You've been waiting for this, haven't you!'

'Carmel, I'm really sorry.' Aisling closed her eyes in distress at the sight of the distraught woman.

'Carmel, come on now,' Brian, the floor manager, spoke gently. 'Aisling's just doing a job.'

'My job!' said Carmel, staggering towards Aisling. She lurched at her and would have scratched her face had Frank not grabbed her arm from behind.

'Be reasonable,' he said. 'You're pissed and Aisling is standing in for you. She's doing you a favour.'

'Some favour,' slurred Carmel but she allowed Frank to lead her away. 'Some bloody friend you are!'

'You'll feel differently in the morning.' Aisling made a last attempt to pacify her.

Enraged, Carmel turned at the studio door. 'I'll get you for this,' she warned Aisling, 'and that's a promise.'

Still upset by Carmel's reaction, Aisling walked over to the presenter's desk and pinned her microphone to her collar. Then she turned to her notes and read them through hurriedly in the few remaining minutes. Almost immediately her professionalism took over and she began to feel less nervous.

'Ten seconds, Aisling,' Frank told her from the box. 'Ready to go?'

Aisling nodded and gave him a thumbs up. She listened to the fading notes of the signature tune. In a few seconds, her face would be seen on thousands of screens throughout the country. She saw the red light on top of the camera that was trained on her and experienced a brief moment's panic. Then she smiled into the lens, all her fears forgotten as she spoke the words she had dreamt of uttering for so long.

'Good evening and welcome to *Ireland Today*.'

Michael and Aisling sat in the living-room of his flat.

'You were great!' Michael told her, popping open a bottle of champagne. 'I couldn't believe it when I switched on the telly and there you were with my esteemed colleague. You certainly kept him on his toes!'

'I'm sorry for being late but I knew you'd understand.'

'Of course I understand.' He filled the glasses

and raised his in a toast. 'Here's to you, darling.'

'It was sweet of you to buy the champagne,' she said, clinking her glass against his. 'I know how broke you are on a ministerial salary!'

'I'll be in the tuppence halfpenny place, now you're taking over from Carmel. I'm so pleased for you, Aisling.'

'Thanks, but I don't know for sure that I'll be made presenter. Frank has to OK it with the Head of Current Affairs.'

'It's in the bag. They won't want a lush like Carmel fronting a programme like *Ireland Today*.'

Aisling looked at him with gratitude. None of the men she had dated before had ever taken a genuine interest in her career. But Michael was sufficiently successful himself not to be envious of her. She wished with all her heart that he wasn't married and that she could be seen with him in public and introduce him to her sisters. As it was, they rarely met outside this little flat. Michael had to guard his reputation carefully and at the start of their affair had made her promise to keep their relationship a secret. But they had also promised to be honest with each other and she felt it only right to tell him of her sisters' suspicions.

'I think Nora and Frances have sussed that I'm seeing a married man.'

'What?' Michael's tone was suddenly sharp, shattering their intimacy. 'You haven't mentioned my name, I hope.'

'Of course not!' She was hurt that he could even think such a thing. 'But the three of us are usually very open with each other. They find it odd that I don't say who I'm meeting.'

'All the same – you'll have to keep this relationship absolutely to yourself.'

'You know I will,' said Aisling and she noted the look of relief on Michael's face. She understood the need for secrecy but was learning that it wasn't always pleasant being the 'other' woman. 'Only I don't like telling lies.'

Aisling wondered how many other women had told similar lies for Michael's sake. As though reading her thoughts, he leaned across the table and took her hand.

'You think you're just one in a line, don't you?'

'Well, aren't I?'

He hadn't hidden his previous infidelities from her.

'I promise you, Ash. You're special.'

Aisling nodded, wanting to believe him.

'It's the truth, my love. But I can't be seen to cheat on Cliodna. It would ruin my career.'

'Why did you marry her when you didn't love her?'

'You know why.'

Aisling was aware that Michael had married for reasons of political expediency. His career had been all important to him and Cliodna was the daughter of a prominent businessman who was a large contributor to his party's coffers. Their marriage had helped him in his climb to the top.

'I was ambitious. I thought you approved of ambition!'

She felt suddenly angry. Was she doomed to be his guilty secret for years to come, hidden away but never seen? It wasn't the kind of relationship she would have wanted, and yet she loved Michael more than she had ever loved anyone, except maybe her family.

He kissed her passionately, disarming her objections. She could hardly blame him for possessing the same hunger for success that was her own driving force. In a few moments, she was in his arms and he was carrying her into the bedroom. He lay her down on the bed and unzipped her dress, fondling her breasts and kissing the bare flesh of her stomach as the dress slid to the floor.

'I want you,' he murmured and he pushed her gently backwards on to the bed and began to make love to her. She closed her eyes and allowed herself to be drawn into an intensity she had never experienced before. Afterwards Michael pulled her into his arms, cradling her, and they lay close together in an intimate silence.

Some time later, Aisling slid reluctantly from under her lover's encircling arms and sat up.

'Don't move away, darling,' he mumbled sleepily.

'Sorry, love, but I have to check on something in my diary. Now that Carmel is out of action, I'm going to be up to my eyes.' She bent down to pick up her handbag from the floor. Michael ran his finger seductively along her bare back and she wriggled with pleasure.

'Oh don't start that or I'll never get up!' As she turned to smack him playfully, she knocked a large invitation off the bedside table. Made of thick cream parchment, it was bordered by intricate Arabic scrolls.

'Looks interesting.' She picked it up and read, 'Mr and Mrs Michael Whelan are cordially invited to the opening of the Phoenician on Wednesday 27 April at 7.30 pm.'

Michael opened his eyes. 'A friend of mine, who owns a chain of middle eastern restaurants in London, is starting up in Dublin. This one will be Lebanese, with the best chef from Beirut in charge. I'm quite looking forward to it.' He lay back with a contented yawn.

Aisling felt a surge of pain and resentment. It wasn't fair. She shared Michael's bed, his thoughts, his dreams, but when it came to normal everyday living and socialising, his wife was the one by his side.

'I suppose Cliodna is going with you?'

Her voice had an unfamiliar bitter ring which caused Michael to sit up in bed.

'That's how things are, Aisling. You know the score.'

'Yes, I know the score but I don't have to like it.' She turned towards him and tried to soften her words. 'It would mean so much, just for once, to go out with you normally, like other couples do. You can't blame me for wanting that, can you?'

'No darling, I don't blame you at all. I wish things could be different.'

He made a quick decision.

'As it happens, Cliodna won't be in Dublin that evening. She's going to visit her sister in Galway. Maybe I could arrange that you can come with me.

Are you free next Wednesday?'

Aisling's face lit up. 'Michael that would be terrific. And you don't have to worry. I'm incredibly discreet – positively pokerfaced. They'll think I hate you!'

'Don't carry it too far!' he warned. 'That can be a dead giveaway.'

TWELVE

Frances put down the phone, an angry expression on her face.

'Of all the cheek!' she told Aisling, who had just come into the kitchen where Frances was preparing breakfast.

'Who was it?' Aisling put some muesli into a bowl and poured on low fat milk.

'The guy who runs Too Hot To Handle – you know, the people Nora's been working for.'

'At this hour?' Aisling was incredulous. It was only seven fifteen.

'He sounded drunk – like he'd been up all night.' Frances sat down opposite her sister and buttered some toast, 'and he was very abusive about Nora. Called her every name under the sun.'

'I'm glad you didn't get her to the phone, then. The nerve of some people!'

'But the reason he was angry is because apparently she hasn't been in touch with them for nearly a week. She was meant to do a party last night and she never showed up.'

'That is odd,' Aisling agreed. They both knew that Nora had been out of the house for the past few nights, returning only in the early hours of the morning. Aisling felt herself blush. She wondered whether Nora had acquired a married lover too.

'What's she been doing?' Frances wondered aloud. 'If she wasn't at work, where was she? You don't suppose it's a man?'

Before Aisling could reply, Nora came quietly into the kitchen in her dressing-gown. Her eyes were heavy from sleep but she had a glow about her that Aisling felt sure could signify only one thing. In childhood, she and Nora had frequently been in competition with each other, but now she felt suddenly protective of her baby sister. She herself was beginning to realise how difficult life could be with a married lover and she sincerely hoped that Nora hadn't made the mistake of falling in love with one.

Frances and Aisling gazed at Nora quizzically but she was too sleepy to notice. 'The bloody phone woke me,' she said with a yawn. 'I'm going to grab a coffee and take it back to bed.'

'The call was for you,' Frances said. Something about her tone startled Nora out of her somnambulant state.

'Who was it?'

'Too Hot To Handle. They want to know where you've been.' And so do we, she nearly added but she bit her tongue. After all, Nora was a grown woman. What she did with her life was her own business.

Sweeping her long hair out of her eyes, Nora gave an embarrassed laugh, ' Oh, I've finished with them. I was fed up being a glorified striptease artist.'

Her two sisters exchanged worried looks.

'Nora, how are you going to live, if you don't

work?' Aisling's tone was concerned.

'And more to the point, where have you been for the past few nights?' Despite the twinkle in Frances's eyes as she asked the question, she also feared that Nora might be involved with a married man.

Nora turned to put on the kettle. She found it hard to look into her sisters' eyes as she told them a bare-faced lie. 'I was with Fintan and the gang. We've been taking in some plays, doing a bit of partying.'

'Do you think that's wise – given your financial state?' asked Aisling.

Defensively, Nora turned on her, flicking back her hair in the way that was so familiar to her sisters and which always signified anger.

'Just because you're a workaholic, doesn't mean I have to be,' she told Aisling. 'And I don't have to explain my every move – after all you don't,' she added meaningfully, causing Aisling to blush for the second time.

'We're not lecturing you, love,' Frances tried to pour oil on troubled waters. 'We just don't want you getting yourself in debt. After all, this place doesn't come cheap.'

Nora spooned some coffee into a cup and poured on boiling water.

'Well, that's all right, because I went to see Daddy a couple of days ago. He's going to tide me over till I get an acting job.' Nora was shocked at how easily another lie came to her.

'He's given you money?' Aisling was surprised. Whatever their father's virtues, generosity wasn't one of them. 'Maybe Madge is having a good effect on him after all!'

'How is he?' asked Frances. Since his marriage he had all but vanished from their lives. They had phoned several times to invite himself and Madge to see their house but on each occasion she had found some excuse to refuse. She was evidently intent on keeping her husband on a tight rein.

'He's fine.' Nora was beginning to regret what she had said about the loan from her father – it wouldn't be very hard for her sisters to check it out and then she'd have yet another set of questions to answer. She wished she could be honest with them about Patrick and save herself this shameful lying.

'We must ask them over again,' Frances suggested. 'Madge can't keep him to herself forever.'

'I wouldn't do that just now,' said Nora, buttering a thick slab of bread to go with her coffee. 'Madge said something about wanting to be alone with him for a while longer.'

'So love *is* sweeter the second time around,' Frances smiled.

'I'm going back to bed now.' Nora saw an opportunity to escape. She was exhausted after a night of lovemaking with Patrick.

'Will you be home tonight?' Frances asked her.

'I don't know,' Nora shrugged, although she was well aware that Patrick was expecting her at nine. 'It depends what the gang are doing.'

With a sweep of her dressing-gown, she was gone.

'Well,' Frances looked at Aisling, 'do you think she was telling the truth?'

'I'm not sure.' Aisling piled some papers into her briefcase and stood up to leave. 'I need to get in to work early.' She didn't want to discuss the possibility that Nora might be keeping a secret from them. It made her too uncomfortably aware of her own situation.

'I'm sure she was lying,' said Frances. 'I just hope she's not going to land herself in trouble. You know how reckless she can be.'

'Don't worry about it.' Aisling gave Frances a peck on the cheek. 'After all, she's a big girl now.'

'I suppose so,' Frances agreed, but she couldn't help worrying. All through their childhood, she had assumed responsibility for her sisters and the habit was difficult to break. But now she had herself to think about, her own life to lead. With a determined air, she stood up from the table. If she didn't hurry, she'd be late for work and Patrick, Mark and Aoife would be waiting for her.

Patrick and Nora thrashed about in pleasure on the four-poster. The phone rang on the table beside the bed, shattering their passion. 'Ignore it,' said Nora, as Patrick put on an arm to answer it.

'I'd better take it,' he said, 'in case it's something urgent.'

As he placed the receiver to his ear, he was assailed by a hearty male voice speaking in a mid-Atlantic accent.

'Have you ever considered how much heat you

[129]

lose through conventional windows?' the voice asked. Patrick felt like laughing.

'I'm losing heat right now!'

'I'm not with you, sir,' the caller sounded bemused. 'But if you put in double-glazed windows, you could cut your heating bills by . . . '

Patrick slammed down the phone.

'A bloody salesman,' he told Nora, resuming his caresses. 'At this hour of the night!'

'Take it off the hook,' advised Nora. 'We don't want to be interrupted again, do we?' She smiled at him seductively.

Patrick obediently removed the receiver from the cradle and pulled Nora back into his arms. But the call had rattled him and he was on edge. He told himself that there was nothing to be nervous about. It was ten o'clock and Mark and Aoife were safely tucked up in bed. Even so, he was a little wary lest Nora's cries of excitement should rouse Mark, who was a light sleeper. He had never experienced a woman who enjoyed sex as audibly as Nora. She was totally without inhibition and uttered loud groans of pleasure both before and during climax.

'Ssshhh,' he warned, as she let out an especially loud cry.

'Sorry, but you turn me on so much.'

He kissed her open lips in order to silence her. Anxiety had dulled his passion, making him temporarily impotent, but Nora slid down his body to suck his penis and eventually he was fully aroused. He had laid her on her back and was about to enter her when he heard it – the unmistakable sound of footsteps on the stairs.

'My God – there's someone in the house,' he warned. Nora continued writhing in his arms, which had suddenly stiffened with horror. Only one other person had a key to the house. Mary couldn't be trusted to have one since she was always losing keys but he had given one to Frances so that she could come and go without disturbing him when he was in the studio. He could hear the footsteps advancing along the corridor towards Mark's bedroom. What was she doing here at this hour of night?

'It's Frances,' he hissed at Nora, who finally got the message. She sat up straight in bed and, to his horror, started to giggle.

'Be quiet! She'll hear you.'

He was already out of bed, and was throwing on his dressing-gown.

'So what?' Nora whispered. 'Isn't it about time she knew?'

She had told him what had happened that morning and how she disliked lying to Frances about her financial situation.

'I'll be the judge of that.' Patrick left the room and walked along the corridor to Mark's bedroom. As he turned to enter it, he almost bumped into Frances coming out.

'Oh, there you are!' she said. 'I tried to phone, but the line was engaged for ages, so I came around.'

'Yes, I was on a rather long call,' Patrick mumbled.

'I called when I let myself in but you mustn't

have heard me. I thought you might be up here with Mark. I hope I didn't give you a fright,' she added, noting his startled expression.

'No, no,' he assured her, praying that his dressing-gown hid his fast-fading erection. 'I had a migraine. I had to lie down.'

Her face filled with concern and he felt a sudden surge of guilt. There was no doubting the affection, perhaps even love, she felt for him.

'I'm so sorry, Patrick. Why don't you go back to bed? Is there anything you'd like me to bring you?'

'No, nothing. In fact, I feel a little better now. I think I'll go down and have a cup of tea.'

'I'll make it for you.'

They turned back down the corridor and approached his bedroom door. He was terrified that Nora would suddenly appear but they passed safely and made their way downstairs.

'Why did you . . . ?' Nervousness had made him almost inarticulate but fortunately Frances didn't seem to notice.

'I've lost my purse. I only noticed it was missing when I went to my bag for my glasses. I wear them when I'm watching television.'

'Ah.'

'There was rather a lot of money in it so I thought it best to come back and see if I'd left it here. If it's not, I'll have to report it to the gardai.'

'You think someone might have stolen it?'

They were in the kitchen now and Frances was looking on shelves and under the table for the missing purse.

'I hope not. I walked through Dun Laoghaire

shopping centre on my way back from work. I'm afraid someone might have lifted it from my bag.'

'Let's hope it's here then.'

While Patrick sat feigning illness, Frances filled the kettle, then searched the other downstairs rooms for the missing purse. After what seemed to Patrick like an aeon, she returned with it in her hand.

'It was under the sofa in the living-room,' she told him with a smile. 'Aoife must have taken it out of my bag, the little minx.'

Patrick heaved a sigh of relief.

'Well, all's well that ends well,' he told her. 'I'd invite you for tea, but I think I'll take this back up to bed. I feel a bit queasy again.'

'You poor thing,' Frances's voice was full of sympathy. 'I get the odd migraine, myself. They're really horrible.'

'I'm sure I'll be better in the morning,' he said, wishing she'd go.

'If there's anything at all I can do?'

'No, no.' He stood up to see her out to the door. As he did, he saw Frances give him a strange look. Had she guessed something?

'I'll see myself out.' She sounded as cheery as ever. Obviously, guilt was making him jump to conclusions. 'You go back up to bed.'

'Thanks,' he said with a smile. 'See you tomorrow.'

He kissed her gently on the cheek and she was gone. He darted back upstairs to where Nora was waiting impatiently.

'What kept you?' she asked. She had showered

in the *en-suite* bathroom and was dressed and ready to leave.

'Frances left her purse here. It took her a while to find it.'

'Look, Patrick . . . ' Nora wore her most determined expression. 'We can't go on like this. It's one thing hiding the fact that we're having sex from your kids but why can't I tell my own sister about us?'

Patrick hesitated. He didn't like telling Nora that he had kissed Frances. He feared that she'd be angry with him for leading her sister on. He knew the three girls were very close and that Nora wouldn't approve of anyone who hurt Frances. On the other hand it had been only a kiss. It wasn't his fault that Frances was obviously a deeply frustrated woman who had read more into it. Making it seem as casual as he could, he told Nora what had happened.

'I was drunk,' he concluded. 'It didn't mean a thing.'

Nora sat back down on the bed.

'But it meant something to Fran.'

'Yes, it may well have. But there was just the kiss, Nora. Nothing more.'

He neglected to mention that he'd invited Frances to visit the States with him.

'Frances is old-fashioned – a kiss would be significant to her.' Nora's face was filled with a concern that he found very disquieting. He was filled with a sudden dread.

'You're not going to let it make any difference to us? I mean, it's not as if I slept with her! Surely she's been kissed before?'

'Of course she has. She had a boyfriend a couple of years back.'

'Only one?'

'She was just fourteen when Mum died and she took over the running of the house. Dad depended on her so much and she had school to cope with as well. No wonder she'd no time for boyfriends. David was her first but it didn't work out.'

'Why not?'

'She never really told us. One minute they were an item and the next he was off to Africa to work with some aid agency. He's a doctor.'

'I don't want this to affect you and me.' Patrick made a sudden decision. 'If you want to tell her about us, go right ahead.'

Nora's brow furrowed.

'You mean, I can do your dirty work for you!' she said angrily. 'If you want to tell her, then do it yourself.'

'Nora . . . ' Patrick began, but she had marched out of the room and was heading downstairs. He ran after her and caught her in his arms at the hall door.

'Will I see you tomorrow?' he asked, desperately trying to kiss her averted face.

'I suppose so.' She disengaged herself from his arms and was gone.

Frances watched the concluding minutes of *Ireland Today*, but though she admired Aisling's professional presentation, her mind wasn't on the programme. Patrick had a woman – or at any rate, was sleeping with one. How could she have been so stupid as to think that he could care for her?

When he had told her about his migraine she had felt her heart surge with sympathy for him. From her own occasional attacks, she knew how debilitating a migraine could be. She had cursed herself for having disturbed him when he was ill but she'd cashed her monthly wages cheque that afternoon and she simply couldn't afford to lose such an amount of money. Besides, she had welcomed the chance of seeing Patrick at night and had half-hoped that he'd invite her to stay for a drink. But of course, with the migraine that was out of the question.

And then, as he had stood up to see her out, the collar of his dressing gown had moved slightly and she had noticed a lipstick mark on his neck. With a shock of horror, she realised he had been lying to her. He didn't have a migraine at all. He'd been in bed with a woman. Somehow, she had managed to compose herself, bidding him a cheery farewell as she left. But now, sitting alone at home, she acknowledged the pain she was feeling. The casual kiss he had planted on her cheek had made it even worse. How could he treat her with such detached affection, when she loved him so deeply? She reminded herself that, after all, Patrick owed her nothing. They had kissed once, passionately, it was true, but he had been drunk. She shouldn't have read anything into it but she had. And now she was consumed by a feeling of intense jealousy towards the woman who was sharing his bed.

Removing her glasses, she stood up and gazed

into the oval mirror above the mantelpiece, assessing her face critically. Her frank grey eyes seemed to her to be dull and lack-lustre and her fresh complexion, devoid of make-up, made her look plain and uninteresting. Standing back from the mirror she thought about the kind of woman Patrick had made love to: a tall, stately blonde or a voluptuous brunette of the kind she had occasionally seen in his portraits.

She was still in this gloomy frame of mind when Nora arrived home.

'Hi,' said Frances, with a false attempt at brightness.

'The gang was doing nothing,' Nora explained in a rush. 'That's why I'm back earlier than usual.' Something shamefaced about her manner sent a shudder of dread down Frances's spine.

Their eyes met. Nora turned away but in that instant, Frances knew that she had been with Patrick. It all fell into place – Nora's night-time disappearances from the house and the fact that she had given up her job. Why had she not seen it until now? She wanted to cry out in pain but something, pride or perhaps an unwillingness to distress Nora, prevented her.

'I'm going to bed,' Nora was saying. 'I'm whacked.'

'Yes, you must be,' Frances murmured, but she couldn't be certain whether Nora had heard.

As she listened to Nora prepare for bed, she sat numbed, staring at the television screen. After a time, when she judged that Nora was asleep, she began to cry quietly. Her mind was awash with conflicting emotions. Nora was still her little sister and she loved her dearly, but at this moment she almost hated her too, for the ease with which she had obviously enraptured Patrick. It didn't seem fair that the one man she had ever loved, apart from David, had been snapped up by Nora, who would probably discard him as soon as she got tired of him. She was filled with a sense of her own failure; she had neither Nora's beauty nor Aisling's intelligence to help her through life.

Then Frances rebuked herself for being so self-pitying. Maybe Patrick would never love her but at least she loved him and didn't they say it was better to have loved and lost than never to have loved at all? She would continue working for him because in that way she could still be close to him. If he and Nora didn't want to tell her about their relationship – and they obviously didn't – she'd live with that too. And one day, when Nora had tired of him and he had got over his infatuation for her, then maybe, just maybe . . .

Drying her tears, Frances went up to bed.

Nora heard her going into her bedroom. She was not, as Frances had imagined, fast asleep, but was staring, wide-eyed, into the darkness. She wanted to tell Frances about herself and Patrick but fear of hurting her had kept her silent. Patrick was too big a coward to tell her himself, so she guessed the relationship must remain a secret, at least for the time being.

Despite her earlier anger with him, Nora did not want to give Patrick up. There was little enough in her life right now and at least Patrick offered a kind of stability. Having seen evidence of Patrick's possessiveness, she guessed it would probably be a problem in the future. She couldn't see them together on a permanent basis, but for now, she was happy to be his girlfriend.

If only Frances weren't involved! Nora desired Patrick physically but she didn't love him as Frances probably did, and this knowledge made her feel guilty. Frances had always looked after her and now she was rewarding her by grabbing the one man she wanted. But perhaps the relationship would just fizzle out eventually, in which case Frances need never know about it. With this consoling thought in her head, Nora eventually drifted off to sleep.

THIRTEEN

'What's the matter, Nora?'

Frances ran quickly up the stairs in response to her sister's scream. Despite her feelings of jealousy about Patrick and Nora, all her protective instincts came to the fore. She opened the bathroom door in panic and then began to laugh. Nora was sitting on a stool trying vainly to peel a thick layer of wax from one long elegant leg.

'Oh shit!' she moaned, looking up pathetically at Frances. 'Poverty is hell. It doesn't hurt like this in the beauty salon.'

'Take it easy.' Frances knelt down to inspect the situation. 'Close your eyes and I'll give one quick tug.' Without waiting for agreement, she took a deep breath and, ignoring Nora's screams, whipped off the layer of wax. 'Now give me the other leg.'

'What's going on?' Aisling, who had just arrived home from work, poked her head round the door. 'Uggh! Revolting! Finish that off and come downstairs for a drink. I've got something to celebrate.'

A few minutes later in the sitting room, Nora, still moaning, gratefully accepted a glass of champagne.

'Just what I need! What's it in aid of, Ash?'

Aisling lifted the bottle to fill her own glass. 'You're looking at the new presenter of *Ireland Today*. They told me this afternoon.'

'Fantastic, Aisling!' Frances put down her champagne and went over to hug her sister. 'Nobody deserves it more.'

'Yeah . . . ' Aisling sounded rueful. 'but I don't feel great about Carmel losing her job.'

'That's showbiz,' Nora waved her hand dismissively. 'She couldn't hack it . . . '

'She was the best till she started boozing,' Aisling interrupted. 'I believe she's gone into St Pat's to dry out.'

'The demon drink!' Nora gulped down the contents of her glass. 'Fill this up again.'

Aisling handed her the bottle. 'Finish it between you. I've got to fly. I need to change and be back in town by seven.'

'Anything interesting?' Nora was all ears. She and Frances were still curious about Aisling's 'secret lover', although, since the episode in Patrick's house a few nights ago, they had not discussed anything that might slide into the dangerous area of romantic intrigue.

'Oh it's just a restaurant opening that some of us from Channel 3 were asked to.' Aisling felt it was best to stick as close to the truth as possible. 'I must dash.'

She ran upstairs, had a quick shower and sprayed herself with Opium. Then she took her best black dress from the wardrobe. She had invested almost a month's pay in the beautifully cut black Italian sheath from Private Collection. It fitted her perfectly and, with its high neck and very low-cut back, was seductive without being too obviously sexy.

Glancing at her watch she grabbed her small suede handbag. She was due to meet Michael before they went to the restaurant and was looking forward to his delight when she gave him the good news about her appointment. She had wanted to tell him as soon as she heard, but he had been in the Dáil all afternoon. Well, it would be even better to tell him in person. This was going to be a special night; there was so much to be happy about. Giving a final glance at herself in the hall mirror, she went into the sitting-room to say goodbye.

Nora looked at her in admiration. 'You look fantastic! Bet you get your picture in the papers.'

'You probably will, Ash,' Frances said, 'once it's out that you've taken over *Ireland Today*.'

Aisling was startled. She felt sure that Michael wouldn't want photos taken at the Phoenician. But the news wasn't general yet, so perhaps they'd be safe.

'Don't worry if I'm not home tonight. If I have a few drinks, I'll stay with Denise.' Denise was a colleague in Channel 3 that her sisters had never met, so there was no fear of exposure. 'Mind you,' she lied pointlessly, 'it may be so boring that I'll be back before midnight.'

Aisling met Michael in a scruffy bar within walking distance of the Phoenician, where, to the surprise of the barman, who was generally asked for nothing more exotic than a sweet sherry, he ordered champagne to celebrate her new appointment.

'I'm not at all surprised you got the job.' He lifted his glass. 'You were the perfect choice.'

They talked about her plans for *Ireland Today*. She hoped to include more foreign reports and to alter the programme's format slightly to give more in-depth coverage to their main story. Michael agreed with her ideas and made various suggestions of his own. They chatted for so long that by the time they arrived at the restaurant it was after eight, and the guests, about fifty in number, were just about to sit down to eat.

The Phoenician was in a converted mews off Baggot Street. It had been lavishly furnished in Eastern style. The impression created was of the private chambers of an Arab potentate. The old stone walls were covered in tapestries and crimson drapes and the brilliant turquoise tablewear contrasted with the simplicity of starched white cloths and silver vases of cream tulips. Hundreds of candles provided a soft and flattering light.

Michael's friend Willie called them over to his table where he had kept two seats. Michael introduced Aisling as someone he knew from Channel 3 and there were murmurs of recognition and polite platitudes from the group at the table about how much they enjoyed *Ireland Today*.

'Aisling is interested in middle eastern cookery,' Michael explained to Willie, 'and since Cliodna is away, it seemed a good idea to bring her along.'

'I hope you don't mind . . . ' Aisling began.

'Not at all. I'm delighted. I wouldn't want

Michael to be all alone.' He gave Michael a shrewd glance and looked at Aisling in open admiration.

The Lebanese waiter placed a menu in front of her.

'I'm not too sure what *mihshi kousa b'lubban* is . . . ' she began. She paused, conscious that she had made a gaffe. Here she was, displaying her ignorance after Michael's pronouncement on her imaginary culinary interests! Fortunately, nobody but the waiter appeared to be listening.

'It's stuffed courgettes with yoghurt sauce,' he explained smoothly. 'Absolutely delicious, madam.'

'Sounds good. I'll have that.'

'Perhaps baked sea-bass to follow?'

'Fine.'

Aisling sat back and watched as the others at the table ordered. Apart from Michael, Willie and his attractive young wife, there were two couples connected with the restaurant business and a good-looking man on his own. Willie introduced him as Hugh Jameson, a solicitor.

She felt relaxed and happy. Perhaps this was just the beginning of a difference in her relationship with Michael. She could feel the pressure of his thigh against hers and she thought with pleasure of the night ahead.

Hugh smiled across the table at her and began to discuss her choice of food. She realised with surprise that he found her attractive and she noted with pleasure that Michael was not too happy about this. He smoothly interrupted their conversations and touched her shoulder from time to time in a gesture that was almost proprietorial.

She had finished her courgettes when the evening began to fall apart.

'Willie, I hope I'm not going to mess up the party.' The woman's voice was strong and clearly heard over the polite murmuring at the tables.

Willie stood up and hurried across the room.

'Cliodna! I'm delighted you could make it after all!' He kissed her warmly. 'Come and sit beside your husband. We'll organise another setting.'

Aisling could just hear Michael mutter 'Christ' under his breath. She looked up and saw a tall, elegantly dressed, rather attractive middle-aged woman smiling down at them.

'Surprised, Michael? At the last minute I decided to wait and go to Galway tomorrow morning. Kate rang and said the weather was dreadful in the west. I didn't fancy driving into it. Then I remembered Willie's invitation. Sorry I'm late.'

A chair was provided and she sat down on the other side of Michael. Everyone moved a little closer and Michael leaned towards Cliodna so as to create a gap between himself and Aisling. Noticing this, Aisling felt a wave of helpless anger. He must have told Cliodna about the invitation. Maybe he wasn't even surprised that she had come. It must be some ego trip, she though bitterly, to have your wife and mistress at the same table.

'I don't think you know Hugh Jameson,' Michael indicated the young man opposite Aisling, 'and this is Aisling Davis. You probably recognise her from TV.'

Cliodna smiled pleasantly at the two of them and Aisling got a strong impression that Michael was hoping that his wife would assume she was with Hugh. She felt a mixture of embarrassment, anger and distress. She wished the floor would open and swallow her or, better still, swallow Michael's surprisingly elegant and confident wife. Where was the homely matron and mother that Michael portrayed when he spoke of her? Cliodna was tall, not particularly slim but certainly not fat. Her clothes were well-cut and carefully chosen and her faded blonde hair was beautifully groomed. She put her hand on Michael's arm. Aisling looked away but she could hear the intimate tone of her voice.

'Mike, why don't we stay in the flat tonight? You leave your car here. I can drive and I'll drop you back to pick it up in the morning on my way to Galway. OK?'

Michael mumbled something that sounded like agreement and Aisling felt that she was going to be sick. She knew it was stupid of her but she had never thought for a moment that his wife ever visited the flat.

'I really liked that report you did – just before Christmas, I think – on loan sharks.' Hugh leaned across the table to Aisling. 'It was a subject well worth airing and it was great television.'

'I'm glad you enjoyed it.' Aisling knew her only hope of surviving this nightmare was to take advantage of Hugh's obvious interest in her. He began to discuss his holiday plans for a trip to Vietnam and she struggled to concentrate on his conversation.

'I believe they're putting a lot of effort into developing tourism, so I'd like to go there before they ruin the place!' Hugh refilled Aisling's glass.

'I shouldn't,' she protested. 'I'm driving.'

'Have you far to go?'

When Hugh heard where she lived, he suggested that, since he was going in the same direction, they could share a taxi. Their cars would be safe overnight in the restaurant's car park. Aisling was relieved. With a bit of luck she could leave shortly with Hugh, and the agony of sitting opposite Michael and his wife would come to an end.

'Would you like cream in your coffee?' Cliodna leaned across Michael to talk to Aisling. 'I can't touch it. I've a desperate problem with weight.'

Aisling mumbled how lucky Cliodna was to be tall since tall people always looked well.

'You do a great job on *Ireland Today*. I envy the way you can handle people, especially politicians when they're trying to avoid the issue.' She laughed and squeezed Michael's hand affectionately. 'I hope you never have to interview Michael. He's a very difficult man to pin down.'

'I think Aisling would be well able for me.' Michael appeared more relaxed now. He was probably pleased that Hugh Jameson was there to camouflage the situation. Aisling was furious with him. His coolness was concrete evidence of practised adultery.

She looked across at Hugh. 'Would you mind awfully if we left a little early? I've a lot to do tomorrow.'

He seemed delighted and Aisling felt a pang of

anxiety. He probably thought it was a come-on. Never mind, she'd use pressure of work as an excuse to avoid any unwanted intimacy. She didn't want to hurt his feelings; he was a nice guy and very attractive. It was bad timing that he should turn up in her life a bit too late, because a few weeks ago she would have been very interested.

They both stood up. Aisling gave Cliodna a firm handshake and brushed her fingers against Michael's hand with an icy touch.

'Maybe we'll meet again some time,' Cliodna murmured politely.

'I hope so,' echoed Aisling, praying that hell would freeze over before that happened.

Hugh seemed disappointed when she insisted he leave her straight home. He took her telephone number and promised to ring. She half-hoped he would because although the only person she desired was that bastard, Michael Whelan, she was praying for the strength to give him up.

She closed the front door. It was only just after midnight and Frances and Nora were still up, looking at a late night film. She wanted to go to bed and cry, but she knew her sisters would think it odd if she didn't say goodnight, so she stuck her head around the sitting-room door.

'I'm off to bed,' she said brightly.

'Was it a good evening?' Frances asked, turning around.

'Any nice men?' Nora didn't look away from the screen.

'Yes and no,' said Aisling. 'Goodnight'. She closed the door. As she passed the phone on the hall table, she had a wild urge to ring the flat and scream abuse at Michael. She picked it up and began to dial. If Michael were still in the restaurant, she would leave her message on the answering machine.

She put down the receiver before she finished dialling. She wasn't going to descend to that level. Tomorrow she would ring him and bring the affair to an end.

Sitting at her desk in the next morning, Aisling looked stressed and tired. She had hardly slept. Scenes from the previous night had flashed endlessly across her mind. She felt a fool; she had been used by a man who wanted everything – money, power, status and women.

She reached for the phone and dialled Michael's private number in Leinster House. After what seemed like an age, his secretary put her through. Hearing his voice, she took a deep breath.

'Michael?'

'Aisling, how are you?' He sounded full of concern. 'I'm so sorry about last night. It was lousy luck. It won't happen again.'

'No, it won't, Michael. I don't want to see you again. I can't cope with it.' Her voice broke. 'Let's just forget we ever met.'

For a moment there was silence and then Michael began to entreat her. 'Please, Aisling, we can't finish like this. Not on the phone. Meet me. We'll talk.'

For some time Aisling resisted his pleas but eventually she gave in.

'OK. I'll see you this evening but not in the flat.'

He agreed to meet her in the small dark pub where they had been the previous night because it was unlikely that anyone he knew would be in such a place.

By the time she arrived, he had already had two whiskeys.

'I'm sorry I'm late,' she said coldly and sat opposite him. He leaned across and tried to take her hand.

She pulled away. 'It's no use. This has to end. I can't be just a bit on the side.'

'You know you're not that, Aisling, but I can't break up my marriage for you.'

'I'm not asking you to,' she answered quickly, trying unsuccessfully to hold back her tears. 'But I don't want to hide away like a criminal and then the one time we appear in public, look what happens! It's unbearable.'

'That was unforeseeable, but it won't happen again.'

'Because you won't produce me in public again, unless you can pretend I'm with someone else! Otherwise you'll bring me to some awful hole like this where you feel nobody knows you.' The barman put a glass of wine in front of her, and looked at her tear-stained face with blatant curiosity.

For a while Michael was thoughtful, then he leaned across and took her hand. This time she made only a half-hearted attempt to resist.

'It *is* hard on you, Aisling. I realise that. Maybe we can find a way to be together for a while, away from all this.' He looked at her with such passion and intensity that she felt her resolve melt away.

'How?' she asked, hating herself for giving in so easily.

'I thought perhaps we could have a weekend away. Somewhere special, like Amsterdam. What do you think?'

Aisling made a last attempt to resist him. 'A weekend! Fine, and then we come back and everything is as bad as ever again. Except that we'll have nowhere to go, because I'm not setting foot in your flat again. I never thought about your wife being there. How stupid of me! Of course, she'd be there.'

'Hardly ever,' Michael tried to hold on to her hand but she pulled it away. 'And I swear I've never made love with her there. We've been in the same bed . . .

'Like last night . . . '

'But nothing happened, Aisling. We've no physical relationship at all.'

Aisling was silent. She wanted to believe him. Michael seized the opportunity.

'Darling, let's get away and then we can talk about the future.' He kissed her face. 'I'll organise the tickets for the weekend after next, if that's OK with you?'

'I guess a weekend can't hurt and I definitely need some kind of break.'

Michael gave an inward sigh of relief. Everything was going to be OK. He had already checked out his schedule and knew the weekend would fit in with his political commitments; besides,

Cliodna was going on a bridge weekend with some of her friends, so there would be no problem there.

'That's settled.' He put a finger gently to Aisling's lips. 'Come on then, Aisling, give us a smile!'

Despite her gut feeling that she was doing the wrong thing and that she should end this relationship once and for all, Aisling looked into her lover's blue eyes and smiled.

FOURTEEN

Nora stood in the hall chatting to Fintan on the phone. He was telling her about an audition for a new play that was taking place in town that evening.

'My bloody agent never told me,' complained Nora. 'Do you think I should go along?'

'It's just an audition. You've as good a chance as any.'

'When does the play open?'

'July. And it's an eight-week run. You'd be working for the summer.'

'Thanks a million for thinking of me. I'll see you there at six. Bye.'

Nora hung up the phone and rushed upstairs to see what was clean in her wardrobe that might be suitable for the audition. The part she was interested in was a small but interesting one. Maybe her luck was about to change.

Her bedroom looked, as usual, as if someone had departed in a great hurry on hearing of a nuclear explosion. Clothes were strewn everywhere and books, magazines and half-empty cups of coffee were scattered about on all available surfaces. She cursed as she tripped over the hairdryer on the floor. Opening the wardrobe door, she found a pair of reasonably clean 501s. The white linen shirt that she had thrown into the wash last week and had forgotten about was on a hanger.

'I love you, Frances,' she mumbled in gratitude, guessing that her sister had ironed it.

Just as she was about to step into the shower, she remembered that she had told Patrick she would be around at eight that evening. She was very likely to be delayed at the audition and Patrick would be furious if she were late. Lately, his possessiveness was really getting her down. He insisted on knowing exactly where she was and what she was doing. For the sake of peace, she had better ring him. Frances would still be in his house with the kids but she had his mobile number and could dial direct to his studio. Wrapping a towel around her, she went downstairs to telephone.

'Hi, it's me.'

'No problem about tonight, I hope?'

'Not really, but it might be better if you meet me in town and we eat out. I've an audition at six and I can't count on getting away until about eight. I'll be ravenous if I've to wait till I get back to Monkstown.'

'An audition for what?' She caught a hint of irritation in Patrick's voice.

'A small part in a new play – *Vicarious Living*. It could be a great way to break in to the Irish scene. I just need one chance.'

'For God's sake, Nora, you don't need all that hassle. It means I'll hardly see you. You'll be working every night.'

'We can be together at weekends,' she protested, trying to sound reasonable, although she
felt very angry. Patrick was so damn selfish.

'With the kids around all the time! Great!'

A worrying thought struck Nora. Mark was
bound to tell Frances if he saw her with Patrick
every weekend.

'We can organise something,' she said weakly.
Then she tried to assert herself. 'Anyway, I have
to think of my future. You're an artist, you should
be able to understand what acting means to me.
You take your own work very seriously.'

'It's not the same thing. I'm supporting a
family,' Patrick paused. 'And I'm supporting you!'

Nora was furious.

'I didn't want to take that money. You made
me.'

'For your modelling services!' Patrick's tone
was bitter. 'And so far you haven't done a single
sitting.'

'Well whose fault is that?' Nora felt guilty as
well as angry now. They had both known the
modelling was just an excuse to allow her to take
the money. 'You're making me feel like a kept
woman!'

'Isn't that what you are?'

Nora was about to slam the phone down when
Patrick added quickly, 'I take that back, Nora. I'm
sorry.'

'So you should be.'

Patrick's tone became petulant. 'It doesn't have
to be like this. Why don't you tell Frances about
us? Maybe she'll have forgotten all about that kiss

by now. Then it will be easier to be together – you could come here during the day.'

Thinking of how Frances would feel knowing that her sister was in bed with Patrick while she did nursemaid in the kitchen, Nora shuddered. She couldn't inflict that kind of pain on her.

'Absolutely not. That stupid kiss has complicated everything.' She changed the subject. 'Look, Patrick, are you meeting me in town tonight or what?'

'All right,' he agreed ungraciously. 'I'll meet you in Café en Seine at eight and we can decide where to eat.'

'Fine, see you then.'

'Don't be late,' he warned.

She hung up. Just as she did, the phone rang. It was her father.

'Hello, pet,' he said casually, as though two days rather than two months had elapsed since they last spoke. He went through the usual litany of asking about her sisters, apologising for not keeping in touch and then invited the three of them around for a barbecue on Sunday.

'Aunt Cathy and Uncle Pat are coming and, of course, Seamus and Una and some of the other neighbours. Madge and I are looking forward to it. We've hardly seen any of them since the wedding.'

Nora was surprised to hear from her father because she had assumed that Madge was still keeping him all to herself. She definitely didn't want to go to the barbecue and she hoped that Aisling and Frances wouldn't go either, because there was always the danger that the subject of her imaginary loan would come up.

'I'm not sure if I'll make it, Daddy. I might be rehearsing if I get the job I'm after.'

'On a Sunday?' her father sounded disbelieving.

'I'll tell the others,' Nora promised. 'They'll be in touch, OK?'

'Don't forget now, Nora. I know what a scatterbrain you are!'

'I'll write it down. Have to fly now. Love you.'

Nora put the phone down and looked around for a bit of paper. 'Fran/Ash,' she wrote, 'Da phoned. Barbecue next Sunday. All the poxy relatives and neighbours will be there. I don't want to go.'

Leaving the note beside the phone, she went to take her shower.

Nora arrived at half past five at the Agora, a tiny theatre in the basement of a Georgian house off Merrion Square. She had come early to give herself plenty of time to read the script. She was really anxious to get this part. Of course, there would be very little money in it because the Agora was an experimental theatre that operated on a shoestring but it had a good reputation with the people that mattered and many influential critics, including some from London, attended the openings. Some of the big names in international theatre owed their success to a début in this unimposing looking building.

She slipped in the side entrance and, with a word of thanks to the receptionist, took the few pages of script that she would read for the audition. There were several others in the green room waiting to be called on stage. Some of the faces were familiar and she nodded at them in a friendly fashion. They all looked nervous. Then she spotted the most familiar face of all.

'Fintan, how's it going?'

'Don't ask!' He made a dramatic gesture. 'I've just finished. I was terrible. I've definitely blown it!'

Nora smiled. Fintan was always steeped in gloom after an audition. It didn't mean anything.

'Don't be so negative, Finn.' She gave his arm a squeeze. 'I've a feeling you're going to get it.'

A young girl put her head around the door.

'I think it's you next,' she said, nodding her head at an established actress in her thirties whom Nora recognised.

'She's a bit long in the tooth now,' Nora whispered to Fintan when she'd gone in. 'Do you think she's going for the same part?'

'Could be. It's not for an *ingénue*.' He laughed. 'You should have stayed out on the town and got some rings under your eyes. You look too young and virginal!'

'Maybe that's why my agent didn't tell me about it. I'm probably wasting my time.'

'It's never a waste of time. Even if you don't get this part, you'll probably make such a huge impression on them that they'll bring you in to play Juliet.'

'God, Fintan, you're always so optimistic about everyone except yourself!'

'I know.' He shrugged his shoulders. 'I'll have to go. I've to meet Phil. The best of luck, love.' He gave her a kiss. 'See you soon.'

'Sure. I'll give you a ring. I owe you a lunch.'

When Fintan left, Nora began to study the script. As she read, her heart sank. The part was Ruby, a woman in her thirties. Still, maybe with a more sophisticated style of dress, she could look older.

By the time she was called it was nearly seven o'clock and she had read the pages of dialogue a dozen times. Her heart pounding, she stepped on to the stage. It was dark in the theatre. A desklight shone on a pile of papers in front of a woman and a man sitting at a table in the auditorium. Nora recognised the woman as Kate Campbell, the owner of the theatre. The man looked up and Nora did a double-take. It was the gorgeous looking director, Tim Mulcahy, with whom she had briefly chatted on the day she was fired from *Docklands*. He smiled in recognition.

'Right, Nora,' said Kate Campbell. 'You can start.'

The selected piece was a telephone monologue in which Ruby tells her lover that she is pregnant. Nora knew she was doing it well, with just the right mixture of vulnerability and defensiveness in her voice.

'That was excellent.' Tim spoke first and Kate echoed his words of praise. Nora began to relax and had a second look at Tim. He was even more attractive than she remembered from the brief meeting in London. Tall and slim, he had that particular brand of understated 'English' good looks, despite the fact that he was one hundred per cent Irish.

'Nora,' said Kate, who knew her well from auditions in the past. 'This is Tim Mulcahy; he's going to be directing the piece . . . '

'I met Nora in London,' Tim interrupted. 'Well, brief encounter would be a more accurate description. It's very nice to see you again, Nora. That was an exceptional performance. Whatever way things go, I have to say you're definitely in the right profession.'

Nora felt a glow of pleasure. Acting was so insecure that, no matter how often people told her she was good, she never quite believed it and always needed more reassurance. She reflected that, for an artist, praise was like a Chinese meal, you were hungry again after a couple of hours.

Kate was looking rapidly through her papers. 'Looks like Nora's the last tonight. Can we talk later on the phone, Tim? I've to pick someone up and I'm dead late.' Tim nodded agreement and, with a quick smile at Nora, Kate rushed out of the theatre.

'Poor Kate spends her life dashing from one appointment to another.'

'And you?' Nora asked teasingly. She knew she was being flirtatious, but she couldn't help it. She really would like to spend some time with Tim and it was not entirely because she wanted to impress him with her acting ability.

'I keep busy,' he said, 'but I usually find time for a drink after work. That's what I'm going to do right now. Do you fancy a pint to wash away the theatre dust?'

'I'd love it.' Nora glanced at her watch. It was seven-twenty. She'd suggest a pub near Dawson Street and she could dash down to Café en Seine at eight or thereabouts.

The evening sun was dazzling when they came out on to Merrion Square.

'Can we go to Neary's?' asked Nora.

'Great. It's a nice evening for a stroll.'

By the time they got to the pub, it was ten to eight and Nora, determined to have her drink in peace, was resigned to facing an irate Patrick. She was enjoying herself with Tim. They had chatted as they walked and she had found out that he was a jobbing director and was delighted to get a chance of doing *Vicarious Living* for the Agora. He had tremendous respect for the contribution that Kate made to theatre in general and was impressed by the way she always managed to attract the most talented actors and directors. Now as they sat upstairs in Nearys he referred to Nora's performance at the audition.

'To be honest, Nora, having seen you only in *Docklands* I didn't realise you had such depths of communication.' His hazel eyes looked straight into hers. 'If only you were ten years older, I'd give you the part of Ruby this very minute.'

Nora's heart sank. She guessed what was coming next. 'Does that mean what I think it means?'

'I'm afraid so. You're just too young. It would take a hell of a make-up job to make you look thirty. Be grateful,' he smiled reassuringly. 'You'll be glad of that in a few years' time.'

Nora felt a great wave of disappointment wash over her. Not only was she not going to get the part but she'd probably never see this man again. After only an hour in his company, she knew that there was something special about him.

Noting the expression on her face, Tim touched her arm encouragingly.

'You're a good actress, Nora,' he said. 'You may even be a great actress in time. Stick with it. I know you've got what it takes. Come on, have another drink.'

Although she knew she should go – it was already half-eight – she accepted and sat back to chat about the theatre in general. At nine o'clock she stood up in a panic.

'God, I must go. I'm over an hour late.' She dropped a kiss on his forehead. 'Hope we meet again soon.'

'I hope so too. Maybe you'll come to the opening?' he suggested.

'I will,' she promised magnanimously, 'especially if Fintan gets a part.'

'Fintan Doyle? Strictly off the record, that's pretty well a certainty.'

Nora felt a mixture of joy for Fintan and renewed disappointment for herself.

'That's great. I'm off. Thanks for the drinks.'

She took off down the stairs, almost falling over in her haste. Outside the bright evening had turned dark and rain clouds were gathering in the sky. She ran across to Dawson Street and in through the wide doors of the café. It was crowded as always, and it took her some time to find Patrick, sitting in a corner opposite the long brasserie-style bar. He was reading a book and his face was like thunder.

'Hi,' she stood nervously above him.

He didn't look up for some time and then he gave her a hard, cold stare.

'I assumed something had happened, but I suppose you were just playing your usual casting couch games.'

She was astounded. She knew Patrick was possessive and jealous but he had no right to speak to her like this.

'How can you say that?' Suddenly she didn't want to sit with him. 'I've lost two jobs because I wouldn't play those games.' It was all so unfair that she was afraid she was going to cry. She stood there feeling helpless. Patrick's face was like a mask. He was hardly recognisable in his blind rage.

'Strange,' he said bitterly, 'that within the space of as many months two producers are trying to get into your bed. It seems reasonable to suppose that you give them some encouragement.'

'Christ, how can you say that, especially when one was a woman!'

'You're an ambitious girl, Nora. Maybe you'd encourage anyone who might give you a part!'

For a moment, Nora wanted to hit him, but with a tremendous effort she controlled herself. 'Have your dinner alone. I'm going.'

At that he stood up, realising that he had gone too far.

'Come back, Nora. I'm sorry.'

But she tossed her head and strode down the length of the café, tears stinging her eyes.

Sitting on the DART on her way home, Nora was still trembling with rage and also with a kind of fear. She felt trapped by Patrick. She now deeply regretted having taken his money; she would have to become independent and struggle to overcome her sexual reliance on him. By the time the train reached Glasthule, she was determined that she would escape, in every sense, from him. Yet, resolute as she was, she felt a sense of physical loss, knowing that she would sleep alone tonight.

Aisling's car was pulling into the driveway as she arrived at the house.

'Hi.' Aisling got out, locked the car door and glanced at her watch. 'Ten-thirty. You are the early bird tonight! Nothing wrong I hope?' She looked with concern at her sister's sad face.

'I'm fine. I'm just tired and a bit fed-up. I missed out on a great part because I look too young.'

'I'm sorry, love.' Aisling put her key in the door. 'But don't worry. Just give it time.'

Nora didn't answer. Time looked like it was going to take care of the problem with Patrick. Perhaps tonight had finished off the affair and she could stop worrying about Frances but she suspected that Patrick was not a man to let go easily of anything he desired and, anyway, she had to admit to herself that she would miss him terribly in bed. Sighing heavily, she followed Aisling in.

Frances was ironing in the kitchen.

'Hi,' she said brightly when the sisters came into the kitchen. 'Hope you're not looking to eat at this hour – there's nothing in the house. We'll have to do a big shop tomorrow.'

'Count me out for the weekend.' Aisling picked up a jumper hanging on the back of a chair. 'I'm off to Amsterdam tomorrow morning. We're doing a feature on Irish people working in Europe, so we're starting with Holland.'

'Lucky you!' said Frances.

Nora said nothing. Something about Aisling's tone made her sure she was lying. She was certain that Aisling was going away for the weekend with her secret lover, while she'd just lost a good part and the opportunity of getting to know the first man she'd ever really cared about.

'Cheer up, love.' Aisling gave her arm a squeeze. 'There'll be other parts. I'd better run up and pack. I'm leaving first thing in the morning.'

When Aisling had gone upstairs, Nora sat down at the kitchen table, trying to control her desire to blurt out the whole sorry story of Patrick and herself to Frances. But she knew that would be foolish because there was a good chance that by tomorrow night she would be back in Patrick's bed.

'Fran, did you see the note about Sunday?' she said to distract herself from her conflicting emotions. 'I'm not going. Aisling will be away and I bet you don't want to spend the evening with the bloody neighbours.'

Frances put down the iron. 'Aisling has a

genuine excuse, but I think we'll have to go because Dad will be really hurt if none of us turns up.'

Nora sighed.

'I suppose so. But I hate the thought of spending an afternoon with Madge. Hey,' she added, 'don't say anything about the money I borrowed. I'm sure she doesn't know and she'd go spare if she thought her new husband had started dishing out dosh to his family.'

Frances gave her a knowing look. 'I won't say anything,' she promised.

FIFTEEN

The alarm clock bleeped beside Aisling's bed. She leaned over to switch it off. Six o'clock. She and Michael were flying out of Dublin for Amsterdam at eight, hence the need for an early start. Aisling gave a slight groan. She was looking forward to the trip of course but she was scared of flying and now the insides of her stomach felt as though they were doing somersaults.

'Wakey, wakey!' Frances knocked on her bedroom door and came in. She always woke early herself and had promised to give Aisling a call, just in case something went wrong with the alarm clock. 'Are you all right?' she asked, seeing her sister's white face.

'It's OK. Just my usual fear of flying.'

Frances laughed.

'Aisling, flying is statistically the safest form of transport.'

'I know, I know,' Aisling got out of bed, and almost keeled over with dizziness.

'Are you sure you're all right?' Frances asked with some concern.

In response, Aisling darted past her to the loo, where she was violently ill. This couldn't simply be fear of flying! Then she remembered the dodgy hot dog she'd eaten yesterday. *Ireland Today* had been covering a protest by postal workers in the city centre and Frank had brought her a hot dog he'd bought from a street vendor. At the time she had been grateful; it had been a long, hard day and she'd been very hungry. Now she was paying for her stupidity. She'd been so looking forward to this weekend away with Michael; it would be just her luck if she were too sick to go. But having emptied her stomach, she felt a lot better and went downstairs feeling able to eat the breakfast that Frances had prepared for her.

'Do you have to go?' Frances asked, as she sat down at the table. 'Can't the programme send someone else, if you're ill?'

Once again, Aisling felt guiltily aware of the lies she was telling in order to protect Michael.

'I'm better,' she assured Frances. 'See – I'm eating my muesli. It was just a mild dose of food poisoning, I'd say.'

'You're sure that's all it is?' Frances gave her a strange look, and it occurred to Aisling that she was thinking of something else.

'You think I'm pregnant!'

Frances blushed.

'Aisling, I'm sorry – it's just that you're so secretive about, well, about your private life, and Nora and I wondered if there was someone – I mean, this trip to Amsterdam . . . '

She trailed off, embarrassed.

'It's business,' said Aisling firmly, 'and there's no-one in my life. I'd tell you if there were.'

'Fine,' said Frances, pouring out coffee for both of them. 'Have you got everything?' she asked.

'Tickets, passport, money?'

Aisling nodded. In fact, Michael had insisted on paying for the trip and would have her ticket for her at the airport when they met. She had packed a sensible weekend bag which contained casual clothes for sightseeing, a crush-proof silk dress for evening wear and a toilet bag into which she had carefully placed her contraceptive pill. They'd only be gone for one night, but she wasn't taking any chances.

'Needless to say, Nora's still in the Land of Nod,' said Frances.

'Tell her I'll bring her back a Dutchman!'

'I doubt if she'd want one,' said Frances but Aisling was too excited to notice the dryness in her tone.

'See you tomorrow night,' she said, grabbing her bag.

'Don't work too hard,' said Frances, as they kissed each other goodbye. 'After all, it's your first trip to Amsterdam. You must see the sights.'

'I'll try,' said Aisling, wanting only to be gone now, away from all the necessary lies.

As she parked her car at the airport, she worried that Michael wouldn't be waiting for her, as arranged. Suppose Cliodna or one of his children were ill and he'd been unable to come? She could almost hear an announcement calling her to pick up the nearest telephone, down which Michael's apologetic voice would explain the unfortunate circumstances necessitating the cancellation of the trip. But as she walked into Departures he was there, his back to her as he perused the departure board. His blond hair curled slightly over his collar, and she longed to grab him in her arms and embrace him. Instead, she sneaked up behind him and, rising on tiptoe, put her hands over his eyes.

'Guess who?' she asked. Michael turned around abruptly and gave her a warning look. He glanced around him cautiously, checking to see if they were being observed. She felt a twinge of irritation. Was it going to be like this in Amsterdam? 'Michael, you've told your wife you're going to Amsterdam on government business. Surely you can relax?'

'Ah, but I didn't tell her I was going with a beautiful blonde,' he said, making an effort to smile. At that smile, all her anger with him dissipated. Soon they'd be in a foreign city, away from everyone and she would have him all to herself for a whole weekend. Her sudden illness had vanished and, with Michael beside her, even her fear of flying seemed to have diminished. She felt that she had never been so happy in her life.

The trip was everything she had hoped for. They stayed in a small but comfortable hotel close to the Rijksmuseum which housed Rembrandt's famous painting, *The Night Watch*. At the reception desk, Aisling noted with pleasure that Michael had booked them in as man and wife. When the receptionist had given them their key, they climbed a narrow staircase to their bedroom and made love slowly and languorously for several hours. Eventually, they washed and dressed and wandered round the city, marvelling at the narrow streets filled with tiny shops selling everything from luxury chocolates to pornographic magazines. Michael bought her a bunch of tulips from a street vendor and presented them to her with mock seriousness.

'With a heart that's true, I'll give to you, tulips from Amsterdam,' he sang, making her laugh.

They clambered on to a waterbus and took a trip round the canals. Michael put his arm around her shoulder as he pointed out various landmarks. Then they visited the Van Gogh Museum, where that sad genius's work made Aisling want to cry. They each bought a poster of his *Sunflowers*. Aisling would frame hers and put it up in her bedroom at home. Michael was going to give his to his son Eoin, who was fourteen and just beginning to appreciate art.

That night, they dined in an Indonesian restaurant, where they savoured the spicy foods of the rice table while making plans for the next day.

'I'd like to see Anne Frank's house,' said Aisling. 'Her diary is so moving.'

'And we'll go to a diamond factory. Amsterdam is famous for its diamonds.'

'And shouldn't we see the red light district?' Aisling suggested. 'After all, it's famous for that, too.'

'Who needs that, when I've got you?'

Aisling smiled, remembering their lovemaking. Never had she felt so right with a man, so physically and emotionally connected as she did with Michael. If only they could be together like this all the time!

'Eat up,' Michael was telling her now, 'I can't wait to get back to bed with you.'

Arms thrown around each other, they wandered back slowly to the hotel. Every so often, they would stop and kiss deeply. This was a city for lovers and they didn't feel in any way embarrassed about behaving like a couple of infatuated teenagers. Returning to their bedroom, they made love once more, with the curtains pulled open and the room lit only by the light of the moon. When they had finished, Michael drew her into his arms.

'I love you, Aisling Davis,' he whispered in her ear.

Aisling felt she would explode with joy. It was the first time that he had said he loved her.

'Oh, Michael,' she sighed, 'I love you too.'

He took a lock of her moonlit hair and wrapped it round his finger. 'And some day,' he promised, 'some day soon, we'll be together properly.'

Aisling was astonished. She recalled how adamant Michael had been when he had told her he wouldn't leave his wife.

'But Cliodna – that night in the pub, you said you wouldn't . . . '

Michael interrupted her.

'Ah, but I did also say we'd talk about the future. I've done a lot of thinking in the last few days, and you were right. We oughtn't to have to hide out in dark pubs or foreign countries. You're the one I want to spend the rest of my life with, and that's what I intend to do.'

'And the party . . . ?'

'To hell with the party,' said Michael carelessly. He stroked her breast. 'There's a reshuffle coming up in a month or so. I expect to move upwards, maybe into Foreign Affairs. Once I get that . . . well, they can hardly remove me from it, just because I've left my wife.'

Aisling felt her heart fill with love. Michael had hinted that he had aspirations to be party leader but that was a goal he'd be unlikely to achieve, at least in the current moral climate, were he to leave his wife. She realised that he was willing to sacrifice his most cherished ambition in order to be with her! She was sorry for Cliodna and his children, who would suffer when he left, but she told herself that theirs had been a marriage of convenience and that such marriages were based upon a lie. Their love, on the other hand, was something pure and true and with that as a basis, surely they would be safe?

Sunday was their second and final day in Amsterdam and Aisling was determined to get in as much sightseeing as she could. They visited Anne Frank's house, an experience which she found both uplifting and depressing. It was hard not to smile at the posters of forties' movie stars that lined the young girl's room, but Aisling's spirits dropped when she remembered that Anne Frank never made it to freedom, dying as she did in a concentration camp in the closing months of the war. Emerging from the house, she felt chastened. How small her concerns seemed when set beside the tragic life of the Jewish girl.

'A penny for them,' said Michael, noting her pensive mood as they walked back towards the city centre.

'It was such a tragic story,' she said. 'In her diary, Anne Frank was usually cheerful and optimistic. I think she assumed she'd survive but she didn't.'

'Well, none of us can tell what the future will bring.' Michael kissed her on the cheek, hoping she'd snap out of this reflective humour.

Aisling shivered slightly. She felt as though someone had walked over her grave. As if to mirror her mood, the fine weather they had enjoyed the previous day suddenly broke, and rain poured down on them, soaking them to the skin. Michael hailed a cab.

'I know what will cheer you up,' he said as they climbed into the back seat. He instructed the driver to take them to a diamond factory.

'Feeling better?' he asked, as sped towards their destination.

Aisling leaned her head against his shoulder.

'Yes, but not because we're going to see some diamonds. I love being with you, Michael. I wish this trip never had to end.'

'So do I, but we'll be together soon. And now,' he said, as the taxi drew up outside the factory, 'we're going to get our engagement ring!'

They dashed through the rain to the factory's reception area, which obligingly remained open on Sundays, so that tourists could spend their money. A sharp-faced saleswoman showed them the various precious stones which were mined in South Africa before being brought to Holland, where they were carefully cut using the latest laser technology.

'Choose one,' said Michael, when the saleswoman placed a tray of rings in front of them.

'I couldn't,' said Aisling, noticing the exorbitant prices on the tags.

'What the lady is saying,' said the saleswoman, smiling insincerely at Michael, 'is that she'd like you to choose one for her.'

'Then I choose this one,' said Michael, lifting a magnificent sapphire in a setting of amethysts. He slid it on to the third finger of Aisling's left hand.

'Like it?'

'I love it,' Aisling was thrilled that he was buying her such a beautiful ring but more important was the commitment he was making to their future together.

'I'm sure you'll both be very happy,' said the saleswoman, somewhat sardonically. Aisling had already seen her glance at the wedding ring on Michael's hand.

'Oh, and I'll take these as well,' said Michael, as the receptionist was placing the ring in its box. Aisling saw him indicate a pair of diamond earrings from another tray. She guessed that he was buying them for Cliodna, and, though she knew she was being foolish, she couldn't help feeling hurt that he should be thinking of her at this moment. But she reasoned that he could hardly return from Amsterdam without a present for his wife and she was too happy to entertain gloomy thoughts for long. As they left the factory, Michael handed her the ring box.

'I don't think you should wear it in public just yet,' he warned. 'People would be bound to ask questions. Keep it hidden away safe somewhere until the reshuffle has happened.'

'Right,' Aisling promised, accepting the box. Again, she felt a downrush of disappointment but rebuked herself for being impatient.

'And now what?' said Michael, as they stood in the pouring rain. 'Maybe we should forget about sightseeing and go back to the hotel.'

'We still haven't seen the Rijksmuseum,' Aisling reminded him, 'I can't go back to Dublin without seeing *The Night Watch*.'

'But we're sopping wet! We'll drip all over their *objets d'art*. And besides, who wants to waste time looking at boring old paintings and sculptures when there are much more interesting things we could be doing?'

'Philistine!' said Aisling happily, 'But you've sold me. We'll go back to the hotel.'

They hailed cab after cab, but it seemed that every one was taken. They stood on the pavement, soaking wet but happy. A drop of rain, which had run down the lock of Michael's hair that hung over his forehead, was now balanced precariously on the end of his nose, making Aisling laugh.

'What's so funny?'

'Your dripping nose!' she told him, giggling. 'If they could see you in the Dáil now!'

Michael grabbed her in his arms and embraced

her. Suddenly, over his shoulder, she saw a familiar face looking at them from the other side of the street. What on earth was Carmel Rafferty doing in Amsterdam? The laughter froze on Aisling's lips, and she pulled away from Michael quickly.

'What is it?' he asked, noting the startled expression on her face.

'Carmel Rafferty,' she told him, indicating the figure, which was, even now, lurching away from them. 'What on earth is she doing in Amsterdam?'

'But she knows me,' said Michael, horrified. 'She interviewed me, remember?'

'I don't think there's anything to worry about, Michael,' Aisling said quickly. 'She seemed pretty drunk – she may not even have recognised us.'

'Let's hope you're right,' Michael's blue eyes were suddenly as cold as ice. 'I wouldn't want anything to happen before the reshuffle.'

'She's not on the programme any more,' Aisling reminded him. 'Last I heard, she was in St Pat's being dried out.'

'Well, it obviously didn't work, if she's still pissed now.' Michael shrugged. 'Let's forget about her.'

Aisling wished she could do just that. But she still remembered Carmel's threat on the day she had taken over from her on *Ireland Today*. She decided not to tell Michael about it. She didn't want to worry him any more than he already did.

At last, a cab stopped for them and they climbed into it gratefully. As they sped back to the hotel, Aisling told herself that Carmel could probably not hurt them. Although technically still employed by Channel 3, she was no longer a force within it. And, besides, when the reshuffle happened, Michael would be leaving Cliodna. By then, nothing Carmel could say or do would make any difference to them.

SIXTEEN

It was raining in Dublin as well as in Amsterdam that Sunday morning and Nora, relaxing on the couch with the papers, was speculating that, with a bit of luck, the barbecue would be cancelled.

'Who'd want to have a barbecue in this?' she complained to Frances. 'I'm sure we won't be going.'

'Dad's not going to put people off at this stage. He'll cook outside under an umbrella and we'll eat indoors. We've done that loads of times.' Frances gave her sister an affectionate pat on the head. 'I'm afraid you're just going have to put up with the "poxy" relatives!'

'Yeah, well, you'll have to suffer "Uncle" Seamus!'

Frances's irrational dislike of their father's neighbour was a standing joke in the family. She knew that Aisling and Nora found her attitude to him odd; she found it odd, herself. Seamus O'Connor was certainly pompous – typical of a certain type of civil servant – but he had always been generous, especially to her, giving her expensive Christmas presents when she had babysat for his children. But she couldn't conceal her dislike, her loathing for him. She was not looking forward to the afternoon and she would stay only as long as necessary to keep her father happy. She picked up one of the newspapers strewn across Nora's legs.

'Hold on,' Nora protested, 'I was about to read that one.'

'You can have it in a minute.' Frances settled down in the armchair with the *Sunday Independent.* 'After all, I was the one who bought them!'

The telephone rang and Nora jumped up. 'I'll get it.' The papers slid on to the floor. She went out to the hall and with some trepidation picked up the phone.

'Nora?'

As she had suspected, it was Patrick and she didn't know how to react. She hadn't heard from him since she had run out of the Café en Seine on Friday night and she had been a little surprised that he hadn't rung yesterday, because usually his bad tempers were shortlived.

'Yes?' Her voice was cool, in contrast to his conciliatory tone.

'Nora, I'm sorry about the other night. We were both a bit uptight and I over-reacted. Am I forgiven?'

Nora could visualise the 'little boy lost' look that he would have automatically adopted. Usually she melted immediately but, this time, she wasn't so ready to give in. She had been really hurt by his domineering attitude and the insinuations about a casting couch had been terribly unfair. More significantly, Patrick was not the man uppermost in her mind at the moment, because since Friday her mind had been on Tim Mulcahy and on what bad luck it had been that she hadn't got the part in the play. She would have had plenty of opportunity to get to know him better. Nora sighed. Things were definitely not going her way, these days.

'Darling!' Patrick mistook the nature of the sigh. 'Don't be upset. I'll make it up to you. I promise!'

Nora said nothing.

'Come around later. The children are in Greystones with their aunt. We can talk over a quiet drink. Please!'

Nora thought quickly. She would like to sort things out with Patrick. She hated to be on bad terms with anyone and especially with a man whose bed she had been sharing. He was so repentant at the moment that he might listen to her when she asked him to stop acting like a medieval husband. Also, it would be a reason not to go to the barbecue, although she'd have to invent a cover story, since she couldn't tell Frances where she was going.

'Well, I suppose we should talk.'

Patrick gave a sigh of relief. 'About four o'clock?'

'That's too early. I'll be there at five.'

She hung up and thought for a few moments before going back into the sitting-room.

Frances looked up from the paper.

'I suppose that wasn't Dad cancelling?' she asked hopefully.

'No, it was poor Fintan on the verge of tears. Phil's walked out on him. They had an awful row.'

The story had come to her easily because Fintan's relationship with Phil had always been tempestuous and Nora was used to providing a shoulder to cry on. 'I'll have to meet him this afternoon. I'm sorry about the barbecue.'

Frances felt her heart sink. She wasn't looking forward to seeing Madge installed in what had been her domain and on top of that she would have to make polite conversation to the man she couldn't bear to be in the same room with. It would be even more difficult without either of her sisters there.

'It can't be helped, I suppose.' Frances knew she sounded ungracious but, apart from everything else, she wasn't at all sure that Nora was telling the truth. She had her suspicions about where she was going. 'What'll I tell Dad?'

'Tell him the truth. He'll be sympathetic, but,' Nora added hastily, giggling, 'keep it strictly hetero! It's Fintan and Phillipa. I don't think Madge could cope with a gay romance!'

By five o'clock the rain had stopped and pale sunshine drifted through the window of the kitchen, where Frances was gift-wrapping a bottle of wine to take to the barbecue. Nora stuck her head around the door.

'So long. I'm off to do my Oprah Winfrey bit. Give them all my love.'

Frances heard the front door close as Nora left. She finished wrapping the wine, feeling suddenly lonely and depressed. Perhaps Nora was really going to comfort a distraught Fintan, but an inner voice insisted that her sister would shortly be lying in Patrick's arms.

It would take a long time to get to Donnybrook from Sandycove on the bus and, since it was after five, Frances indulged herself and ordered a taxi. The evening ahead would be difficult and she felt entitled to a bit of luxury.

The taxi pulled up in Marlborough Road. Frances opened the newly painted gate and walked up the long garden path to the front door. The garden looked well cared for, but Frances was a little amused by the extravagance of over-filled flowerpots and hanging baskets which made it almost impossible to stand in the porch. She rang the bell and Madge, dressed in lime-green silk, opened the door.

'Wine? How nice of you.' Her stepmother took the bottle and gave her a peck on the cheek. 'All on your own? Your father will be disappointed.' She sniffed disapprovingly.

'Aisling's away – Dad knows that. And at the last minute Nora couldn't come.' Frances was still standing on the doorstep when her father appeared. Madge moved back and he enveloped his daughter in his arms. 'It's lovely to see you, pet. Come out to the back. Where's Nora?'

Frances explained about Fintan and his romantic troubles and her father murmured sympathetically as Nora had envisaged he would.

'A lover's tiff. She'll be back tomorrow. Still,' he mused knowingly, as he opened the French doors to the patio and ushered Madge and Frances out, 'it's very upsetting at the time. It's kind of

Nora to go and talk to him.'

'Frances?' Pat Fagan, her father's partner and best man at the wedding, put down his tankard of beer and gave her a hug. 'Let me get you a glass of wine. He was genuinely fond of John's eldest daughter and remembered with admiration how, when little more than a child herself, she had looked after her father and sisters when her mother died. He didn't ask about Aisling and Nora. 'They get all the attention,' he often said to his wife, Betty, 'and Frances is worth more than the two of them tied together.'

'Thanks, Pat,' Frances took the proffered glass. 'It's not a bad evening now. I think we'll be able to eat outside.' She looked around. Her father had returned to his cooking post and was busy controlling the flames. A delicious smell of grilled steak and spices wafted across the garden. Aunt Cathy was hovering beside him issuing orders and Frances smiled as she watched her father nod his head in agreement and then totally ignore his bossy sister. It was a familiar scene from past summers. She noticed with relief that there was no sign of the O'Connors.

'Hi, Frances, good to see you.'

She turned and saw her cousin Peter.

'Peter, what a surprise! I didn't expect you to come all the way from Cork for a barbecue?'

'We were up for yet another wedding yesterday, so it fitted in nicely. Here . . . ' He tried to take her almost full glass. ' . . . let me top that up.'

'Hang on,' Frances laughed, 'I've only arrived, I'll be on my ear and I should give a hand.' She gestured to where Madge and Pauline, Peter's wife, were coming out from the kitchen carrying bowls of salad and platters of garlic bread.

'Relax, it's not your problem now. Enjoy yourself.'

She leaned back against the wall, warm now from evening sunshine and cradled her glass in her hand. Maybe it wouldn't be such a bad evening after all. She tried to put the vision of Nora and Patrick out of her mind. It could be true about Fintan. She would make herself believe it was true.

'Isn't it a perfect evening now, thanks be to God.' Frances heard Seamus's deep voice resound across the patio and she froze with anxiety.

'Well, how's my favourite girl?' Seamus came forward, holding both hands out to Frances like a visiting dignitary.

'I'm fine, Seamus.' She tried to move further back against the wall. She looked around anxiously for Peter but he had wandered off to start picking at the food on the table.

'Seamus? Am I no longer an honorary uncle?' He smiled.

'I'm glad it's stopped raining,' Frances ignored his question. She wished that Nora and Aisling were here to handle the situation. They didn't particularly like Seamus either but he didn't upset them. 'I must go and give Madge a hand.' She tried to move past him but he held out an arm to stop her.

'Don't rush away from me. I never see you at all these days.' Then, abruptly, he took his arm away and let her pass. 'Run off and help then, but make sure you sit beside me at the table.'

Frances moved away gratefully, promising herself that Seamus would be the last person she'd sit beside that evening.

'I said I was sorry, Nora. What more can I do?'

Nora looked intently at the flute of white wine on the wooden table in front of her. They were sitting outside in Patrick's slightly overgrown back garden. The angelus from a local church rang and the strains of the last movement of Bruch's Violin Concerto became almost inaudible.

Nora didn't answer Patrick's question. The bells and the music came to an end.

'Will I put on another disc? What would you like, Nora?' Patrick was trying very hard.

Nora took up her glass and took a long drink.

'Patrick, we have to talk properly.'

'I thought we sorted everything out when you arrived,' he began.

She looked at him in disbelief. 'Sure,' she said sarcastically, 'you took me in your arms, kissed me and hugged me, opened a bottle of wine and now we're sitting in the sun pretending everything is just fine.' She crossed her arms. 'Well, it isn't. For one thing, I've been here nearly an hour and you haven't even asked about the part that was so important to me.'

'I'm sorry, Nora.' Patrick's handsome face showed impatience. 'I was thinking about us, not about work. Well, did you get it?'

'No, I didn't.' Nora's eyes began to smart. She was really upset about not getting that part.

'Don't worry about it,' he tried to take her hand.

'At least we'll have more time together if you're not working.'

Nora pulled away from him and stood up. 'You insensitive bastard! You're so selfish. It doesn't matter how I feel just so long as you can have what you want.'

'Maybe you're the selfish one?' Patrick's expression hardened and, noticing this, Nora began to cry. She couldn't face any more scenes.

'Darling, you'll get a part soon.' He stood up and put his arms around her and she nestled in against his chest, still feeling miserable but glad of the comfort of his body. She probably would get a part soon but not with Tim Mulcahy as director and that was what really mattered.

'It's getting a bit cold,' Patrick said, 'let's take the wine upstairs and we'll make up properly in comfort.'

Nora obediently allowed herself to be led up to the familiar four-poster bed. No matter how much Patrick and she fought, she couldn't resist him sexually. She loved the way he explored her body, patiently waiting for her every response to coincide with his.

Now he moved gently down her body. She felt the slight abrasiveness of his beard between her thighs and sighed with pleasure as he gently used his tongue to massage her clitoris. Nora wished she could love this man who understood her needs so well but all the time she was imagining herself with someone else and, when she came, she had to stop herself from crying out 'Tim'.

SEVENTEEN

Aisling sat in her office and tried to work. She had notes to prepare for an interview with a government minister, one of Michael's colleagues, who was involved with a construction company which was applying for planning permission to build in an area which had been designated recreational land. The minister was accused of trying to influence the rezoning decision and was threatened with demotion. He seemed determined to hang on to his position but Aisling reflected that with public pressure mounting against him, the reshuffle Michael had spoken of would come sooner rather than later.

Everything came back to Michael. She knew she should be concentrating on her work but all she could think about was the weekend. Apart from seeing Carmel, it had been perfect in every way. After their trip to the diamond factory, they had returned to the hotel and ordered lunch in their bedroom, where they had stayed, making love, until it was time to catch the plane. At Dublin airport, Michael had arranged for a delivery of two dozen red roses, which were presented to her as they walked through Arrivals.

'How will I explain these to Frances and Nora?' she asked.

'Tell them a romantic Dutchman gave them to you on impulse,' he said.

'They won't believe me,' she warned.

'Let them believe what they like!'

She had been thrilled at his apparent ease with the situation. He no longer seemed to mind that her sisters might suspect her of having an affair.

He had seen her to her car and she had driven home on a cloud of euphoria and love. On arrival at Sandycove, she had put the roses in the boot of the Golf, where they remained until that morning, when she impulsively took a few of them into the office to put on her desk. She would rather have brought them home but it was easier to lie to her workmates than to Frances and Nora. It had been a struggle to contain her happiness when telling her sisters about the trip and she was sure they had noticed her dreamy eyes and the little involuntary smile that crossed her lips every now and then. She couldn't wait for the time when she'd be able to tell them everything.

She took the ring box from her bag and slipped the sapphire on to her finger. Soon she would be able to wear it openly but for now it had to stay hidden, only taken out for those private moments when no one was around.

The phone rang on her desk.

'Aisling? It's Hugh Jameson. We met at the Phoenician?'

'Oh, Hugh.' Aisling had completely forgotten the charming man who had brought her home that awful night when she had thought her love affair was over.

'You gave me your number and fool that I was, I lost it. Then I remembered you work in Channel 3. Would you like to go to dinner some time?'

'I don't think so, Hugh.' She felt genuinely sorry at turning Hugh down, but after Amsterdam, she couldn't imagine ever looking at another man. Hugh backed off instantly.

'That's fine. I'll see you around then.'

'Sure,' she said, putting down the phone. A moment later, it rang again.

'Darling, it's me.'

'Michael!'

She was thrilled to hear his voice. He hardly ever called her at work, and it she felt it was a sign of his growing commitment to her.

'I couldn't wait to talk to you again,' he said. 'I'm in my office. But my heart's still in Amsterdam.'

She smiled.

'Mine too. As a matter of fact, I've got your ring on now.'

There was a pause at the other end of the line.

'Don't worry,' she assured him, quickly. 'There's nobody to see it.'

'Well, be careful.'

'I will. How did things go when you got home?' she asked, changing the subject.

'Fine. Cliodna was still in Navan with her bridge party. The nanny was minding the kids.'

Hearing Cliodna's name, Aisling felt a moment's guilt. How would she feel when Michael told her he was leaving? After all, she was the mother of his children and even if they no longer had sexual relations, he was still her husband. But she put this uncomfortable thought to the back of her mind.

'You've heard about O'Brien?' she asked, referring to the government minister. 'The reshuffle may happen sooner rather than later.'

To her surprise, Michael disagreed.

'No, he's going to hang on in there. He has the Taoiseach's backing and it's not as if he kept his involvement in the company a secret.'

'But he tried to pull a fast one!' Aisling was incredulous. 'Surely he can't get away with that?'

'It was his brother who did the lobbying. He's covered his ass well.'

'Not well enough!' All the same, Aisling felt a moment's disappointment. She had hoped the reshuffle would happen at once and that she and Michael would be together.

'There *will* be a reshuffle, Ash,' he said, sensing her mood. 'But like I told you, it will happen in a month or so.'

'Oh, well,' Aisling tried to be philosophical. 'I suppose I'll just have to wait. Mind you,' she added, 'I'll give O'Brien a roasting on tomorrow's programme.'

Michael laughed.

'I wouldn't doubt you.' He lowered his voice. 'I can hear my secretary moving about outside, I'd better hang up. See you tonight?'

Aisling could hardly wait.

'Of course.'

'My flat,' he said, and then he was gone.

Aisling put down the phone, slipped the ring

from her finger and replaced it in her bag. Telling herself that it would only be eight hours before she saw Michael, she returned to her notes and forced her brain to absorb them. She had been studying them for about five minutes when Geraldine came in to brief her on an item they were doing on Cuban immigrants. Aisling had to struggle to look interested as Geraldine talked her through her the research.

'There's something odd about you today,' Geraldine said suddenly. 'You've asked me the same question three times.'

'Sorry.' Aisling struggled to look interested. 'I'm just a bit tired.'

Geraldine gazed at her quizzically.

'If I didn't know better, I'd say you were in love. You've a silly grin on your face and your mind is miles away.'

'It's just that Monday morning feeling. Don't mind me.'

'Well then, why don't we go and have a caffeine fix? Maybe that will help you get your act into gear.'

'Great. I owe you a coffee.'

At the cash register, Aisling opened her bag to pay for the coffees. As she pulled out the purse, the ring box came with it and fell to the floor. Geraldine picked it up and before Aisling could stop her, had opened it.

'An engagement ring!' she exclaimed. 'So I was right!'

'Shhh!'

Aisling grabbed the box from Geraldine and

quickly shoved it back into her bag. She didn't think anyone had heard, except perhaps the cashier, who looked so dull and dour that she'd hardly be interested in a mere romance.

'Who is he?' Geraldine persisted when they sat down at a table. 'And if you're getting married, why are you being so damn secretive about it?'

'All right,' Aisling made a snap decision. 'I'll tell you. But it's strictly confidential for now.'

Geraldine understood instantly.

'Ah. That means you're in the same boat as I was. He's married.'

Aisling lowered her voice so that nobody in the vicinity could hear.

'It's not quite the same as you and Billy. He's a politician. If the word got out now it could affect his career.'

Geraldine's eyes widened.

'It's Michael Whelan!'

'How did you know?' Aisling was astonished.

'You obviously fancied him that time he was on the programme and whenever you talk about him you become sort of . . . ' She struggled for the word. ' . . . sort of reverential. You badmouth every other politician except him.'

Aisling rebuked herself mentally. Had she made it so obvious!

'Don't worry, Aisling; no one else has noticed.'

'Thank God they're not all as perceptive as you!'

Geraldine smiled. 'I've been in the same boat myself, remember?'

'Well then, you understand the need for discretion. There's a reshuffle coming up and once he gets his promotion we'll go public.'

Geraldine's expression became serious.

'Are you sure of that?' she asked.

'Of course. He's going to tell his wife and the party.'

'It's just that . . . ' Geraldine tried to find a tactful form of words. 'Well, you know you're not the first woman he's been involved with.'

Aisling nodded.

'But I'm the last,' she said. 'And that's what counts.'

The doorbell rang in Geraldine's flat. 'Shit!'

It had been a long, hard day and Geraldine wanted to relax. Billy was out covering a news story and she had just settled down for the evening with a gin and tonic and a romantic video. She didn't relish any interruption. For a moment, she flirted with the idea of pretending she wasn't at home, but the caller would have seen her car parked outside the flat and would know she was there. The bell rang again.

'Coming, coming,' muttered Geraldine, hauling herself up from the beanbag on which she was reclining. She spoke into the intercom.

'Yes?'

'It's Carmel Rafferty.'

Instantly, Geraldine's exhaustion was overcome by curiosity. Following her dismissal from *Ireland Today* Carmel had been offered a backroom job, but had peremptorily refused it. She had handed in her resignation and was rumoured to be in St Pat's, drying out. Geraldine wondered what on earth she was doing here now. She had worked for many years as Carmel's researcher but the two had never been close friends.

'Come in,' she told her, pushing the security button for the outer door and opening her own hall door to greet the unexpected guest.

'Nice to see you, Geraldine,' said Carmel with a smile that Geraldine could tell was strained. She was wearing no make-up. Her skin was lined and pallid and she looked ten years older.

'Sit down,' said Geraldine, indicating a bean-bag. 'Sorry it's not more plush, but money's tight at the moment.'

That was putting it mildly. Billy's wife had screwed him for a massive separation settlement that left them living almost entirely on Geraldine's earnings.

'Thank you.'

Geraldine could see Carmel eyeing the gin and tonic and removed the glass hastily. She thought she had caught a whiff of alcohol from Carmel's breath when she had greeted her, but perhaps she had been wrong. At any rate, it was unfair to tempt her.

'Would you like a cup of tea?'

'That would be lovely,' said Carmel, with another strained smile.

'So – eh, how have you been?' asked Geraldine, as she made the tea in the little kitchenette that was separated from the living area by a formica-covered counter.

'Oh, fine,' said Carmel, airily. 'I've discovered there is life after *Ireland Today!*'

'What have you been doing?' asked Geraldine, hoping she didn't sound too nosey.

'I've been offered a new job. With Philomel.'

Philomel was a major production company which made documentaries and dramas for both the home market and overseas. Geraldine couldn't help being impressed. 'That's great,' she said enthusiastically. 'I'm pleased for you.'

Carmel accepted the proffered mug of tea.

'You know, I'll actually be earning more than I got from those stingy bastards in Channel 3,' she said. 'That's why I'm here, as a matter of fact.'

'Oh?'

'I'll need a top-rate researcher. We're doing a series of hour-long documentaries for the Beeb.'

'I see.'

'You'd be paid a lot more than you're getting now.'

'But it wouldn't be a permanent job. I'd be on contract?'

'Yes, but almost everyone is, nowadays.'

Geraldine thought rapidly. Philomel was a major company and would certainly pay above the going rate. She and Billy could use the money, no doubt about that, and yet there was something not quite right about the offer. She found it hard to believe that Carmel, with her drink problem, had simply walked into another job. She decided to come straight to the point.

'Do they know about your drinking?' she asked. For a moment, Carmel's eyes flashed dangerously, but when she spoke her tone was casual.

'I'm an alcoholic,' she said. 'But I've dried out

now and I'm dealing with it. One day at a time, and all that.'

Somehow, watching Carmel's trembling hand as she rooted in her bag for a cigarette, Geraldine doubted that she was as much in control of her drinking as she was letting on. She had found Carmel difficult to work with in the past and if she was still drinking, that would probably not improve.

'I think I'll stay where I am, Carmel. Thanks all the same. I quite enjoy working with Aisling.'

'Fine.'

Geraldine had expected Carmel to try some persuasion and was surprised and a little disappointed when she didn't. 'Speaking of Aisling, how's that affair of hers going?'

Geraldine played dumb.

'Affair? I don't know of any affair.'

'Oh, come on, Geraldine,' Carmel's tone was that of a schoolteacher admonishing a very stupid pupil. 'Everyone knows that she and Michael Whelan are an item. They went to Amsterdam together.'

Geraldine was taken aback. Aisling hadn't told her anything about Amsterdam.

'I don't think we should be talking about it,' she said firmly.

'What's the harm?' persisted Carmel. 'It's public knowledge.'

'It's not,' Geraldine insisted. 'And who told you they were in Amsterdam?'

'Oh, someone who knows someone who knows Michael Whelan,' said Carmel. 'From what I gather, it's all round Leinster House.'

'Then I'd better warn Aisling. She thinks nobody knows.'

Carmel smiled.

'Love is blind,' she said, 'and deaf as well, it seems.'

'Seriously, Carmel. If this got to the press, it could destroy Michael's career. And that would devastate Aisling. She really loves him.'

'He's had affairs before,' Carmel pointed out. 'They don't seem to have harmed him.'

'But there's a reshuffle coming up. He's in line for promotion. And he mightn't get it if news of this affair leaks.' She paused. 'I know there's no love lost between yourself and Aisling . . . '

Carmel interrupted.

'Oh, I bear her no ill-will now. As a matter of fact, she did me a favour. If it hadn't been for her, I wouldn't be working at Philomel.'

'Well then, do her a favour and tell the gossips to put a sock in it.'

'I'll try, but you know how people love a scandal.'

Geraldine's brow creased, in concern.

'I'm worried for Aisling.'

'You think he'd sacrifice her for his career?'

'I don't know. He's told her he's going to leave his wife. Once he gets the new ministry.'

Carmel put down her mug and stood up.

'Then she's a fool,' she said. 'Michael Whelan won't leave his wife. Not for Aisling or for anyone.'

Though Geraldine would never have admitted it to Carmel, she was thinking the same thing herself.

Carmel walked a respectable distance from the flat before pausing to take the gin bottle from her bag. She unscrewed the lid and took several swigs. Its bitterness stung the back of her throat, but the alcohol soothed her strained nerves.

She had got what she wanted. It amused her to think that Geraldine could be so gullible. She had played the oldest trick in the book – using a decoy to catch a duck – and Geraldine had fallen for it. There was no job offer at Philomel, not for Carmel and not for Geraldine, it had been merely a ploy to get her into the flat and on to the subject of Aisling. Thanks to Geraldine, she now knew that Aisling and Michael weren't just having a brief fling, they were a definite item, and that was something she could use in the future. She'd show them the folly of their dirty weekend in Amsterdam!

Her own trip to Holland had been made on a drunken impulse. Having discharged herself from St Pat's, she had made for the nearest bar where she had phoned an old drinking buddy who now lived in the Dutch city. It had seemed like a good idea to go and see her but the trip had been a disaster. She and her friend had fallen out and when Carmel had spotted Michael and Aisling she had been on her way to the airport to come home. Mere chance had placed the lovers in her way but the best news stories often came about through chance encounters.

Carmel replaced the gin bottle in her bag and made for the nearest bus stop. She thought how unfair it was that Aisling had a lover and a job (her job!) when she had neither. Since losing out to that bitch, she had even had to sell the BMW that had been her pride and joy. But now she was seeking revenge and didn't they say that revenge was a kind of wild justice? Well, she'd get justice if she played her cards right. It was a pity she didn't have photographs but she had what was almost as good – a recording of her conversation with Geraldine. She had turned on the tape while pretending to hunt for a cigarette and now it was safely in her bag, nestling next to the gin bottle. She'd wait for the proposed reshuffle and once it was announced, she'd sell her story to the press. Carmel's lips tightened in satisfaction. The fragile bubble of Aisling Davis's happiness was about to burst.

EIGHTEEN

Aisling looked out the kitchen window at the sheets of summer rain. 'Can you imagine what the traffic will be like?' She turned to Frances. 'If you're ready to go, I can drop you off at Monkstown. Save you getting soaked.'

'Great.' Frances drained the last of her coffee and stood up. 'We'll leave the breakfast mess for Nora to do when she finally surfaces!'

'Talk about lazy! She'll be in bed till lunchtime.' Aisling stood up and had a quick check in her handbag for tampons; her period was due that day. 'Still, I feel a bit sorry for her. She was really upset about not getting that part.' She glanced at her watch. 'God, look at the time! Hurry up!'

Frances followed her out to the car and said nothing. The more she thought about Nora's mercy run to a heartbroken Fintan a few weeks before, the less she believed it. She had almost certainly been with Patrick. And Nora wasn't the only one with a hidden agenda. She glanced across at Aisling as the car trailed along the line of traffic on the coast road. There had been a air of secrecy about both her sisters for some time now. It upset her that neither of them felt able to tell her about their love lives. In a real sense they were less close under the same roof than when they had been living apart. It was not at all the way she had imagined sharing a house would be; something had to be done before it was too late.

'Maybe the three of us should go out for a drink tonight, Aisling, and have a chat?' she suggested. 'You're right about Nora being upset.'

'Not tonight.' It was Friday and Aisling was hoping to see Michael. 'But definitely soon.' She drew up at the kerb. 'Quick – hop out before the lights change.'

Stuck in the almost stationary traffic, Aisling watched Frances run quickly through the rain to Patrick's house. She should have agreed to her sister's suggestion. It would be nice have a heart-to-heart as they used to have in the old days. The problem was that she would feel a hypocrite listening to Nora's emotional outpourings with her own secret ticking away like an unexploded bomb between the three of them. It wasn't that she didn't trust her sisters but, as a journalist, she knew the dangers of speaking to anyone about a forbidden liaison. She had been horrified when Geraldine told her about Carmel Rafferty's visit but they had reassured themselves that nobody would believe a word that Carmel said. Her gossip would be dismissed as jealousy of Aisling.

She hadn't dared tell Michael about the visit. He'd be furious if he learnt that Geraldine knew about them and would worry unnecessarily about what Carmel might do. She consoled herself with the thought that none of this would matter once the reshuffle took place and the relationship was out in the open. Then she would have the tough job of convincing Frances that Michael's marriage had been over long before she met him. Frances had strong feelings about unfaithful husbands and would be upset to learn that her sister was cast in the role of the other woman.

Still thinking nervously of how Frances might react to the news, Aisling shifted into gear and moved forward slowly. 'Yes,' she thought, 'it's definitely time for confession.'

Frances and Jean had been to a movie and were sitting in Neary's pub enjoying a drink.

'Did you understand any of it?' Jean was alluding to the art-house film they'd just seen. 'All that Swedish agony and *Angst*?'

Frances grinned.

'I quite enjoyed it, actually. But maybe romantic movies are more your line!'

'They certainly are! Especially since meeting Tony!'

Tony was a pilot Jean had started dating a few months before.

'I'm sorry I haven't been in touch, Fran. But he swept me off my feet!'

'Into the clouds!'

'Well, that's where we met. You wouldn't believe it but we air hostesses don't come across that many eligible men.'

'I don't believe it!'

'It's true!' Jean nodded her dark head, insistently. 'The passengers are usually married business types. Most of the pilots are married too. But then I met Tony . . . '

'And it was love at first sight?'

Frances grinned, knowing that for Jean, it always was.

'But that's enough about me,' Jean said. 'Now tell me: what do you think about me?'

Frances laughed. Jean was like a breath of fresh air. She had missed not seeing her for the past few months – so much had happened in both their lives. Hesitantly at first, she began to tell her about her growing love for Patrick and of her belief that he and Nora were sexually involved. When she had finished, Jean took her hand across the table.

'Oh, Fran,' she said. 'I wish I'd been around for you through all this.'

'I just don't know what to do.' Frances admitted. 'I love him but he doesn't love me.'

'And you're sure it's Nora he's involved with?'

'I'm positive. She hasn't said anything but I know.'

'And Aisling? Can't you talk to her about it?'

Frances shook her head.

'Aisling's just not the same lately, either. Nora and I are convinced she's got a married lover.'

'My God, it's like a soap opera in your place!' Jean became serious. 'Maybe you should think of moving.'

'From the house? And leave the girls?'

'Leave everything,' Jean's voice was firm. 'Including your friend Patrick. If he doesn't care about you, it's best to cut your losses.'

'I couldn't,' Frances looked sad. 'And not just because of how I feel about him – his kids would miss me. We've got very close.'

Jean drained her spritzer with typical carelessness, spilling a few drops on to her mohair jumper. She wiped it off, hastily.

'You're doing it again, Fran,' she warned.

'Doing what?'

'Putting everyone else's needs before your own. You did it when you were growing up and you haven't changed!'

Frances sighed.

'Believe me, I don't want to be a martyr. I want to find a nice man, settle down, have kids . . . '

'You had a nice man,' Jean reminded her. 'I always thought you and David would make a go of it.'

'So did I.' Frances looked miserable. 'I wish I could explain why it all went wrong.'

'I know what will cheer you up.' Jean took some tickets from her bag. 'These are comps for Lillie's Bordello. Do you fancy going?'

'I'm not really dressed for a disco,' Frances glanced down down at the skirt and long jumper she was wearing.

'Take the skirt off and wear the jumper as a dress,' suggested Jean. 'We'll put on some war paint and who knows? You could meet a real ride!'

Frances nodded. Jean was right. There was no point moping. She would go out and dance until dawn. It was a long time since she had done that.

'Only five days overdue? That's nothing. The same thing happened me last month.' Geraldine was unconcerned. She handed Aisling a salad sandwich.

'But I'm always spot on, almost to the minute

every four weeks.' Aisling protested. 'I wasn't bothered when it didn't come last Friday, but this is Wednesday and still no sign. I keep running to the loo to check.'

'I noticed that this morning. I thought you'd got honeymoon cystitis!' Geraldine laughed, then became serious again. 'I suppose you're very careful about taking your pill to the minute?'

'I take it at 7.00 every morning when the alarm goes off, no matter where I am.'

'Well then, stop worrying. Maybe the pill has thrown you out a bit. You're not on it long.'

'That's probably it. I'm not going to worry any more. But I had to say it to someone, so I was glad when you suggested a quick sandwich in your place. Much easier to talk here than in the canteen with everyone around. And,' she added with a frown, 'I'm still a bit neurotic about gossip since you told me about Carmel's visit.'

'The bitch was playing me like a fish! Pretending there was a job for me in Philomel!'

'And saying that everyone in Leinster House knows about our affair! If Michael knew, he'd freak!'

'She was just trying to get me to confirm it,' Geraldine looked miserable. 'And I walked straight in!'

'Supposing she tells someone?'

'I haven't heard a whisper from anyone and you know what media people are like for spreading the dirt! I'm so sorry, Aisling. But I did it for the best.'

'Don't worry about it. Anyway,' Aisling added,

'the reshuffle will probably happen now that O'Brien is getting so much stick from the public. I'm certain that Michael will get Foreign Affairs in the next week or so and then we can stop all this awful secrecy.' She ran her fingers nervously through her hair. 'I hope I'm not pregnant, Geraldine, but if I am, it's even more important to stop hiding.'

'You're not pregnant.' Geraldine said with an air of conviction, praying she was right. Geraldine did not share Aisling's optimism about a smooth transition from an adulterous secret to a glorious romance. She knew that rocky road well and her own happy outcome was the result of a great deal of pain.

'Maybe I should check, or is it too soon?'

'It's not too soon with the new testers. Tell you what,' Geraldine hopped down from the stool at the formica counter where they were eating their sandwiches. She believed in making quick decisions. 'I'll run down to the chemist and get one. Then you can relax.' Before Aisling could protest she had picked up her bag and was headed for the door. 'Hang on to your pee. Cross your legs until I get back.'

Aisling picked up *The Irish Times* but the newsprint danced before her eyes. She couldn't concentrate, not even on the item relating to the trouble in the cabinet. It all seemed incidental compared to what might be going on in her body. Her feelings changed from second to second. She wanted to carry Michael's baby even under these circumstances but then she felt frightened. It wasn't the right time for an extra complication but she reassured herself she couldn't be pregnant unless her pills were duds. Then with an intake of breath she remembered the morning she went to Amsterdam and how she had thrown up the remains of that lousy hot dog and almost certainly the small white contraceptive pill as well.

The door opened and Geraldine came in, brandishing a small package.

'Get it over with – the suspense is killing me!' Geraldine handed her the packet and gestured to the bathroom.

'No need. I know I'm pregnant.' Aisling's face had gone pale.

'How?' Geraldine laughed. 'Did it kick – at five days old!'

'I remembered something – quick, give it to me.' Her head reeling, Aisling went to the bathroom and followed the simple instructions. The following few minutes were an illustration of the theory of relativity.

'It must be time now. It seems like an hour,' Aisling pleaded with Geraldine who was watching the clock.

'Three seconds to go . . . two . . . one . . .

They both rushed over to the container. Aisling picked it up.

'I can't see anything,' she said. 'Is it blue? I think I've gone blind. Look, look,' she shoved it in Geraldine's face. 'Tell me.'

Geraldine could clearly see the blue strip. She put her arms around her friend.

'It's positive. I think a good strong cup of tea is

called for before we go back to work.'

Back at the studio Aisling worked with a quiet intensity. Tomorrow's edition of *Ireland Today* would be an important one, given the political scandal about the building contracts. By coincidence Michael would be on the panel, as the acceptable face of the party and to field the attacks against the government.

She took a break at four and rang Frances at work. Her sister was delighted to stay in for a chat that evening and she promised to contact Nora to ask her to be around. Then Aisling rang Michael in the Dáil but, as usual, he was unavailable.

Aisling put down the phone feeling lonely. She wanted desperately to tell Michael the news about the baby and be reassured that everything would be all right but, when she had made no contact by half-five, she gave up. They were meeting for lunch tomorrow anyway; it could wait until then. The most important thing now was to see her sisters and tell them most of the story.

Aisling looked into the expectant faces of her two sisters. She felt nervous and didn't know how to begin. On the way home she had stopped to buy a bottle of wine and now, playing for time, she handed Frances and Nora a glass each. She poured herself a half-glass. Anything more might be bad for the baby.

Frances gave her an opening. 'Is this a celebration?'

'In a way.' Aisling wondered could it be

regarded as a celebration; she had contemplated champagne rather than wine but then had thought better of it. She fell silent for a few moments.

'Come on, sis,' Nora was perched on the kitchen table, looking as if she was about to run off somewhere any minute. 'I've got to go into town to meet Fintan.'

'I'm in love with someone,' Aisling blurted it all out quickly before she lost her courage. 'He's a wonderful man and we're going to be married as soon as we can, but there's a complication.'

'You mean he's already hitched?' Nora looked at her sister with a knowing eye.

'Is she right?' Frances's face was aghast. 'God, Aisling, how could you get involved in that?'

'I didn't get involved deliberately, it just happened. Anyway,' she protested, ' his marriage was in trouble long before I met him.'

'Yeah,' said Nora cynically, 'his wife doesn't understand him!' Then seeing the tears well up in Aisling's eyes, she jumped off the table and put her arms around her sister. 'I'm so sorry, I'm a stupid bitch. It must be awful for you. Is it anyone we know?'

'I can't say who it is just at the moment. He's too well known. We agreed we'd keep it quiet for a while. I'm sorry.'

'But you can tell us,' Nora protested, moving away. 'We're your sisters, for God's sake.'

'I promise I'll tell you as soon as I can.'

Nora persisted.'Have you told anyone else?'

'No,' she lied. They would be hurt if they knew about Geraldine.

Frances had said nothing for some time. Now she began to speak very quietly.

'Aisling, I know what it's like to be in love. I know how you feel but there are some things you can't do, not even for love.' Her voice broke with sympathy for her sister. 'You can't break up a family. You'll never forgive yourself – think of the kids. I suppose there are kids?'

'Yes, and he loves them. But they'll be better off,' she insisted. 'It's miserable for kids in a broken marriage. And it *is* broken,' she added firmly. 'It was broken ages ago.'

'If you can't think of his family, think of yourself.' Frances begged. 'Second relationships often don't work out. You're going to throw everything away and then you'll be left, like he's leaving his first wife.'

Aisling looked at the two faces that, after Michael, she loved best in the world. Nora's expression was sympathetic if cynical and Frances looked worried and angry.

'I thought that even if you didn't understand, you'd support me no matter what.' Aisling began to sob. She felt sick with anxiety and repressed emotion.

'Don't cry, love,' Frances took her hand. 'Of course we'll support you through anything. If you murdered someone, we'd support you! It's just that we're concerned for you.'

'And the fact that you won't tell us who it is. Our minds are running in all directions. Hey,' Nora tried to lighten things up. 'Is it someone famous? A pop star?'

Aisling smiled in spite of everything. She looked with affection at her sisters and felt guilty. They shouldn't be kept in the dark any longer. 'I'm sorry, Michael,' she thought, 'but they have a right to know.'

'It's Michael Whelan,' she announced. There was no reaction. 'You know, the Minister for Social Welfare.'

Aisling watched their faces as they took in the implications of an extramarital political affair. 'And, I may as well tell you – I'm pregnant.'

'Darling, come in.' Michael opened the door. It was one o'clock the next day and Aisling had arrived at the flat for lunch. He took her in his arms and kissed her and all her anxieties melted away. Everything would be all right.

Coffee and sandwiches were on the table.

'Not much of a lunch, I'm afraid,' Michael apologised. 'I have to rush back fairly soon.'

Aisling's heart fell. This was not a situation that should be rushed. 'It doesn't matter about lunch . . . ' she began.

'No?' his voice was teasing. 'That's fine with me.' He took her by the shoulders and, leaning towards her, kissed the side of her neck.

Aisling nervously twisted the sapphire ring she always wore when she was with Michael. 'I've something important to tell you.'

'Come into the bedroom, love, it's more comfortable.'

Obediently, she followed him in to the room that she had vowed she would never return to, but that had been some weeks ago and things were different now. It was hard to know how to begin.

'Amsterdam was so wonderful . . . ' she began.

'Yes, indeed,' he laughed. 'But it can be just as wonderful here.' Gently he began to unbutton her cotton blouse.

To his surprise she put up a hand to stop him.

'Michael,' her face was radiant, although her voice trembled. 'I'm pregnant.'

'What? How could you be pregnant?' He stood up and moved back from the bed, staring at her in disbelief.

This was not what she had anticipated. A cold feeling settled in her stomach and she began very quickly to tell him about the bad hot dog, the vomiting, the late period and the test yesterday. Then she sat waiting for him to take her in his arms.

'The test could be wrong.' His blue eyes were sharp with anxiety.

'I'm sure it's not. But Michael, what with the reshuffle and everything, it will be all right. You'll be free to be with me and . . . ' her voice trailed away. She was still waiting for him to take her in his arms.

He sat beside her on the bed and spoke in serious, measured tones.

'Of course I'll be free to be with you but not if you're pregnant. Don't you see? A minister who leaves his wife is accepted – eventually – but a minister who is busy getting a mistress pregnant while he's still with his wife is not accepted – ever.'

'I don't understand . . . ' Aisling's voice faltered.

He took in his arms and held her close, assuring her of his love. Dimly she heard him talk about starting a baby later when they were living together.

'But we have started a baby. It won't wait.'

'No, but there'll be another baby – other babies. I promise you, my darling. And I'll look after everything and be with you all the time.'

She realised what he meant by 'looking after everything' and a wave of nausea swept over her.

'You mean . . . you mean an abortion. You don't want this child, our child?'

She pulled away from him.

'Of course, I want our child, Aisling, but later, for both our sakes.'

He looked at her beseechingly. 'I promise I'll make it up to you.'

She recognised that he was adamant and, in that instant, she knew clearly that, although he loved her, he would not sacrifice his career as well as everything else for her.

'Michael, I'll have to think . . . give me time to think.' Her eyes filled with tears.

He moved towards her again and kissed her tearstained face. Then he made love to her with tremendous tenderness. Afterwards, they lay in each other's arms and Michael whispered assurances of love. He did not mention the pregnancy again. Later, standing at the door of the flat, he appeared unwilling to let her go but held on to her, repeating over and over again.

'I love you, Aisling. I love you so much.'

She left him and walked to her car. The day

had changed. Clouds were gathering and a chill wind made her shiver in her summer clothes. She shivered again and then remembered that there was an old sweater in the boot. In a trance she opened it and stared at the roses that lay dead and forgotten in the shadows.

NINETEEN

'I'm sorry, Nora, but there's nothing in at present.'

Nora had phoned Eleanor Turner, her agent, in the hope that some auditions might be coming up.

'Not even for an ad?' she asked, desperate to find some sort of acting work.

'I don't think you should go for ad work.' Eleanor was insistent. 'You're a serious actress, you don't want to ruin your image.'

'What image?' Nora felt angry with Eleanor. Didn't she realise that, since her return to Ireland, she had not had a single acting job?

'Be patient, Nora. The big break's probably just around the corner.'

'Sure!' Nora slammed down the phone and made herself a coffee. She hated being unemployed. Each day seemed to stretch endlessly before her, with only the prospect of meeting Patrick at night to break the monotony. She almost envied Aisling the drama in her life; not that she'd fancy being in her shoes, with a married lover and a pregnancy to cope with, but at least Aisling was living, whereas her own existence seemed to be one long, tedious wasteland. If only she'd got that job with Tim! She'd be in the theatre now, working under his direction and maybe getting close to him in other ways as well. It just wasn't fair.

She picked up a copy of the previous night's *Evening Herald* and studied the Situations Vacant column. She had to find work of some sort, and soon. She no longer wanted to be financially dependent on Patrick and since there were no acting parts available, her only option was to find another stop-gap job to tide her over. The one thing she drew the line at was singing telegrams. Thinking of the strip she'd done, she gave a shudder. She'd certainly not get involved in that line of business again!

An ad for waitressing caught her eye. A newly opened city centre bistro was looking for staff. She didn't relish the thought of waiting at tables but she'd done it before in London when times were hard and anything was better than relying on Patrick. What was more, the ad specified that flexible working hours were available and that would suit her nicely. If an audition came up, she'd be able to get off and do it. She read the ad through again. There was an open interview at seven o'clock this evening. She'd be there.

She glanced at her watch. It was two o'clock and she had a whole afternoon to put in before the interview. She decided to take a long, bracing walk but first she'd have to phone Patrick to tell him she might be late this evening. There could be hundreds of applicants for the jobs and heaven only knew how long it would take.

'You're doing what?' From Patrick's tone, you would have thought she'd told him she was going to work in a bordello rather than a bistro.

'It's a job, Patrick. I need to work.'

'I'll give you whatever money you need.'

'But can't you see? I don't want to be dependent on you. I need to make my own way.'

'And what about us?'

She'd expected that question and was ready for it. 'I'll still be able to see you.'

'Not if you're going to be in that place every night.'

'The ad said the hours were flexible. I can work days and still see you in the evening. Besides, I probably won't even get it.'

'Maybe it's not a job you're going for at all.'

A nasty insinuating tone had entered his voice.

'I beg your pardon?'

'You've been different lately. It's as if your mind is somewhere else. Or maybe on someone else.'

Nora blushed guiltily, knowing he was right. Her thoughts were increasingly focused on Tim, though she hoped she had hidden it from Patrick. But he was so possessive that she should have guessed he'd pick up on it.

'I don't know what you're talking about.'

Patrick changed tack suddenly.

'And who holds interviews at seven in the evening?'

Nora's green eyes blazed with anger.

'It's a restaurant, Patrick. They're probably busy during the day. And I don't give a damn what you think, it's the truth!'

For the second time in ten minutes Nora slammed down the phone. She was shaking with rage. How dare Patrick question her this way? For the past few weeks, there had been harmony between them, and, although her mind was on Tim, she had made a positive effort to make things work with Patrick. After all, she hardly knew Tim and might not see him again for ages. Patrick had his faults, but at least he seemed to love her and didn't they say a bird in the hand was worth two in the bush? Now, after that jealous outburst, she wasn't so sure.

She glanced out the widow. The sun was glistening on the sea and there were children playing on the beach. It was a beautiful day and she was going to enjoy it. She put on a pair of black lycra cycling shorts and a matching T-shirt. She was going out for a healthy walk and she wasn't going to let Patrick or anyone else destroy her pleasure.

Nora stood in a long line of people waiting outside the office that was situated above the lively Bistro Boules in Dame Street. She was wearing the only suit she possessed, a smart navy-blue Quin and Donnelly number, and had tied her hair back because she figured that hygiene would be very important when working as a waitress. Now she wondered if it was worth the bother. There were so many people going for the jobs that she was sure she was wasting her time. She had been here for almost an hour already and there were still several people ahead of her. The door opened and one applicant emerged while another went in.

As she waited for her turn, Nora amused herself by creating histories for the people around her. That dark-skinned little man with the balding head was an ex-Mafia gofer who'd left Sicily after being sickened by the violence of the family he worked for. The woman with the tired, haggard expression had escaped from the husband who had physically abused her for years and was making a new start. And the young girl who was reading *War and Peace* was a student who was putting herself through university.

After another three-quarters of an hour, Nora had reached the head of the queue and was ushered into the room. A pleasant looking woman in her forties sat behind an untidy desk.

'You're very welcome,' she told Nora. 'And I'm sorry about the delay. We honestly didn't expect so many people to turn up.'

Nora smiled, responding to the woman's warmth.

'The recession may be over but unemployment seems as bad as ever.'

'Too true. My name is Imelda Harding. I'm the manageress here.'

She leaned across the desk to shake Nora's hand.

'Nora Davis.'

'So tell me about yourself, Nora.'

Nora gave a brief account of the waitressing work she had done in London.

'And what brought you home?'

'I missed my family.'

She would have liked to have told Imelda Harding the truth but she knew that she'd never get taken on if she were to admit that she was an actress who would throw up the job at the first opportunity.

'If you don't mind my saying, you don't exactly fit the type of applicant we've been looking at. To put it bluntly, you look like you should be a top model!'

Nora groaned inwardly. It would be just her luck to lose out on the job because she looked too attractive.

'I don't see why that should matter . . . ' she began, but Imelda Harding interrupted.

'I think you'd make an excellent assistant manageress,' she said. 'Bistro Boules is a three-hundred seater. When we opened a few weeks ago, we had no idea it was going to take off the way it has. I've been working every hour God sends and I'd appreciate a second-in-command.'

'Oh!' Nora couldn't help being pleased.

'With your past experience, I think you'd fit the bill.'

'Thank you.'

'We open from noon till midnight. You'd work days one week and nights the next.'

Nora smiled.

'That sounds grand.'

She could imagine what Patrick would have to say about it, but he would just have to put up with seeing her every alternate week.

'The salary is two hundred a week. So when could you start?'

Nora was a little taken aback. She hadn't expected to be offered the job right away.

'Could you make it tomorrow?' Imelda asked.

'The sooner the better as far as I'm concerned.'

'Fine,' said Nora, brightly. If only getting acting work were this easy!

'Then I'll see you at noon. Just to show you the ropes.'

They shook hands and Nora left the office. Despite the fact that the job wasn't what she wanted, she couldn't help feeling pleased. It would be good to be doing some work that wasn't sleazy like the singing telegrams and to be earning her own money without reference to anyone else. She glanced into the bistro on her way out and saw that it was buzzing with activity. She'd enjoy being here and if an audition came up on a day that she was working – well, she'd find some way around it.

She walked down Dame Street and on to Nassau Street where she'd catch a 7A or a 8 bus that would leave her to Patrick's. She wouldn't get there until almost ten and he'd probably be in a sulk but she didn't care. She was doing something positive with her life and that made her feel good.

Lost in her thoughts, for a moment she didn't notice the green Saab car that pulled up alongside her. Then she heard a familiar voice. 'Nora!'

Tim had lowered the electric window and was leaning across the passenger seat to speak to her. 'Can I give you a lift?'

Nora felt her heart jump with joy. Only a few hours ago she'd been gloomily telling herself that it could be ages before she saw Tim again, and now here he was. She climbed into the car, gratefully.

'Where to?' he asked, as the car purred off through the night time traffic.

'Oh, I was just going home,' Nora said airily. She certainly wasn't going to ruin things by telling Tim she was on her way to see her lover. Besides, after the way Patrick had spoken to her earlier, she didn't really want to see him now. Let him wait until tomorrow.

'And home is . . . ?'

'Sandycove.'

'That's on my route,' he said. 'I live in Dalkey.'

As they headed out the Merrion Road he told her about the rehearsals for *Vicarious Living* which were now in progress. Fintan was doing well in his role as a sexually ambiguous accountant but the actress who had got the part of Ruby, for which Nora had auditioned, was proving more problematic.

'She just won't take direction,' Tim told her. 'She plays for laughs at serious moments and misses the laughs when she ought to be getting them.'

'You should have cast me!' Nora couldn't resist telling him, with a sideways glance at his handsome face.

'Believe me, Nora, I would have if you'd been the right age. But don't worry. There'll be other parts.'

'That's what my agent said,' Nora said. 'But I got fed up waiting, so I've just got myself a job in a restaurant.'

'That's a good idea,' Tim said. 'There's nothing worse than sitting home waiting for the phone to ring. Believe me, I know.'

'But surely you're never out of work?'

'Not nowadays, thank goodness. But there were some pretty lean times in the past.'

They chatted all the way to Sandycove. Nora felt totally at ease with Tim in a way she never had with Patrick. He seemed intuitively to understand her and, of course, they had a lot in common. She felt sorry now that the drive was coming to an end.

'Fancy a quick drink?' asked Tim as they drove into Sandycove. 'We could go to the Eagle House.

'Great!' said Nora, thrilled at the chance of spending a little more time in Tim's company.

The pub was full and smoky and Tim had to push his way to the bar to order their drinks. Nora found a couple of bar stools in a corner and they sat and talked, sipping their drinks, until closing time. She wished the night could have gone on for ever, and couldn't help wondering if Tim would ask to see her again when he dropped her home.

They pulled up outside the gate of the town-house. There were no lights on in the hall or living-room, so Aisling and Frances were either in the kitchen or in bed.

'Would you like to come in?' she asked Tim. 'For coffee?' she added, with a nervous laugh. She liked Tim so much and for perhaps the first time in her life, was terrified of rejection.

Tim didn't answer immediately. Instead, he turned off the engine and switched on the car's interior light. Then he turned to her and cupped her face in both his hands. For a gorgeous, heart-stopping moment, she thought he was going to kiss her.

'You're so beautiful,' he said. 'And I love being with you. But . . . '

'There's another woman?' Nora couldn't control the quiver of disappointment in her voice.

Tim nodded.

'Things aren't great between us but I'm not going to give you a sob story. We're still together and while that holds, I'm going to play by the rules.'

Nora nodded. She appreciated his honesty but she couldn't help wishing he was more like Aisling's lover, Michael Whelan, who apparently had no trouble being unfaithful. Suddenly, she felt tears well in her eyes. She didn't want Tim to see her crying.

'I'll see you,' she said, kissing him quickly on the cheek before getting out of the car. He seemed to hesitate a moment, then he switched on the engine and drove off.

Nora opened the gate to the house and was walking to the door when someone grabbed her arm from behind. It was twisted up behind her back so that she cried out in pain. For a moment, she thought it was a mugger; then she heard Patrick's voice.

'Bitch!' he said, in a soft, but furious tone. 'You weren't at any job interview!'

'Yes, I was!' She was furious at being spied on.

'With that guy in the Saab?' Patrick asked. 'I saw you, through a gap in the hedge. You kissed him!'

'It was only a friendly peck on the cheek,' said Nora. 'He dropped me home.'

'Oh yeah?' Patrick clearly didn't believe her. 'Then why was he holding your head in his hands and gazing into your eyes?'

He twisted her arm back further. For the first time, Nora felt really scared of him. He'd obviously been skulking around the house waiting for her to return. He didn't seem to care that either Frances or Aisling could have seen him.

'Let go of my arm,' she pleaded, 'and I'll tell you.'

Patrick released his grip and Nora turned to face him. She could barely make out his features in the darkness but the obsessive rage that had brought him here tonight was almost palpable.

'How long have you been here?' she asked.

'Since ten o'clock, when it was obvious that you weren't going to come. I asked a neighbour to mind the kids,' he added, as though trying to show that he was perfectly in control of the situation. Well, he plainly wasn't in control of anything and nor would she be, as long as she was involved with a man like him. 'It's over, Patrick,' she told him, trying to quell her fear as she spoke. Would he lash out and hit her? Might he be carrying a knife? She wouldn't put anything past him.

'So you *are* two-timing me, you cow!'

'No, Patrick, I'm not. Tim's the director of that play I went for. And yes, I'd like to be involved with him but it's not going to happen.'

'You slut!' he said, shouting now, seeming not to care who heard. 'You threw yourself at him but he turned you down. Serves you right, you bloody whore!'

'I'm going inside,' she told him, in as even a tone as she could muster. 'And if you ever bother me again, I'm going to call the police.'

She walked towards the front door, praying he wouldn't follow. Fumbling to turn the key in the lock, she could hear him breathing heavily behind her, but he didn't do anything and as she let herself into the house, she saw him turn and walk from the front gate.

Shaking from the fright, she went to the kitchen to pour herself a stiff drink. Frances was seated at the table, listening to classical music on the radio. As soon as she saw Nora's white face, she knew there was something wrong.

'What is it love?' She was on her feet in a moment, and had turned off the radio. 'You look like you've seen a ghost.'

'Oh, Frances!' Nora collapsed into her arms in tears. 'He frightened me!'

'Who frightened you?' asked Frances, though a voice inside her was saying that she knew exactly who.

'Patrick Comerford.' Nora didn't mean to blurt out the name, but she couldn't help herself. 'I've been seeing him for a while and now he's making my life a misery. He came here tonight. He was lying in wait for me.'

'He didn't . . . ' Frances could hardly bear to say the words, ' . . . he didn't hurt you?'

'He twisted my arm, that's all.'

Frances said nothing, just held Nora closely to

her. After a few minutes Nora's sobs subsided and she pulled away from her sister.

'I'm sorry,' she said, looking Frances in the eye. 'I should never have got involved with him. I know how much you care for him.'

'Yes, I care for him, but I've known for some time that you and he were . . . ' She paused, unable to say the word 'lovers'.

'You knew?' Nora was incredulous.

'Oh, Nora, Nora,' despite her distress, Frances couldn't help but smile. 'You may be a great actress on stage, but off it . . . '

'Well,' Nora said, 'It's all over between us now. You can have him and welcome!'

Frances shook her head.

'If only life were that simple, love. But I'm afraid it isn't.'

TWENTY

It was a Saturday morning and Aisling, Frances and Nora were having a leisurely breakfast on the patio. The sun was shining and the marigolds that Frances had grown from seeds in large, glazed pots created a glorious splash of colour. The old stone walls were bright with purple and white passion flowers which, this hot summer, had produced soft apricot-coloured fruit which the sisters had picked and eaten.

'More toast, Ash?' Frances pushed the plate towards her sister.

'I couldn't,' said Aisling. 'I feel quite ill.'

Nothing had prepared her for the experience of morning sickness, which had begun almost as soon as she knew she was pregnant. That had been six weeks ago now and since then, she had agonised over whether or not to have an abortion. The pragmatic side of her told her she should. After all, she had her career to consider, not to mention Michael's. It made sense to delay having a baby until he had got his ministry and had left his wife. And her own career wouldn't exactly be helped by a maternity break. It would be better to wait until she had indisputably established herself as the unrivalled presenter of *Ireland Today*.

And yet, she couldn't help thinking of the tiny

life inside her. Even the ghastly morning sickness was a sign of its presence. She had read up about the stages of growth in pregnancy and knew that now, at just eight weeks old, her baby had ears as well as tiny fingers and toes. Try as she might, she just couldn't think of it as a mere bundle of cells, an embryo or a foetus; it was her baby.

'What should I do?' she asked Nora and Frances for the umpteenth time.

Frances regarded her frankly.

'I think abortion's wrong, Ash. I don't care what Michael says. It's just not right to kill off human life.'

Nora dipped a spoon into her runny egg.

'It's not a baby yet,' she objected. 'And it has to be Aisling's decision.'

'I know that,' Frances turned to Aisling. 'But I honestly believe that if Michael is serious about you, he'll support you whatever you decide.'

'It's not that simple,' Aisling objected.

'Isn't it?' asked Frances.

Aisling sighed. She valued the opinions of both her sisters but it was her decision, her choice. If only she could make up her mind.

The phone rang in the house, and Nora uncurled her bikini-clad form from the sunchair she was sitting on to run in and answer it.

'It's for you,' she told Aisling, coming back out. 'I think it's Michael's secretary.'

Since she had told Michael about the pregnancy he had phoned every day, hoping to hear that she'd decided to have the abortion. But when he rang her at home, he never made the call himself, fearing that Frances or Nora might recognise his voice.

'Will you hold for Mr Whelan?' his secretary asked. Aisling couldn't help wondering what she made of these calls. She must surely realise that Michael and herself were more than acquaintances; but then as a reliable, discreet secretary, she would undoubtedly keep any suspicions to herself.

'Aisling?' Michael sounded nervous. She knew that her inability to make a choice was causing him much personal stress, and because she loved him so much, she wanted things to be right for him. If only she could turn back time and have the pregnancy never happen.

'Hi,' she said, trying to sound bright.

'Have you made up your mind yet?'

Aisling hesitated. She hated to disappoint him but she had to tell the truth.

'I just can't decide.'

'Well, events may overtake us,' he warned. 'I've spoken to someone from O'Brien's camp and apparently they recognise that he'll have to go. The reshuffle may happen at any time.'

Aisling reflected that, only a couple of months ago, the reshuffle had been something she had longed for. Now she dreaded it.

'I don't want to have to choose between my career and you,' he said. 'Please, Aisling. Try to see sense.'

Aisling hesitated.

'Can I see you?' she said. 'Maybe if we could talk it over?'

'There's nothing to talk over!' Michael snapped. 'And I have to go home. It's Saturday, remember?'

'I'll call you on Monday,' she promised. 'I'll have made up my mind by then.'

'Right.'

Without another word, he was gone. Aisling returned to the patio, her heart heavy. The pregnancy had put a huge strain on their relationship and today, for the first time, Michael had almost lost his temper with her. She could see his point of view but it hurt her that he seemed unwilling to consider hers.

'I'm going to let him know on Monday,' she told her sisters.

'Well don't let him browbeat you into anything,' warned Frances. 'If you do decide to go ahead and have the baby, you know we'll be here to help.'

'Absolutely,' echoed Nora.

'We'll support you whatever you decide,' Frances added. She wanted Aisling to know that, although she was personally opposed to abortion, she'd still be her sister, no matter what. She smiled and took Aisling's hand. At the small kindness, Aisling felt tears prick at her eyes. Nora had told her about her disastrous love affair with Patrick and of its effect on Frances. Aisling had been astonished to learn that Nora had kept it a secret for so long and was even more surprised to learn of Frances's deep affection for Patrick. She was aware that each of her sisters had had difficulty in dealing with the aftermath, but they hadn't allowed their own problems to prevent them from being there for her.

'Thanks,' she said with heartfelt gratitude. 'I love you both.'

Carmel hated the small bedsit that was her most recent home. She thought with longing of the luxury apartment she had lived in for almost twenty years. The landlord had flung her out when she'd failed to pay the rent for two months running. Now, the bedsit's drabness was somewhat blurred. Although it was only eleven in the morning, she was already half-way through a bottle of gin and was feeling its effects.

She leafed erratically through the pages of a newspaper she had bought earlier on. It was the only luxury she allowed herself these days, apart from booze which wasn't really a luxury, more a necessity. The paper was full of speculation about the future of the errant minister but he was still hanging on to office and though the editorial hypothesised about a possible reshuffle, there was no confirmation that it would definitely happen.

'Shit!' As she turned another page, Carmel knocked over the glass of gin. It fell off the cracked formica covered table on which she was reading and the contents spilt on the dirty linoleum floor. Carmel picked up the glass and refilled it, without bothering to clean up the spillage.

It irked her that she was, as yet, unable to take her revenge. Bitterness ate through her like acid through metal. She longed to hurt Aisling; yet the one means she had for doing that seemed to elude her. What if this man O'Brien hung on to his post? She supposed that she could still go to the papers with the tape, but there was no guarantee that Michael would dump Aisling if the carrot of a senior ministry were no longer available. She itched for some kind of instant revenge, but what?

She glanced briefly at the personal column on the back page of the paper. A lover was sending birthday greetings to his girlfriend. Carmel's lips twisted cynically. Her own ex-lover had once placed just such an advertisement for her birthday, carefully coded so that his wife wouldn't understand it. But he had eventually dumped her, just as she hoped Michael would dump Aisling.

And then it came to her. Why hadn't she thought of it before now? With trembling fingers, she dialled the paper's classified advertisements number. The phone rang for a long time without being answered. It was Saturday morning, so they were probably operating a skeleton staff.

'Come on, come on!' Carmel muttered, impatiently. Eventually she got through.

'I want to place an ad,' she said. 'In the personal column of your paper. Am I in time for Monday?'

'Yes, you are,' the voice replied.

'Good,' said Carmel. 'Now here's the wording . . .'

Michael and Aisling sat in the scruffy bar where they had met on the fateful evening when they had visited the Phoenician. Aisling hated the pub, because it reminded her of Michael's wife and of how she had felt that night on seeing him with her. But at least it was safe and safety was of paramount importance right now.

'It could only mean us,' Michael told Aisling,

pointing at the ad. He had phoned her at work as soon as he saw it and had insisted on their meeting to discuss a plan of action.

Aisling read it through again. It was worded as a warning.

Michael and Aisling – hope you enjoyed Amsterdam.
A big announcement can be expected soon.
Love, C

'It has to have come from that Rafferty woman,' Michael said. 'That would explain the reference to Amsterdam.'

Aisling nodded miserably.

'I thought you said she wouldn't do anything?' Michael's tone sounded accusatory.

'I know she was upset that I got her job . . . ' Aisling took a deep breath, 'She threatened to get back at me for it, at the time.'

'Why didn't you tell me that, when we saw her in Amsterdam?'

'I didn't want to worry you,' Aisling said, hopelessly.

'And the 'big announcement' means she's going to spill the beans about us. Well, she's not bringing me down. She can't know for certain we're having an affair. All she saw was one hug. You could have been anyone – a mere acquaintance.'

'She does know, Michael,' Aisling said, and in a trembling voice, she told him of Carmel's visit to Geraldine. For a few moments Michael was silent but when he spoke it was in a cold, measured way she had never heard from him before.

'You told your friend Geraldine about us?'

Aisling nodded, miserably.

'She guessed there was something going on, and then she saw the ring . . .'

'I warned you never to show that ring to anyone!'

'It was an accident. It slipped out of my bag. And I was so happy, Michael. I needed to tell someone.'

Michael's lips tightened.

'Who else knows?'

'Just my sisters.'

Michael's eyes had turned to ice.

'You betrayed a trust. You swore you'd never tell anyone.'

Aisling wanted to cry. She knew she had been stupid and that Michael had every right to be angry with her.

'OK, I shouldn't have told them but they're the people in the world I'm closest to, apart from you. And they'd never breathe a word.'

'They don't need to.' Michael gave a bitter laugh. 'Geraldine's done it for them! She told the very woman who has it in for you.'

'Carmel just wants to make trouble for me. And she's certainly succeeded. But she probably won't do anything more. No journalist in town would believe her.'

'I wouldn't be too sure. Even if it's just a rumour, they'll want to run with it. And where does that leave me?'

'You can deny it.' She made a quick, agonising decision. 'I'll have the abortion and nobody need know. It would be her word against ours.'

Michael reflected on this.

'I suppose we can ride it out. But if she does talk, I'll have to keep my distance from you for a while.'

'How long?' Aisling asked, in a small voice.

'Until I'm secure in the ministry. Then I'll tell Cliodna the marriage is over – that's if she doesn't end it herself when she hears this story!'

'And then we can start seeing each other again?'

'Yes, but Aisling you must see how vital this abortion is now. If you were to be walking around pregnant, it would lend credence to the gossip.'

Aisling nodded.

'So long as I know I'll have you, in the end.'

'You'll have me,' he promised, but his tone was bitter. 'Unlike you, I don't break my word.'

TWENTY-ONE

'Daddy, help me, please.'

'Not now, Mark. Can't you see I'm reading?'

Frances looked at Patrick in surprise. His tone of voice was unusually harsh and, seeing Mark's hurt expression, she went to look over his shoulder at the colourful drawing of Tigger that he was trying to finish.

'That's lovely, Mark. Tigger will be pleased.'

'But, Franny, he's no eyes. I forgot his eyes.' He put down his crayons and looked pleadingly at his father, who continued to read the newspaper, oblivious of his son.

It was almost lunchtime in the Comerford household and Patrick was not out in the studio working. He had been hanging around the house for most of the morning. For several weeks now he had been distracted and depressed and many times Frances had wanted to take him in her arms and comfort him but she knew that it wasn't her arms he wanted. It had not been an easy time for Frances. She could see how much Patrick missed Nora and she felt sick with jealousy. Then suddenly she would feel angry with him because of how he had treated her little sister. Lying in bed at night, unable to sleep, she was overwhelmed by the mixture of emotions that spun through her head. But in the mornings she would think about Mark and Aoife and would put on a cheerful face for their sakes. 'Patrick,' she said sharply, 'Mark needs a bit of help.'

Patrick put down the paper and moved across to his son. With just a few dextrous strokes, he gave Tigger flashing expressive eyes and Mark was satisfied.

'Thank you, Daddy,' he beamed. 'I'll go and show it to Tigger.' He clambered down from his chair and, clutching his masterpiece, left the room.

Patrick gave Frances an apologetic look. 'You're right to tick me off. I've been neglecting them both. I've something on my mind.'

'Do you want to talk about it?' Seeing the sad look on his face, Frances once again longed to comfort him for the loss of her sister.

'I'm afraid not, thanks all the same.' Patrick's immediate response was to avoid any kind of intimate conversation with Frances. He had had trouble over that before. Then he thought again. At least he would be able to get some information about Nora, who put down the phone whenever he telephoned. He had given up trying to contact her but he couldn't get her out of his mind. He looked very directly at Frances. 'Maybe I should talk to someone.'

'Why not me?' Frances took a deep breath. 'Anyway, I think I know what's wrong and . . . '

At that moment Mary, the housekeeper, came in with Aoife, who was clutching a large yellow duster.

'We're finished upstairs. Aoife has everything

spick and span.'

'Me do spick spam.' Beaming with pride, the little girl ran into Frances's arms.

'I'd better get down to some work.' Patrick stood up. 'Frances, could you stay on this evening and we'll talk about that other matter when the kids are in bed?'

'OK.' Frances's eyes followed Patrick as he left through the French windows. She held little Aoife close to her. She was both excited and apprehensive about the coming evening.

'Nothing wrong, is there?' Mary's sharp antennae had picked up the signs of strain in the household over the past few weeks. She was hoping that Frances wasn't thinking of leaving the Comerfords. Her own work had been much easier since she had come and she was fond of the quiet girl who was so good with the children.

'No, it's nothing at all, Mary,' Frances lied.

Frances poured a cup of coffee for Patrick, who took it silently.

It was nine o'clock that evening and the two children had been in bed for some time. Patrick and Frances had finished eating and, having exhausted all trivial topics of conversation, they knew that the real issue must now be faced. The silence in the kitchen had become an almost solid presence that had to be broken. Suddenly they both spoke together.

'How about a . . . '

'I think I should . . . '

Patrick laughed. 'I was going to suggest a

brandy?' Without waiting for a reply he fetched the bottle and poured out two large measures. 'Now, go ahead with what you were saying.'

Frances took a gulp of the brandy. She had already had several glasses of wine but she was so nervous that she felt totally sober.

'I was going to say that I know what's upsetting you. It's Nora, isn't it?'

Patrick nodded his head. He wasn't surprised that she knew because he had guessed that, by now, Nora would have confided in her sisters and would probably have painted a very dark picture of his behaviour. 'She told you?'

Frances nodded.

He put his head in his hands. 'I want her back. I don't know why. She's been an absolute bitch, using me, seeing other men . . . '

'And you, what about you? Threatening her, hurting her . . . ' Frances's voice trailed off. She didn't know whether she was angry with Patrick for hurting her sister or for loving her.

'I know I shouldn't have been so aggressive but I didn't hurt her, did I? I hope to God I didn't hurt her!'

'She's fine.' Frances felt a wave of jealousy sweep across her again. Everyone was always concerned about her sister, who in many ways was so irresponsible. Just for once she wanted to be like Nora, to take life in both hands and not give a damn about the consequences.

'Has she got another relationship – that director?' Patrick asked, afraid of the answer.

Frances shrugged. 'I don't think so. But how

would I know? She didn't tell me about you.'

'It could have been difficult, with you working here.'

Frances looked him straight in the eye. She was impatient with all the deceit.

'It was difficult anyway.' She looked down at her glass. 'I knew she was in bed with you that night I lost my purse. I'm not an idiot.' For a moment she felt she was going to cry. 'I care about you, Patrick. Nora's my sister but I really care about you.'

She's trying to say she loves me, Patrick thought. He took her hand, compelling her to look into his face. Her eyes, softened by emotion, looked almost as beautiful as Nora's. 'I'm glad you care about me, Frances, I care about you too. I'd never want to hurt you or Nora. But the last few years . . .' He stopped, unable to talk about Deirdre and his overwhelming grief and guilt.

'Your wife?' Frances stood and moved automatically to his side to comfort him.

He put his arms around her waist and rested his head against her breast. He spoke of the terrible months after Deirdre's death when he had lain awake every night, suffering the physical pain of loss; and, even worse, remembering the distress he had caused his wife because he would not trust her, because he wanted to possess her totally. 'Those same feelings came back with Nora. I think I was half-mad with grief, I don't know what I felt for Nora.' For the first time, Patrick wondered if he really loved Nora at all. He lifted his head to look at Frances.

Without stopping to think, she bent down and kissed his lips. Filled with a need for the comfort of a woman's body, he stood up and took her properly in his arms. For some time they embraced and, almost automatically, he slipped his hand under her teeshirt and, loosening her bra, caressed her breasts. She did not object but when he tried to undo the zip of her jeans she pulled away.

'Patrick, this isn't a good idea.' The protest rang hollow because Frances desperately wanted to feel Patrick's naked flesh against her skin. There was an inevitability about this moment that made resistance absurd.

Certain that she wanted sex as much as he did, Patrick led her into the sitting-room and gently laid her down upon the long sofa. He tried to block out the memory of Nora sitting there that first night, her beautiful dark hair piled on top of her head, laughing as she insisted that they find a proper bed to make love in. He sensed that if he suggested to Frances that they go upstairs, she would be frightened. Patrick had an intuitive understanding of women and he was aware that Frances was on a knife-edge. The wrong movement, the wrong words and she would back away from him.

Frances did not back away. She allowed Patrick to undress her and she helped him to remove his clothes. Then they lay down together and she closed her eyes in pleasure as he kissed her breasts and the curve of her stomach.

As he lifted himself to lie on top of her, Frances went icy-cold. Patrick was not there any longer.

There was nothing. Only a terrible weight of darkness that pressed down on her and took the breath from her body. The memory of a red-hot curve of pain ran through her. With all her strength she pushed the darkness away.

'What is it?' Patrick was taken aback at the violence of her reaction.

'I don't know, I really don't know but I do want you.'

He held her close to him. Soon she became aroused again and, whispering endearments he moved her hips towards him so that he could enter her without covering her body.

The darkness began to press down and Frances felt she would scream. But she stopped herself and tried to listen to his words of love. This was the man who had given new meaning to her life, the man she had almost lost to her sister. She felt the softness of his beard on her face, and, relaxing, she let him move into her. When he came, although she did not experience any great physical pleasure, the darkness almost vanished and, lying in his arms, she felt as if she could fall asleep without fear.

Looking at her closed eyes Patrick felt protective. He did not love Frances, he did not even greatly desire her because he still ached for Nora's passionate responses. But he felt grateful for the comfort Frances had given him. Although he was chauvinistic and possessive, he was not a cruel man and he sensed that she had done something that had been very difficult for her, despite the fact that she was not a virgin. He remained holding her in his arms as she fell into a light sleep. He would stay awake to be there when she opened her eyes, so that she would not be frightened again.

Frances was dreaming, deep troubled dreams that she would not remember for some time to come. And when that time came she would need to be brave once more.

TWENTY-TWO

London was overcast but unbearably hot and muggy as Aisling and Nora walked towards the clinic. It was situated on the broad tree-lined avenue of a prosperous London suburb. Well-heeled businessmen and women hurried along carrying briefcases. The cars that purred by were large and sleek and the houses themselves were imposing redbrick Victorian buildings that spoke of affluence.

'There it is,' said Nora, as they stopped outside the Rita Hobbs Clinic. 'How do you feel?'

Aisling shrugged. She wasn't feeling anything at the moment; only a blessed numbness. But she was grateful to Nora who had insisted on accompanying her. Michael had explained how impossible it would be for him to come with her under the present circumstances. Aisling had tried to understand – if he were seen flying out of Dublin with her, it would only serve to fuel Carmel's story. But when Nora heard about it, she had been mad.

'Who cares about his bloody career? You're doing this for him and he should be with you!'

Aisling reflected that Nora was maturing. Only a few months ago, she'd have been too busy pursuing her relationship with Patrick to bother about anyone else's concerns. Yet when when the chips were down, it had been Nora, rather than Frances, who had sprung to her assistance.

'I'm coming with you,' she had told her. 'You're booked in for a Monday and the restaurant's closed then, anyway. I'll get the Tuesday off and we'll be back home in the evening.'

Tearfully, Aisling had agreed. She had been a little hurt by Frances's silence on the matter and had read it as disapproval.

They walked up the steps to the clinic and entered a plush reception area. A well groomed woman was sitting at the desk.

'Welcome to the Rita Hobbs,' she spoke in a polite but businesslike manner. 'May I show you to the waiting room?'

Aisling and Nora were ushered into a room off the hall. Some women were seated around a large mahogany table flicking through copies of *Vogue* and *Tatler*. A large tropical fish tank took up most of one wall and there was a coffee-making facility beside the marble fireplace. It was a typical consultant's waiting-room, though more expensively furnished than any Aisling had been in before. Of course she knew that abortion clinics weren't seedy back rooms lit by naked bulbs but she was a little taken aback by this anonymous luxury. The clinic seemed to offer no hint of the painful realities that were being faced by the women who entered it daily.

Michael had made the booking for her.

'Done this before, have you?' she had asked him bitterly. Michael had looked hurt.

'I know one of the consultants who works there,' he told her. 'We were at college together.'

In a few short days the whole thing had been arranged. Michael had insisted on paying for everything, including Nora's expenses. Aisling had heard of clinics from which women were discharged just a few hours after their abortions but here she would be required to stay overnight for observation, while Nora was booked into a nearby hotel. Aisling was aware that the cost involved must be considerable but Michael had been more than willing to pay.

'This must be costing Michael an arm and a leg!' Nora said, reading her thoughts. She spoke in a near-whisper but even so, the sound of a human voice somehow broke an unspoken rule in this silent room. A couple of the women glanced up from their magazines, then returned to them quickly, as though embarrassed at having witnessed a social gaffe.

One by one the women were ushered out by the receptionist, while other women arrived. After about half an hour it was Aisling's turn.

'Ms Davis,' the receptionist said, 'this way, please.'

Aisling stood up.

'Come with me, Nora,' she said and despite the receptionist's quiet disapproval Nora followed. The receptionist led them up the richly carpeted stairs to another room where a nurse was waiting.

'This is Ms Davis,' said the receptionist, 'and a friend.'

'Her sister, actually,' said Nora but the

receptionist had already gone.

'I'm Patricia Lynch,' the nurse announced in an unmistakeable Cork accent.

'You're Irish!' Aisling said.

'Does that surprise you?'

'I suppose not.'

'I just want to take some details,' she told Aisling. 'But first of all, we have to make sure you're happy about having this termination.'

'I am,' Aisling said. 'It might damage my career to have a baby now . . . ' She paused. ' . . . and there are personal factors, as well.'

'Right – well that's the counselling bit over,' Nurse Lynch laughed. 'It's just a formality but we have to observe it.' Aisling said nothing. If she were to express her real feelings about the abortion, the clinic might well refuse to go ahead with it. 'I'll just explain the procedure to you,' Nurse Lynch was saying. 'There's no need to be frightened,' she added, kindly. 'Nobody likes having a termination but it's a very minor operation.'

Aisling answered Nurse Lynch's long list of questions automatically. Had she any history of miscarriage, previous abortions or pregnancies? As she made her responses, she was thinking of the feature she had done on abortion – it seemed like years ago now! – for *Ireland Today*. How easy it had been for her to express her sympathy for Laura, the young girl who had travelled to Liverpool to have one. With hindsight, there had been something almost patronising in her attitude. She had never for a moment considered that she might find herself in the same position. Yet here she was, about to terminate the life of her unborn baby. Aisling pulled herself up sharply. There was nothing wrong with termination – it was simply a matter of choice and she was making hers. But was she? Was it not Michael who had made the choice, Michael who had decided? She had had no real say at all. If she didn't end the pregnancy, then she would lose him and that was an outcome she couldn't bear to consider.

'That's about it,' Nurse Lynch was concluding. 'Have you any questions?'

'What?' Aisling realised that she hadn't heard a word that had been said.

'Aisling . . . ' Nora looked concerned. 'Are you all right?'

'Yes. Yes, I'm fine. What happens now?'

'As I was saying, we take you down to pre-op. You'll be given a fairly mild general anaesthetic and when you wake up, you'll be free as a bird.'

'Right.'

Nurse Lynch looked at her perceptively.

'Are you quite sure you're happy with this?' she asked.

'Yes, quite sure.'

'Well then, I'm afraid I have to ask your sister to leave now. She can come back and see you this afternoon, when you're awake.'

Nora hugged Aisling.

'I'll be back later,' she assured her. 'And don't worry, you'll be fine.'

As she watched Nora's figure retreating down the stairs, Aisling suddenly felt like crying. She wanted to run after Nora, to forget the abortion and spend the rest of the day in the London shops. But of course she didn't. Instead, she obediently followed Nurse Lynch into yet another room, full of cubicles, where she changed her clothes for an operation gown. When she was ready, Nurse Lynch led her into the pre-op room, and helped her on to a trolley which would later be wheeled into the adjoining theatre.

'The anaesthetist will be here in a minute,' Nurse Lynch said, 'And I'll see you later.'

Aisling lay on the trolley. She looked out the sash window at the grey sky. The window was slightly open and she could hear the traffic moving below. And then she heard another noise. The sound of a child's laughter, echoing upwards from the pavement. A sound full of happiness and joy, as though the child (and she couldn't tell if it was a boy or a girl) had just been given some wonderful new toy. It was the sound of life and of hope and at that moment, Aisling knew that she couldn't let go of her baby. She sat up on the trolley and looked around for her clothes. Nurse Lynch hadn't brought them into the room; they would probably be placed in a locker beside the bed she would occupy after the operation. She was clambering down from the trolley when the anaesthetist arrived. He was a tall man, dressed in a surgical gown.

'Back up, please Miss Davis,' he indicated the trolley. 'It's time for the anaesthetic.'

'No!' Aisling shouted, running past him. 'I'm not going through with it!'

She rushed back to the cubicle room where Nurse Lynch was folding her clothes.

'Give them to me!' Aisling pulled the garments from her roughly. 'I've changed my mind.'

She dashed into a cubicle and flung her clothes back on. Nurse Lynch was waiting for her when she emerged.

'Would you like to talk some more?' she asked Aisling. 'Lots of women have doubts before this operation and it's as well to discuss them.'

'There's nothing to discuss,' Aisling was already half-way out the door. 'I'm not going through with it.'

She ran down the stairs past the receptionist, whose mask-like expression never altered. Out on the street, she paused and inhaled deeply. She knew that she was effectively ending her relationship with Michael. He would distance himself from her and would strenuously deny whatever gossip Carmel circulated about her pregnancy. But perhaps, once he was well established in his ministry, they could start seeing each other again. It was a risk she would have to take. She looked up at the sky and saw that the sun was beginning to pierce the July cloud. Its warmth on her face seemed like an assurance that she was doing the right thing. The rain that Londoners were longing for was not going to arrive just yet but Aisling welcomed the sunshine. She stood for a moment, relishing it, then turned and headed off in the direction of Nora's hotel.

'You're quite sure about this?' Nora asked, as they

sat in the hotel lobby eating cream cakes.

'Absolutely!' She didn't tell Nora about the child's laughter. It might have seemed absurd to her and, besides, it had been a private moment.

'Well then, I'm delighted!' Nora smiled. 'I knew you weren't happy about going ahead and you might have regretted it later.'

Aisling nodded. 'I think I would have.'

'But what about Michael? What will this mean for you and him?'

Aisling paused a moment before speaking.

'Nora, only an hour ago, I was sure I couldn't live without him. But now . . . well, what's meant to be, will be.'

'If he cares about you, he'll stick around.' Nora took Aisling's hand. 'If not, then you're better off without him. And since he's paying for this trip, let's enjoy ourselves! We'll book you in here for the night, then go and see the town.'

Aisling felt tears well in her eyes.

'You've been so good, Nora. How can I ever thank you?'

'You don't have to,' Nora assured her. 'After all, what are sisters for?'

TWENTY-THREE

'Fanny, me want more dink.'

'Please!' Frances reminded Aoife, as she took the plastic beaker from her chubby brown hand. She poured out some orange juice from the pottery jug on the kitchen table.

'There you are, pet.'

'Ta, ta, please, tank-oo.'

In spite of all her worries, Frances laughed and gave her a hug as the little girl slid off her chair and toddled out the kitchen door into the garden.

Looking through the window, Frances could see Mark watering the flowers in the terracotta pots. It was only mid-July and already the earth looked parched and Mediterranean. It seemed as if this glorious summer would go on for ever. She thought anxiously of Aisling and Nora in the stifling heat of London. They had left very early that morning and Aisling had given her a wan smile as she picked up her overnight bag.

'I know you think what I'm going to do is wrong, Fran, but . . . '

'Don't,' Frances interrupted. 'Whatever you do, you're my sister and I love you.'

Frances wished she had not been so distracted with her own troubles over the past few days because she should have spent time with Aisling.

Now she kept thinking about her. Sometimes she thought of the baby but she tried to put that out of her mind. It was too distressing.

She looked at her watch – it was nearly one o'clock. Maybe it was all over by now.

Suddenly she felt very lonely. On an impulse she picked up the phone on the kitchen wall. There was a possibility that Jean might be free this afternoon.

'Hi, it's Frances.'

'Everything OK, love?'

Jean's voice was concerned and Frances was quick to reassure her. 'I'm fine.' She knew why Jean was worried. Frances had told her about sleeping with Patrick and how worried she was that it would be difficult to go on working for him as if nothing had happened. But in some strange way, having sex with Patrick had cured her obsession with him. It was less than a week since that fateful night and already she felt nothing stronger than affection for him and gratitude that he had helped her to overcome her sexual fears. He did not preoccupy her at all.

What did preoccupy her were the memories surfacing in her mind. Pictures swept across her consciousness – the indistinct features of a man's face, a narrow bed, the sound of children shouting and laughing. She had lain awake for hours last night, worrying over Aisling but also praying these fragments in her head would come together and that she could remember the something important that was eating away inside her.

'Jean, are you free this afternoon, by any

chance?'

'Sure, I'm off till Thursday. What have you got to offer?'

'Two small children, buckets and spades and a swim.'

'Sounds great. I'll pick you up and we'll go to White Rock.'

They made arrangements and Frances hung up and went out to the studio to tell Patrick that she was taking the children to the beach. She took a long cool drink of orange with her.

He looked up from his work when she opened the door.

'Just what I needed.' He took the glass gratefully.

'I thought you might be thirsty. It's so hot. I'm going to take the children to the beach.'

'They'll love that.' He drained the glass and handed it back to her. 'Thanks, Frances – for everything.'

They smiled at each other and Frances thought back to the Thursday morning last week after they had made love. She had come to work as usual and instantly sensed Patrick's anxiety that she might expect from him what he was not able to give. That first day they had both been uneasy and embarrassed but that evening Frances plucked up enough courage to talk openly to him about it. She had been quick to reassure him that she knew he didn't love her and, indeed, although, she was very fond of him and adored his children, she didn't love him either.

It had been a wonderful relief to say that and

to know it was true. Now it would be possible to become his friend and she could tell by Patrick's attitude that he felt the same.

The hot jungle smell of the ferns growing by the wayside was overpowering.

'That's so evocative,' Jean sniffed with appreciation, as she got out of the car on Vico Road. 'Remember how we used to come as kids, with Aisling and Nora. How are they?'

'Fine,' Frances felt uncomfortable. She had decided not to say anything to Jean about the abortion. She felt that it would not be fair to Aisling.

'I can carry that,' Mark took the basket from Frances and began to stagger down the steep path to the strand.

'I help,' Aoife toddled after him on her pudgy brown legs.

It was not too crowded on the beach and they found a secluded place quite easily and spread out the towels.

The children settled down near them with their spades and buckets of water that Mark had fetched to slop into the sand. Frances and Jean took off their cotton shorts and T-shirts and lay down in the sun in their swimsuits.

'Will I do your back?' Jean waved a bottle of Ambre Solaire in the air.

'OK, but don't throw it all over me!'

When they were properly oiled, they lay back and relaxed for a while in the afternoon heat.

'Frances,' Jean was never silent for long. 'How

are things at the house?'

Frances sat up and checked that the children weren't listening. She turned to Jean. 'We both seem to be handling it well. It's odd, but I don't have those complicated feelings about him any longer.'

'It's really good that you were able to have sex.'

'Yeah, I'm so relieved about that but,' she added, her eyes darkening with sadness, 'it's a bit late.'

Jean's sympathetic pat on the shoulder indicated that she knew that Frances was thinking about David.

'Come on, Jean,' Frances jumped up. 'Let's take the kids into the water.'

For some time they splashed about with Mark and Aoife at the edge and then Frances, leaving Jean in charge, swam steadily out into deeper water. The sounds of children's shouts faded. She turned onto her back and closed her eyes against the glare of the sun. Disturbing memories began to surface again. She tried to think of something else. Nora and Aisling had said they would ring this evening. She must make sure to be at home.

'Hey, Fran, it's my turn to swim.'

Hearing Jean's shout of protest she headed for the shore and took over the children. It was a struggle to show an interest in their games; she was so tired today that she could barely keep her eyes open. Later, lying back on the hot sand, she could feel herself slipping off into sleep.

She felt a light touch on her arm. Jean was standing beside her, towelling herself dry.

'Fran, you're exhausted. I'll mind these two.'

'You're a pet. Just ten minutes.'

'Come on you two, we'll go down and build a big, big castle.'

'Can I build the moat, Jean, and put shells all around . . .'

Frances smiled as Mark's voice faded away into the echoes of children's laughter. Shifting on the sand she felt the dampness of her swimsuit against the small of her back.

Suddenly she was trembling all over. Paralysed by a weight that pressed down upon her, she was unable to move. She tried to open her eyes but her lids were too heavy. A man's face was very close to her, so close that the features were blurred, but in a flash of recognition she knew who it was. She knew who it had been.

She pushed herself up to a standing position. For a moment she did not know where she was. Then she saw Jean and the children. Mark waved to her. She stood there, unable to wave back. Jean, sensing that something was wrong, came running up to her.

'What's the matter? God, you look like death! Are you getting sunstroke?'

Frances had to be alone and she seized the excuse. 'I *am* hot. I'll go sit in the shade. I'll be OK.'

'I'll get back to the kids. But I'll be keeping an eye on you. Don't go far.'

Frances moved towards the shade of the high cliff and found a flat rock to sit upon. She whispered to herself the name that had escaped her for so long and she allowed the past to return.

'Seamus O'Connor.'

It had been hot that first sad summer after her mother's death and fourteen-year-old Frances had been pleased when the O'Connors had suggested that she go with them to their mobile home in Courtown. She knew she would have to do a certain amount of babysitting for the twin boys, but she didn't mind that because James and Sean were well behaved six-year-olds.

Seamus and Una O'Connor had been very good to the Davis family since their mother's death the previous autumn. Whenever Frances babysat for them, she arrived home with an apple tart or a tray of homemade biscuits that Una insisted she take back to her sisters. She was a gentle, kind woman, very much in the shadow of her more dynamic husband.

'Mrs O'Connor, I'd love to go.' She had responded eagerly to the request. 'I'll have to ask Dad but there won't be a problem.'

'Of course, you can go, pet,' her father said when she told him. 'In fact it suits fine because I'm off to the Derby for that fortnight and I've asked Aunt Cathy to come and stay here, so I'm sure you'll be glad to be out of the house!'

Frances felt a pang of sympathy for Aisling and Nora, who would be left with Aunt Cathy. Nine-year old Nora called her the 'aunt from hell', because she insisted they behave 'like young ladies for a change'.

'You lucky thing!' Aisling whispered to her that

night in the bedroom. 'I really hate the thought of two weeks with the old bat. Una O'Connor's lovely. She'll let you do what you like.'

Maybe, thought Frances but he won't. Mr O'Connor was quite strict with the boys and Frances was a little nervous of him. He had never said a cross word to her but there was something about him that made her fall silent in his presence. Even his wife seemed subdued when he was around.

The mobile home was lovely. The O'Connors had recently bought it and everything was new and sparkling. It was situated right on the beach and you could race down in your togs and be in the water almost as soon as you woke up. The days were long and sunny and the first week passed so quickly that Frances didn't miss the company of people her own age. The children in the other mobile homes were all young, so it was fortunate that she had a good supply of books and tapes.

By the Wednesday of the second week the twins were getting tired of sea and sand and pleading for a trip that afternoon to the funfair in the town. They were all ready to go when Una remembered that she had to put the casserole for the evening meal in the oven at four o'clock.

'Use the timer.' Seamus suggested.

'No timer on this little oven,' she laughed. 'It's OK. You go on. Pity,' she added, 'I was looking forward to a go on the dodgems.'

'I'll stay,' Frances volunteered. She hated funfairs and she was dying to finish the detective story she was reading. 'Honestly, I don't mind.'

'Are you sure? You *are* good.' Una looked pleased. 'It's in the fridge – all ready to go in.'

When they had gone Frances settled down in the sun with her book. At half-three she went for a swim and headed back to the house to sort out the dinner. She was surprised to find Mr O'Connor getting out the car as she arrived.

'You're early.' Frances said. 'Where are the others?'

'I remembered I needed to get some paperwork finished before I go up to the office tomorrow.' He opened the boot and took out a pile of boxes. 'I'll go back later and collect the family.'

Struggling with the boxes he opened the door and ushered her in. 'Looks like it's just the two of us.'

Suddenly, Frances felt cold in her wet suit. She went straight to the cooker and switched the oven on. She turned around and fell against Seamus who was standing right behind her.

'Sorry,' she apologised.

'Don't say anything, don't say anything.' He pushed his mouth against hers and tried to force her lips open. Frances could not believe this was happening. She tried to push him away but he refused to let her go. With a feeling of panic she lifted her leg to hit him where it would hurt but, anticipating what she was going to do, he lifted her up and carried her into her bedroom.

He put her on the bed and held her down with the weight of his body, while he struggled out of his shorts.

'Stop!' Frances tried to scream and his hand went over her mouth.

'Shut up. No one will hear you anyway.'

Frances felt her swimsuit being pulled down her body and a hand forced its way between her legs.

'Relax, this won't hurt. You're such a lovely girl.' Mr O'Connor's voice had lost its harshness and was soft and caressing. 'Don't keep struggling. It'll be easier if you let me. Just let me.'

She tried to turn her head to the side, so that she could not see his awful face. She did not want to feel that hardness that was forcing its way into her body. She could feel the gritty texture of sand in the small of her back. She would not listen to his breathing; she would listen to the sounds of children laughing and shouting on the beach.

A terrible pain went through her body but she couldn't scream.

When he had lifted himself off her, he covered her with a blanket.

'I'm sorry. I couldn't help it.'

Frances could sense him standing above her. Huddled under the blanket, she kept her eyes tightly closed.

'You won't say anything to anyone about this.' His voice was cold. 'Anyway, no one will believe you. They'll call you a liar and a slut. Tell you what . . . ' He leaned over her, his voice was gentle now and she felt his fingers caress the top of her head. ' . . . we'll keep it as our little secret.'

She lay on the bed for what seemed a long time. When she heard the door shut and the car starting, she got up and, wrapping a towel around her, she went into the kitchenette and put the casserole in the oven.

Back in the bedroom she stared for some time at the blood on the quilt. She tried to wash it away with cold water. Then she dressed herself in jeans and a heavy sweater because she was so cold. Picking up her torn swimsuit, she went out to the bin and threw it away.

When the O'Connors came back, they found her shivering in an armchair. Una talked about getting a doctor but Seamus said that it would be ridiculous, that she just had a chill.

Una gave her a warm drink and aspirin and put her to bed. Frances tossed and turned all night, tormented by terrible dreams. The next morning she said that although she felt better she would like to go to home that day. She drove up to Dublin with Seamus, who talked for a long time about loyalty and secrets. But Frances wasn't listening to his conversation. She was thinking about how sick she had been the day before and the only thing she wanted to do was to forget all about it.

TWENTY-FOUR

As soon as she heard the sound of the taxi pulling up, Frances ran to open the front door. She heard Nora's cheery voice talking to Aisling.

'It's OK, Ash, I have the money here.'

The taxi drove away and the two sisters came slowly up the driveway. Aisling looked at Frances and instantly burst into tears. Her older sister rushed over to put her arms around her.

'I don't know why I'm crying,' Aisling protested, 'because I glad I didn't go through with it. I never wanted to have an abortion.'

'I was so relieved when you rang last night and said you'd changed your mind.' Frances let her sister go. 'Come on in. You must be exhausted.'

'We didn't get too much kip last night,' Nora agreed as they went in. 'But it wasn't all misery. We'd a super meal at Michael's expense. Made it all the sweeter!'

Frances looked anxiously at Aisling.

'Have you told him yet?'

'No,' Aisling sat down at the kitchen table. 'He's going to ring this evening but I won't tell him on the phone. I'll see him tomorrow.' She ran her hand nervously through her hair. 'He'll be furious but I know I've done the right thing.' She cradled her arms over her stomach. 'Suddenly this baby is more important to me than any man.'

'Talking of which . . . ' Nora cast an appreciative look at the plate of sandwiches that Frances had prepared in case they were hungry. ' . . . you might feed the poor sod! You ate hardly anything on the plane.' She proffered the plate to her sister.

'Thanks, love.' Aisling took a sandwich and put a hand affectionately on her sister's arm. 'I don't know what I'd have done without you.'

'I feel awful. I should have been with you . . . ' Frances broke off and put her head in her hands.

'Fran, don't be upset. I know how you feel about abortion. It would have been difficult for . . . '

'No, it wasn't that. It was . . . ' She began to cry and Nora and Aisling rushed over to her.

'What is it, Fran?' Aisling handed her a tissue.

Frances looked at their two anxious faces. In the midst of the turmoil they were all going through, the most important thing to hold on to was the love they had for each other. It was time that she told them everything but she didn't know how to begin. She dried her eyes and began to speak in a quiet voice.

'The last few days have been pretty awful . . . '

'You can say that again!' Nora exclaimed.

'I don't mean the baby – something else, to do with me.'

Nora had a flash of intuition. 'Patrick?'

Frances looked away. She wasn't sure how Nora would feel when she told her that she had slept with her ex-lover.

'Yes,' she confessed, 'I slept with Patrick last week.'

There was a long silence. Aisling's eyes were wide with astonishment and Nora's confused feelings were visible on her face.

'It was just once, Nora. It will never happen again.'

'He wasn't horrible to you, was he?' Nora's voice was concerned and Frances could tell that she was trying to overcome the feelings of possessiveness that often linger even when a relationship is over.

'He was kind. It just happened, Nora...'

'Forget it, Fran. I know how much you care about him. And anyway, there's nothing between us any more. If you love him, that's all right with me...'

'I don't love him; I don't think I ever did. It was some kind of obsession. What's important is what it made me remember.' She crossed her arms tightly across her chest, gripping her shoulders with her finger-tips. 'It's so hard to talk about it.' She spoke in a whisper. 'I feel the pain all over again. I really want to tell you but...'

Aisling and Nora exchanged warning glances. They knew instinctively not to put pressure on Frances. They sat on each side of her at the kitchen table and held her hands.

After some time Aisling spoke.

'Who was the bastard who abused you?

Frances looked at her with gratitude. Thank God some one had finally said it for her.

'How did you guess, Aisling?'

'Something about the way you couldn't go on talking, something about the way you were holding yourself so tightly.' She got up and began to walk up and down. 'Christ, I'd love to kill him. Who was it?'

Frances didn't answer. She wished that Aisling could guess who it was. That someone else could put it all in to words and make it real.

'I was fourteen . . . ' she began.

'That long ago and you never said a word!' Nora seemed almost angry as she gripped her sister's hand.

'How could I?' Frances's voice was full of anguish. 'I didn't know. It was all buried . . . ' her voice broke. After a couple of seconds she continued in a calmer tone. 'I suppose I repressed it.' She turned to Aisling. 'That's what happens, isn't it?'

'Yes, love, that's what happens. I read a lot about it for that recent programme on sex abuse.' She saw Frances shudder again as she said the words. 'God, you were only a child! And Mum had just died. Please, Frances, tell us who it was?'

'It was Seamus O'Connor.'

'Christ!' Nora stood up and moved towards the window.

'I should have guessed.' Aisling's voice was cold with rage. 'The respectable family man – pillar of the community. Fran . . . ' She sat close to her sister and took her in her arms. ' . . . you poor pet. How did it happen?'

'Do you remember that summer I went to Courtown with the O'Connors?'

They nodded and, with breaks for tears and for comforting, she told them everything that had come back to her.

'I remember that time,' Aisling said thoughtfully. 'You were very strange afterwards for a while. Even though I was only twelve, I really noticed. In fact,' she added, 'I was upset because I thought you were annoyed with me over something. I cried myself to sleep for nights over it.'

'I'm so sorry, Ash.'

'Don't be daft, you were the one who was really suffering. That bastard O'Connor.'

'You went on babysitting for them for years.' Nora said in amazement.

'But I didn't know what had happened. If I had I wouldn't have gone near him.' Frances could feel herself becoming angry. Was Nora blaming her for what had happened?

'Of course, you wouldn't have.' Aisling's voice was gentle. 'Did anything else . . . ?'

'I honestly don't know. I don't think so.' Frances tried to remember. 'I don't think I was ever alone with him. I was beginning to really dislike him.'

'We often wondered why,' said Aisling.

'We couldn't understand it,' Nora added. 'They seemed to be so good to you.'

'And you put us off babysitting for them when we were old enough, so deep down you felt uneasy.' Aisling became very serious. 'Frances, something has to be done about him. He can't be allowed to get away with it. He could be doing it to other kids.'

'I couldn't face that . . . ' Frances began to cry again. 'It would mean police and courts and everything. I couldn't . . . '

'I don't mean now, Fran. Now you need

counselling. You need someone professional that you can talk to.'

'We'll go with you.' Nora was bewildered by her older sister's tears. She was used to Frances being the one who looked after her; now everything had changed and she wanted to protect her sister. 'I'd do anything to help. I'll go and stick a knife in that pig right now, if you like!'

'There'll be no need for that,' Aisling said firmly, 'he'll be sorted out in time. The most important thing is that Fran gets help. I know some really good people. You will go, won't you?' She looked pleadingly at Frances.

'I suppose I must.' She was terrified at the thought of what lay ahead but she knew her sister was right. 'The most important person in my life is gone because of it. I have to do something.' She suddenly wanted to be alone. 'I'll run up and wash my face. I might feel a bit better.'

When she had gone Nora and Aisling looked at each other.

'I was just thinking . . . ' Nora began.

'I know what you're going to say,' Aisling looked at her shrewdly. 'David.'

'I'm sure any kind of sex was impossible.'

'You can bet on it, Nora.' Aisling looked sad. 'And David was so right for Frances.'

'It's awful to think the pig that caused all that is living happily up the road, in the bosom of his family. I suppose he's looking forward to an early retirement.' Nora gripped the edge of the table. 'I'd like to give him an early retirement with a hatchet in his head!'

'I think Dad still plays golf with him,' Aisling said with a shudder. 'Can you imagine what he'd do if he knew?'

'I hate the thought of telling him,' Nora agreed. 'He's going to feel really guilty, even though it's not his fault. Do we have to tell him?'

'Ssh,' Nora warned. 'Here's Fran.'

Frances came in and, walking over to the french doors, opened them wide and took a deep breath. It was a hot evening, heavy with the smell of summer flowers. She turned around to look at her sisters.

'I feel much better,' she said. She had brushed her hair and put on some make-up. 'Now I know what's been the matter with me all these years and I'm determined to do something about it.'

TWENTY-FIVE

It was Wednesday morning and Aisling was standing outside the door of of the block of flats where Michael had his apartment. She glanced at her watch. Michael had promised to meet her here at eleven but though she had had rung the bell several times she had received no answer on the intercom. She was about to turn and walk away, when his BMW pulled up at the pavement beside her with a squeal of brakes. Michael jumped out, apparently oblivious of the fact that he was parked on a double yellow line.

'I've got it, Ash!' his voice was full of excitement. He was beside her on the pavement now, positively radiating joy. 'I've just come from the Taoiseach's office. You are looking at the new Minister for Foreign Affairs.'

Aisling tried to smile. She wanted to share in his enthusiasm but she dreaded having to tell him that she was keeping the baby.

'How are you?' he asked quickly. 'You sounded a little strained on the phone last night. Did it all go off OK?'

Suddenly, Aisling didn't want to go into his flat for what she knew would be the last time. She thought of the double bed, with the print of *Starry Night* above it, and of all the times they had made love there. Now that their relationship was about to end for good, she didn't want to go in to the flat, with all its memories.

'Can we talk in the car?' she asked.

'I'd better park it.' Michael sounded puzzled now. He must surely suspect that something was wrong.

They drove in silence into the gloom of the underground car park. Michael steered the BMW into his parking space. Switching off the engine, he turned on the interior light and stared in silence at the steering wheel.

'You didn't do it, did you?'

Aisling's eyes filled with tears.

'I couldn't, Michael. I just couldn't kill our baby.'

Michael sighed. When he spoke, his voice was calm but cold and he didn't turn to look at her.

'You know what this means, don't you? Our affair has to end.'

'But some time in the future, Michael . . . when the baby is born and you've settled in your ministry.' She took his arm. 'Please look at me, Michael. Please don't say it's the end.'

Michael turned towards her and the calm blue eyes she had loved so much were as hard as steel.

'It's over. You didn't keep your side of the deal.'

'But Michael, I couldn't . . . '

'You never intended to have that abortion!' Michael was angry now, and wasn't bothering to disguise it. 'You knew what it could do to me, to my family, but you didn't care. If that woman Carmel starts talking to the press about us, I'll deny everything. Now get out.'

He leaned across her and opened the passenger door. Aisling couldn't believe he was doing this to her; he was writing off the love they had shared as though it had never existed.

'I've been a fool, Michael, haven't I?' He wouldn't meet her gaze and was staring straight ahead of him at the wall of the car park. 'You never really intended leaving Cliodna. I'd have had the abortion and you'd have gone on making excuses to stay with her.'

'It's all hypothetical now, isn't it?' Michael said. 'Just get out of here.'

Numbed, Aisling walked from the car park on to the busy street. The sun was shining brightly as though to mock the heartbreak she was feeling. She had truly believed that Michael loved her but she had been deceiving herself. She had fallen for the oldest lie in existence – the man who says his wife doesn't understand him. Michael's track record with women should have alerted her but she had believed that this time it was different. This time he was truly in love. But the way in which he had just ended with her shattered all her illusions.

As she walked towards her car, she felt a tiny flutter, as though of butterfly wings, in her stomach. It was the baby. Soon, the flutters would become nudges, the nudges kicks as her baby grew within her. At least, her affair with Michael had left her something. It wouldn't be easy being an unmarried mother. But she was fortunate in having a good job and plenty of support, even from Frances, who was struggling to come to terms with her past at regular counselling sessions. There would be hard times ahead, but with her sisters' help, she and the baby would survive them. She thought of a line from *Juno and the Paycock* where the pregnant Mary, whose lover has abandoned her, mourns the fact that her baby won't have a father. 'It'll have what's far betther,' says Juno, 'It'll have two mothers.' Aisling gave a small smile. *Her* baby would be better off again. It would have three.

Two weeks had passed and Aisling had come in early to her office to prepare a major feature for that night's programme. She shifted uncomfortably in her seat. The skirt she was wearing was far too tight and no longer really fitted properly. She undid the button and gave a sigh of relief. She would be almost glad when the time came to buy maternity clothes – at least then she wouldn't have to go on pretending. Thus far, she had put off telling Frank about her pregnancy but she had better do it soon, before she began to show.

The phone rang on her desk and she picked it up.

'Aisling Davis?' a male voice asked.

'Yes.'

'I'm Pat Cooney from the *Irish Journal*. We want to get your side of things.'

'I beg your pardon?'

'You must have seen this morning's *Daily Chronicle*,' Cooney said. 'Michael Whelan is going to take a pasting because of his affair with you.'

Aisling froze. Since Michael had ended with her, she had tried not to think about him. Frances and Nora had told her that she was better off without him, and, although she was still very hurt, she was beginning to see that they were right. She hadn't given much thought to Carmel, believing, as Michael did, that she couldn't harm him. True, she had gone to a paper with her story, but surely Michael would simply deny her allegations?

'I haven't seen a paper yet,' she said, cautiously. 'What does it say?'

'Some woman called Carmel Rafferty has sold a tape to the *Daily Chronicle*,' Cooney told her. 'It proves beyond doubt that you and Whelan were sexually involved for some time. I'd like to hear your version of events.'

'No comment.' Aisling slammed down the phone and switched it on to 'answer'. Then she went into the outer office where a file of all the dailies was kept. She found the *Daily Chronicle* and looked with disbelief at the lurid headline. 'Minister Michael's Current Affair'. She read on.

The newly appointed Minister for Foreign Affairs enjoyed an affair of a different kind with Aisling Davis, the presenter of the popular current affairs programme, Ireland Today. *Whelan promised to leave his wife for Miss Davis but not until he secured his new ministry. The Daily Chronicle learnt of the affair when it received a taped conversation between Carmel Rafferty, a former* Ireland Today *presenter and Geraldine Ryan, a close friend of Miss Davis.*

Alongside the report, there was a large photo of a smiling Michael and Cliodna, and a smaller one of Aisling herself.

Aisling put down the paper and groaned. This would destroy Michael. Carmel had taped her conversation with Geraldine and had coolly handed it over to the press. But she hadn't known that the affair was already over. 'This was aimed at me,' Aisling said aloud. She was stunned that Carmel would go to such lengths to hurt her.

Before she could read on, the office door opened and Frank came in, waving a copy of the tabloid.

'Have you seen this, Aisling?' he demanded. 'Is it true?'

Aisling nodded miserably. 'The affair's over now,' she said, 'but you may as well know, I'm pregnant by him.'

Frank smiled.

'Well, you old devil!' he said. He didn't look angry, as she had feared. If anything, he seemed amused.

'My position,' Aisling began, 'will it be affected?'

'I suppose we'll have to give you maternity leave,' Frank said. 'But knowing you, you'll be straight back to work from the labour ward!'

Aisling felt relieved. Thank heavens Frank was not adopting a judgemental approach.

'I don't think the programme will suffer,' he assured her. 'If anything, it will push up our ratings. You'll be even more of a celebrity than you are already.'

'Great!'

'Of course, the management doesn't condone such affairs and I may have to have a word in a few ears up above but I'd say the only one to suffer from this will be Michael Whelan.'

'He may lose the ministry,' she agreed. 'Not to mention what his wife will say.'

'Do you still care about him?' Frank asked.

'He treated me badly,' Aisling said, 'but I can't help feeling sorry for him, so I suppose I do still care, a bit.'

Frank put his arm around her shoulder.

'You'll get over it,' he assured her. 'And Whelan may just hang in there. He's had affairs before. He's well known for it.'

'But none that reached the papers,' Aisling pointed out.

The phone rang again in her office. She heard the answering machine click on.

'That'll be a reporter,' Frank warned her. 'If I were you, I'd take a few days off. Wait until all this dies down.'

'But the programme . . . ' Aisling objected.

'We'll find a fill-in presenter, till you're back,' Frank told her. 'Don't worry – your job is safe.'

Aisling returned to her office and was putting together some papers to bring home with her when Geraldine arrived, in tears.

'Aisling, I'm so sorry,' she blurted. 'My news-agent just showed me the wretched paper. I'd no idea Carmel taped our conversation.'

Aisling smiled at Geraldine.

'Calm down,' she said. 'I know it wasn't your fault. I've told Frank everything and it's OK.'

Geraldine looked relieved.

'Thank heavens,' she said, with feeling. 'I couldn't care less about Michael. It was you I was worried about.'

Aisling had told Geraldine how Michael had ended their relationship. Geraldine had been sympathetic but had admitted that she never for a moment thought that Michael would leave his wife.

'She may leave him now,' Geraldine spoke with glee. 'But Aisling, if she does, I hope you won't take him back.'

'No way!' said Aisling, but inside, she wasn't so sure.

Aisling spent the rest of the day at home with the phone off the hook. She resisted ringing Michael to offer her sympathy. What was the point? He would hold her responsible for what had happened and she would feel worse.

Nora was on a day shift, so both she and Frances were able to stay home that night to support her. They had both heard about the newspaper report and were anxious to help Aisling in any way they could. The three of them sat in the living-room, discussing it.

'That awful woman,' Nora said, alluding to Carmel. 'Little does she know, she's done you no harm at all.'

Frances nodded her agreement.

'And she hasn't done herself any good. Who's going to employ her after this?'

'I hope she drinks herself into the grave!' said Nora.

Aisling looked at her, and smiled.

'You're very loyal,' she said, 'but I don't wish Carmel dead. I wish she'd get help for her drinking. Maybe then she wouldn't be so bitter and twisted.'

The doorbell rang, interrupting them.

'I'll get it,' Nora jumped up from the sofa and went to answer it. Aisling and Frances heard a male voice speaking from the doorstep.

'It's a reporter,' Aisling said. 'They must have found out where I live.'

After a moment they heard Nora's voice raised in anger.

'And I'm telling you, she's not here!'

Then the door was slammed and Nora returned to the living-room.

'That was Pat Cooney from the *Irish Journal*.'

'He rang me at work,' Aisling admitted.

'I told him you weren't here but I don't think he believed me.'

Frances turned to Aisling.

'Maybe you ought to go away for a few days. Until all the fuss dies down. It's not good for you to be under this kind of stress when you're pregnant.'

'But when will it die down?' Aisling wondered. 'It could be ages.'

'I don't think so,' Nora said. 'According to Cooney, Michael has resigned.' She glanced at her watch. 'It's five to nine. Let's switch on the news and see what's happening.'

They turned on the television and waited expectantly for the evening news. Michael's resignation was the top story. The Taoiseach had read a transcript of the tape and was said to be furious at hearing how Michael had planned to keep his affair a secret until after he secured the ministry. He had called Michael to his office and had demanded his resignation.

'Serves Michael right,' said Nora. 'I hope Cliodna flings him out, too.'

'Mr and Mrs Whelan are attending a charity dinner this evening,' the newscaster went on. 'Our reporter spoke to them as they arrived.'

Michael and Cliodna were shown entering an hotel where they were accosted by several reporters. Michael made a brief statement asserting how pleased he was that his wife was standing by him after his unfortunate 'indiscretion'. 'I will not return to the back benches,' he told the reporters, 'I am retiring from politics and will concentrate on managing my farm and whatever other business interests may come my way. I have nothing more to add.'

Then, taking Cliodna's arm, he disappeared into the building.

Frances looked sympathetically at Aisling.

'I know this is hard for you, love. You probably half hoped Cliodna would fling him out and you'd somehow get back with him.'

Aisling nodded, miserably. She had indeed, been hoping just that. But on hearing Michael refer to her as an indiscretion, she realised that the affair was really over.

'Maybe I will go away,' she said. 'Down the country for a few days.'

'We'll talk to Dad and Madge,' Nora informed her, 'I'm sure he's been trying to get through.'

Aisling sighed. She dreaded what her father would think when he heard his daughter had been having an affair with a married man.

'He'll be so disappointed in me,' she said, tearfully. 'And all I ever wanted to do was please him.'

Frances spoke firmly.

'You've tried far too hard, you know,' she said. 'Maybe that's what drove you to make such a good career for yourself. But you have to stop trying to please him now, Ash. You're a grown woman – look after yourself. You don't need his approval.'

Aisling nodded.

'You're right,' she agreed. 'I will stop. And thanks, Frances. God knows, you've enough on your plate without worrying about me.'

'We've all had our troubles,' Frances insisted. 'And we're here to help each other.'

Nora stood up. 'Want me to phone some hotels for you?' she asked. 'What about a few days in the Parknasilla? That's really luxurious.'

Aisling nodded and Nora went out to the hall to phone. She would spend a few days pampering herself. With any luck, the story would have died down by the time she arrived home. When the press learnt that she was pregnant, it would undoubtedly flare up again and there would be much speculation that Michael was the father. But she would maintain a dignified silence and would certainly not 'kiss and tell'. There would be some difficult times ahead but she wasn't going to worry about them now.

TWENTY-SIX

Frances looked round the living room in Marl-borough Road. Since Madge had married her father, it had changed almost out of recognition. The once rather gloomy green walls had been redecorated with a narrow pink and white striped wall paper and the sagging old leather settee had been replaced by a wine-coloured suite which, Frances had to admit, was a lot more comfortable. It was mid-December now and a huge Christmas tree, its tip almost touching the ceiling, was decorated in gold and silver baubles and there was a welcoming fire burning in the grate. The overall effect was a little too perfect for Frances's taste but she had to admit that the room was brighter and more lived-in than it had been for years. She glanced across at Aisling to gauge her response to the changes. 'Not bad,' Aisling murmured, as Madge came in, carrying a large tray that groaned under plates of buttered scones, fruit cake and *petits fours*.

'I'm sure you must be hungry,' Madge turned and smiled at the heavily pregnant Aisling. 'After all, you're eating for two!'

'We didn't expect all this,' Frances told her. 'We really just wanted to drop in and see you.'

Madge smiled.

'We have to make them welcome, don't we, John?' she asked her husband, who had followed her into the room, carrying a large pot of tea.

As they ate and drank, Frances reflected that Madge seemed to have mellowed recently. For a long time she had kept their father to herself, perhaps fearing that her place in his affections would be threatened by his daughters. But when Aisling's affair with Michael had been exposed in the newspapers, she had come into her own. John Davis had been horrified to learn that a daughter of his was involved with a married man and even more shocked to hear that she was expecting a baby by him. But Madge had been philosophical and her attitude had helped stem the rift that threatened to develop between Aisling and himself. 'For heaven's sake, John,' she had told him, 'you'd think she was the first girl ever to make that mistake! Stop playing the strict father and see what you can do for her.'

That had been back in the summer, and now, with Christmas approaching, much of the drama of those sultry months had subsided. When Aisling's pregnancy became public knowledge, some of the newspapers had carried articles speculating that this must be Michael Whelan's baby – but as Michael had now retired from politics, their interest was shortlived. As for Frances, she was still in counselling. It had been a long, painful but ultimately cathartic process. With the help of her counsellor and her sisters, she now felt ready to confront her abuser. But first, she wanted to find out from her father how Seamus

O'Connor was. She needed to do this discreetly, since she had no intention of divulging the true reason for her curiosity. She had decided never to tell her father what had happened her that fateful summer so many years ago; he would only blame himself and what was the point in that? But even the thought of making enquiries about the man she so hated brought up all her childhood fears and Aisling had agreed to come with her for moral support.

Now she was wondering how she would ever raise the subject of the O'Connors. She half hoped that Aisling would do it for her. But, as it happened, there was no need for either of them to ask.

'Did you hear about poor Seamus?' Madge asked suddenly.

'What?' Frances's question was a hoarse whisper but neither her father nor Madge seemed to notice.

'He's had a massive stroke,' Madge said. 'Just a week ago. He's in Vincent's and they don't think he'll be out for Christmas.'

'I doubt if Christmas is in the forefront of his mind,' John Davis commented drily.

'Yes, but it must be awful for Una,' Madge said. 'Still, at least, she has her two sons. I'm sure they'll take care of her.'

Frances glanced across at Aisling, who read from her expression that she simply couldn't deal with this piece of news.

'How bad is he?' Aisling asked, on her behalf.

'Mrs Murtagh down the road was in to see him

and he can hardly talk,' Madge said. 'In fact, they don't even know if he'll pull through.'

'But with strokes you can't tell,' their father said, 'He could make a perfect recovery.'

'Oh, I don't think so,' Madge said. 'Not after a massive one like that.'

'You don't know!' their father snapped, and Frances guessed that Seamus O'Connor's stroke had brought home to him a sense of his own mortality.

Madge hastily changed the subject and began a long discourse on the difficulty of finding exactly the right Christmas presents to buy for everyone. As she droned on, Frances tried to make sense of what she had just been told. She felt a mixture of pleasure and disappointment. She couldn't help feeling glad that her abuser had been struck down by a physical illness and might even be facing death. In the past few months she had even fantasised about killing him herself, though she knew she could never actually harm him. At least now after his stroke he would almost certainly be incapable of harming any one else again. Since remembering what had happened her, she had spent many sleepless nights worrying that, by not confronting him, she might be allowing him to abuse some other young girl. She was sure she was not the only one he had harmed in that way. She recalled that, over the years, Una and Seamus had had a succession of live-in domestics, mostly young girls from impoverished backgrounds on whom Una had taken pity. How many of them had been abused by Seamus, failing to speak out because they would never be believed? Now, all that would stop. But she felt disappointment too, because if Seamus was as ill as Madge said he was, then she might be deprived of the satisfaction of confronting him. And even if she did, maybe he would be too ill to understand what she was saying.

'What do you think, Frances?' Madge asked, intruding on her thoughts.

'About what?'

Madge tutted, irritably.

'The cashmere jumper I'm telling you about. Do you think my niece would like it? She's about your age, so you'd know.'

'She'd love it,' Frances said, managing a smile. 'I want to go and see Seamus O'Connor,' she suddenly announced. 'Do you think that would be all right?'

'I'm sure it would,' her father said, smiling. 'And you're right to go, Frances. He was very good to you.'

'Little do you know,' thought Frances, as they stood up to leave. 'Little do you know that he almost destroyed my life.'

They kissed their father and Madge goodbye, accepting their invitation to Christmas Day drinks.

'You know I'd have you to dinner, girls,' Madge said, apologetically. 'But there are so many relatives on my side of the family that I just *have* to invite, that I'm afraid there wouldn't be room.'

'Don't worry,' Aisling said, as she kissed her father's cheek, 'the three of us like being together.'

When they had got into the Golf, Aisling turned to Frances.

'Are you sure you want to go through with it?' she asked. 'I know you need to confront him but you might not be able to get him to admit to anything, if he's so ill.'

'Even if he were in the full of his health, he probably wouldn't admit it,' Frances pointed out. 'But I want to do it anyway.'

'Right,' Aisling said, 'but I'm coming with you. You're not going to be on your own.'

'No time like the present,' said Frances, as Aisling turned the key in the ignition. 'Let's drive there now. I want to get it over and done with.'

Seamus O'Connor had been moved from Intensive Care into a private room. Frances and Aisling stood outside the door for a moment, uncertain whether to go in. A nurse appeared behind them.

'Visitors for Mr O'Connor?' she asked and they nodded. 'Go on in – it will do him good. But I should warn you – his speech is very slurred.'

Aisling opened the door and let Frances go in ahead of her. Seamus O'Connor lay as still as death on the bed, his eyes closed. Illness seemed to have shrunk him. His large frame looked almost childlike beneath the bedclothes and his cheeks were sunken hollows in his once full face. Aisling looked at Frances.

'I think he's asleep,' she whispered. 'Are you sure you want to stay?'

'Yes!' said Frances, loudly, and Seamus's eyes flicked open. When he saw her, he looked panicked, as though she were an avenging angel suddenly come to show a mirror to his face. He struggled to speak but the only sound to issue from his mouth was an incomprehensible gurgle. All Frances's earlier fear vanished and she was suddenly possessed by an almost unnatural calmness.

'You know why I'm here, Seamus.' She spoke in a low voice but she could see from his expression that he heard her. 'I'm not here because you're ill – I'm not here to offer sympathy, I'm here to remind you that when I was fourteen you sexually abused me.'

Seamus's eyes glanced towards the open door and he raised one trembling white finger to his lips.

'He's afraid you'll be overheard,' Aisling was dismissive. 'He's only worried about what other people might think!'

Frances stared straight into his watery eyes.

'I don't care what other people think,' she said in the same, measured tones. 'You destroyed my chance of happiness with the one man who loved me. And you damaged me in other ways, too. I was never as confident as I should have been, because of what you did. I found it hard to trust people, especially men. I've known what obsession is but I don't know if I'll ever meet anyone I can truly love – and all because of you!'

Seamus closed his eyes, unwilling to hear what was being said.

'Open them!' Frances said, and to her surprise, he obeyed. 'Have you anything to say to all this? Any word of apology?'

Slowly, Seamus shook his head.

'You bastard!' said Aisling, passionately. 'I'd like to kill you for what you did to Fran. And now you won't even say sorry.'

Seamus mumbled something and Frances bent to try and catch his words.

'Sounded like, "I didn't do it",' she told Aisling. 'But he did, he did!'

She was becoming upset now, unable to maintain the confident calmness she'd displayed just a few moments earlier. All the old fear and anger took over and she wanted to run from this room and its hateful occupant. Aisling put her arms around her and held her trembling body.

'You're a family man,' Frances said. 'What if someone had done to one of your sons, what you've done to me? How would you feel if either of them had been ruined for years by a pervert like yourself? And suppose that man was a hypocrite – just like you are? A pillar of the community, posing as the perfect father and neighbour? How would you feel about him?'

'Stop!'

This time the word was clearly audible and Frances pulled away from Aisling's arms to face her abuser. A single tear rolled down Seamus's face, trickling into his opened mouth. For the rest of her life, Frances would wonder whether that tear represented genuine remorse or mere self-pity. But suddenly she knew it didn't matter any more. What was important now was that, having confronted this sick old man, she should get on with her life and put the past behind her.

'I'm going now, Seamus,' she told him. 'And I

intend to get over what you did to me. I'm not going to let myself be your victim any longer. I can't say I forgive you but I'm going to do my level best to forget you. That won't be easy but for my sake and the sake of the other young women I'm sure you harmed, I'm going to try.'

She turned to Aisling. 'I'm finished now,' she said.

Turning her back on Seamus, she left the room. As they walked down the corridor to the main doors of the hospital, they met Una O'Connor, coming in. She looked haggard and worried but assumed a bright smile when she saw them.

'How kind of you to come!' she greeted them. 'Your father told me you were going to. I'm sure your visit cheered Seamus up no end.'

Frances looked at her with genuine sympathy. She was certain that Una knew nothing of her husband's proclivities and saw no reason to enlighten her now. Let her go on believing that Seamus was the caring husband and father he made himself out to be. To tell her the truth about him, in the twilight of her life, would be an unnecessary cruelty.

'He seems a little improved,' she said. 'At least, from what we had heard . . . '

'Thank God,' Una looked relieved. 'I couldn't bear to lose him. And at Christmas time!'

She hurried down to corridor to her husband's room and Frances and Aisling left the hospital. Once outside, Aisling turned to Frances. 'I was proud of you,' she said. 'You were terrific. I hope it hasn't been too stressful for you?'

'It's not an experience I'd want to repeat,' Frances admitted, 'but I'm glad I did it. I am going to put it behind me now, Ash, insofar as one ever can.'

The crisp winter air made her shiver but this time, it was a healthy shiver, not the feverish trembling of a woman who had been abused.

'It's cold,' she said. 'I want to go home and have a nice glass of mulled wine. And then,' she smiled at Aisling warmly, 'I intend to have the best Christmas ever with the two people I love most in this world.' She glanced at Aisling's bump and grinned, 'Or should I say three?'

TWENTY-SEVEN

It was a crisp December day and pale sunshine drifted through the window of the sitting-room in Sandycove.

Nora, who was kneeling on the ground beside a large Christmas tree, dipped into a tea-chest and held up an ugly cardboard star, childishly daubed with red and yellow crayon. 'Remember this, Fran?'

'Do I what!' Frances exclaimed. 'You were so delighted with yourself when you made it that we all lied and said it was beautiful!'

'It *is* beautiful,' Nora said in mock outrage. 'It was a work of genius for a four-year-old.'

Stretching up to the topmost branch of the tree, she placed it where everyone would see it.

Watching Nora, Frances smiled. Madge had suggested that they take the old chest of decorations and use them for their first Christmas in Sandycove and, although everything looked faded when compared to the sparkling new ornaments in Marlborough Road, she was pleased because she was sentimental about the good memories of the past.

As if reading her thoughts, Aisling looked up from wrapping presents and said quietly, 'You were terrific yesterday at the hospital, Fran. I wish you'd been there to see her, Nora.'

'A pity the old bastard wasn't in the morgue but I suppose Fran was right. It was important to look him the eyes and tell him what a shit he is.' Nora reached into the box and pulled out another lopsided star. 'This is an even better one,' she boasted.

'I don't want to drag you away from admiring your childhood masterpieces,' Aisling interrupted, 'but you'd better get a move on if you want to be in time for your audition.'

Nora looked at the clock. 'It's three o'clock!' She jumped up. 'And I haven't changed yet!'

Stopping at the door she looked at her sisters and said with feeling. 'Say a prayer I get this part. I know it's tiny but the play will be on in the Gaiety and there's a great director.'

'We'll keep our fingers crossed.' Frances shouted after her. They heard her light steps run up the stairs. 'I've a good feeling about this audition, Ash. I think she'll get it.'

'I hope you're right. She's been a long time resting.' Aisling rummaged about in the box of decorations and held up a beautiful German glass bauble. She looked at it admiringly. 'That's lovely and there are lots like it in here. I remember when Dad brought them back from Munich.' She picked up Nora's crumpled star. 'We'll use Nora's masterpieces sparingly.'

Frances laughed. 'We'd better leave one or two in a conspicuous place to keep her happy. She'll want everyone to admire her creations tonight.'

To celebrate their first Christmas in the house, they had decided to throw a party. After the trauma of the past few months Frances was really looking forward to letting her hair down.

'What time are they coming?' she asked.

'About nine.'

'I suppose we've enough drink?'

'Plenty. By the way, Jean rang. Tony can't make it. He's flying.'

'That's a pity but it's Jean I really want to see.' Frances stood up. 'If you finish the tree, I'll start making the chilli and there's plenty of Haagen-Dazs in the freezer – that'll do fine for afters.'

'Sorry!' Ashling smiled apologetically at Frances. 'I finished it last night. This baby just loves chocolate ice-cream!'

Nora was lucky; a train rolled into the DART station as she arrived. She found a seat and opened the manuscript of *Fallen Idol*. Turning to the second page, she glanced at her lines. It hadn't been difficult to learn them. There were only forty in all. She was auditioning for the part of a fellow student at the college where Anna, the main character in the play, is studying. Anna becomes disillusioned with her lover, a celebrated poet who adores her as his muse but who doesn't see her a real person. She struggles to break free of him and eventually discovers that she has her own writing talent to develop. Nora loved the part of Anna. She had read the script through several times since her agent had given it to her and would have sold her soul to play her. But, of course, the producers would have some famous name lined up for that, so she was wasting her time even thinking about it. But it was a terrific play and Peter Winters, a God-like figure in the theatre world, would be directing it; even a small part was worth having.

Pearse Street station was full of Christmas shoppers fighting to get down the narrow staircase. Nora stood back and let them go ahead of her. It was only four-fifteen and she wasn't due at the Gaiety until five. Walking slowly along Nassau Street in the crisp December air she thought how great it would be to get back at work again. She glanced in the shop windows as she passed to reassure herself that she looked OK in the new romantic look that she had chosen to wear. Over a silk cream shirt she wore a soft corded jacket and her high black boots were perfect with the green cashmere jodhpurs. Her dark hair was loosely tied back with a velvet bow and bronze antique earrings almost touched her shoulders.

It was two minutes to five when she arrived at the Gaiety. She was ushered straight away into the auditorium, where two men were sitting at a table with their backs to her. One of them turned around and beckoned her to go up on to the stage. The other man was busy writing notes and didn't look up until she was standing centre stage waiting for instructions. She felt an odd sense of *déjà-vu*. Then he lifted his head and her heart did a somersault. It was Tim Mulcahy.

He didn't show any sign of recognition as he indicated that she begin the reading.

When she had finished, he smiled warmly.

'That was great, Nora. Could you wait outside for a few minutes?'

Her head was buzzing with questions as she sat in the cold lobby waiting for Tim to come out. Why was he involved? Was it possible that her agent had been wrong and Winters wasn't the director?

The swing doors opened and Tim came out and walked across to her.

'Great to see you, Nora.' He sounded like he really meant it. 'But I suppose you're disappointed not to meet the famous Peter?'

'I'd much rather see you. But I was told that he was directing.'

'That was the intention but a last minute conflict of interest arose.'

Nora surmised that this was a diplomatic way of saying that Peter had had a major row with the producers.

'So,' Tim continued, 'his loss is my gain. I was very flattered to be asked to step in and luckily I just happened to be free.' He put a hand out and touched her arm. 'Congrats. You have the part. We saw the others earlier and you beat them hands down.'

'Great,' Nora felt like dancing with joy. It was as much to do with seeing Tim again as getting the part. 'And I'm really glad you're directing.'

'Could be fate.' He gave her an intense look that sent tingles down her spine.

'How are things?' Nora was longing to ask him was he free of his romantic entanglement.

'Not so bad. I've just moved out to Clontarf.

I've got a bachelor pad there now that I'm on my own again.'

'I'm sorry,' Nora lied, hoping that her joy was not too obvious.

'Don't be.' he said, 'It was the right thing for both of us. I'd better get back inside. I've to sort out rehearsal schedules with the rest of the team. We hope to start on 28 December. I'll give you a call before then, Nora.' He leaned over and placed a gentle kiss on her lips. 'We'll be seeing lots of each other from then on.'

She said goodbye and, leaving the theatre, headed down Grafton Street. The Christmas lights were twice as bright as they had been earlier on and the flowerseller on the corner of Chatham Street looked radiant with seasonal goodwill. A small child, clutching a giant teddy, toddled along beside his laughing father. Everywhere that Nora looked she found something to smile at. She put her fingers to her lips. She imagined that she could still feel the gentle pressure of Tim's mouth on hers.

A log fire was burning brightly and the soft light from the candles that Aisling had placed around the room was reflected in the baubles and tinsels on the tree. A Bjork disc was playing at full volume on the stereo and the hum of conversation was correspondingly high. The party had been in full swing for a couple of hours and everyone was in great form.

'Have some more punch, Geraldine.' Aisling held out the jug of golden liquid. 'You don't have to worry, Billy's driving.'

'Thanks, Ash.' Geraldine stopped talking animatedly to Fintan and Phil and held our her glass. 'It's wonderful stuff – absolute dynamite!'

'I'll take your word for it. A bit much for Bonzo!' She patted her seven-month bump which was elegantly draped in a bronze brocade maternity suit. The very short skirt showed off her shapely legs and her face was glowing with health.

'Hold on, Ash, I'll have a drop more.' Nora was in high spirts after her successful audition with Tim. She was wearing a tiny scarlet chiffon sheath dress with shoestring straps. Her high-heeled suede sandals were a matching red and the men in the room couldn't take their eyes off her. 'Fintan, darling, I didn't see you!' She flung her arms around him.

'You did actually, Nora. I've had about three kisses already.'

Phil laughed. 'I think you've had a bit too much punch, Nora!'

'What the hell, Phil? I'm so happy tonight. You heard about my part, Fintan?'

'You've told me that too! It's mega!'

Nora took him by the hand. 'Come with me and I'll show you my stars. They've hidden them away at the back of the tree, but we're going to find one and put it on top.'

Aisling nudged Frances, who had just joined the group. 'I knew she'd be looking for those stars!'

'She's the end!' Frances laughed. 'I see Patrick is getting on great with that fellow in the corner. Who is he, Ash?'

'Alan Crowe from our Arts Department. They'd have lots in common.'

Frances leaned over to Aisling and lowered her voice.'I'm glad Patrick came. I thought it might be a bit awkward with Nora but she didn't seem to mind when I said I should ask him.'

Aisling put down the jug on the table. 'I must remember to congratulate him on his autumn exhibition in New York. I believe it was a terrific success.'

Frances nodded. 'He's going over next summer to Cape Cod for a holiday. I have a feeling there might be some romance going there. I hope so.' She glanced at her watch. 'God, it's nearly eleven. I'd better get the food going.'

Noticing her leaving the room, Jean followed her out.

'I'll give you a hand, Frances.'

'That would be great.'

'Give me over that bowl of salad and I'll put the dressing on.'

'Right, and I think the garlic bread is ready to come out of the oven. You could put it on that wooden platter there.' Frances began to lay out large pottery plates on the kitchen table. 'I should run in and get Ash to help.'

'No, don't.' Jean said quickly. 'I wanted a chance to see you on your own.'

'Oh?' Frances looked at her questioningly.

Jean took a deep breath. 'I think you should know that David is home. I bumped into him in town yesterday and we went for a cup of coffee. He asked how you were. I've a feeling he's going to ring you.' She put her hand on Frances's arm. 'How do you think you'll react?'

'He's probably only home for Christmas.' Frances tried to stay calm but her heart was beating rapidly.

'No, Frances. He said he's home for good.'

'Well he may have a girlfriend, or even be married by now.'

'That's not the impression I got. I think you should see him if he rings.'

'I'll think about it. I promise. And thanks.' Frances gave Jean a hug. 'Let's get some chilli into that crowd in there before they freak out on the punch.'

Nora opened the patio doors. 'What a fantastic moon!'

It was four o'clock in the morning and the last of the guests had gone.

'Nora!' Frances protested. 'It's freezing out there.'

'It's beautiful.' Nora was now outside holding her arms up to the heavens. 'Come and look at the stars.'

'We'd better humour her, Fran,' Aisling stood up from her chair and propelled Frances through the patio doors. 'We'll get no peace till we do as she says. Nora is in hyperactive mode!'

'I'm hyperhappy, that's what I am.' Nora put her arms around her sisters and hugged them close. She shivered. 'It is cold but everything looks so beautiful glistening in the frost.'

'Remember how hot it was only a few months

ago.' Frances gestured to the winter-shrivelled climbing plants that trailed the old stone walls. 'Hot enough for fruit to grow on the passion flowers.'

'It'll be just as hot next year,' Aisling said confidently. 'And we'll sit in the sun and eat passion fruit with cream and sugar and talk about everything that has happened to us.'

Nora made a face. 'Lots of sugar, please. They were very bitter.'

'Only in spots,' Frances said philosophically. 'A bit like our lives.'

The three girls looked at each other and smiled.

TWENTY-EIGHT

It was the opening night of *Fallen Idol* and Nora
had arrived at the Gaiety at six o'clock. She had
'run' her lines with the stage manager and had
spent the next hour doing relaxation exercises in
the green room. She was dressed and made up
and in a few minutes the call for 'beginners' would
come through on the tannoy. Then she would walk
out on stage in front of a packed opening-night
audience of critics and friends. Frances and Aisling
were out there with her father and Madge and
would be rooting for her but what would the critics
say? She felt the familiar flutter of first-night
nerves, but tried to dismiss them – after all, hers
was a tiny role and might not even merit a mention
in the reviews.

There were only six characters in the play, so
she had a dressing-room of her own, a luxury she
savoured. Tonight it was full of good luck cards
and flowers. Frances and Aisling had sent a
bouquet and so had her father and Madge. Fintan
was away on holiday with Phil and had sent her a
bouquet through Interflora. Even Sarah, whom she
hadn't seen since working on *Docklands*, had
somehow got to hear about the play and had sent
her a tiny teddy bear holding a banner that said
good luck. But it was the eighteen red roses from

Tim that took pride of place on her dressing-table. Tomorrow was St Valentine's Day and he had enclosed a funny card with the bouquet.

He had phoned her the morning after the party and they had been dating on and off ever since. Once rehearsals began they saw even more of each other – when she was not on stage herself, she sat in the auditorium watching as he directed Deirdre Breslin, the London-based actress who was playing the part of Anna. Often, when work was finished for the day, they would wander down Temple Bar, eating in different restaurants and talking as though they had known each other all their lives.

For the first time ever, Nora felt that maybe she was in love. But she wasn't rushing things and, unusually for her, she hadn't slept with Tim at once. Somehow, she had wanted to take things slowly – to savour a precious friendship before the relationship moved on to a more physical level. They had been to bed for the first time only the previous week and Tim had been everything she wanted in a lover. He wasn't quite as passionate as Patrick but then Patrick had been obsessed. With Tim, sex was more than mere lust; it was a deepening expression of their growing affection and it left her feeling more fulfilled than any of her previous affairs. She knew the relationship mightn't last, but for now, she was enjoying it.

A knock on the door interrupted her reflections.

'Nora?' she heard Tim's voice on the other side of the door. She was a little surprised, as Tim had already wished her good luck and was planning to go for a quick pint in Neary's pub to steady his nerves. As soon as she saw his face, she knew that something was seriously wrong.

'Deirdre's sick,' he said. 'The stage manager called a doctor and he thinks it's probably glandular fever. She definitely can't go on.'

'My God,' Nora said, 'can she really not do it? The audience is out there, waiting.'

'She thought it was just a flu bug – apparently she's been fighting it all day but now she's in a fever and it's out of the question.'

'She should have let you know,' said Nora. 'She should have said something.'

'There's no point in worrying about that now,' said Tim. 'Do you think you can play Anna?'

'What?' Nora looked at him, in amazement.

'You're about the same age – and you know the part, you were there all through rehearsals. Please, Nora – I know it's a lot to ask but we don't have an understudy and if you don't do it, we'll have to cancel.'

'But what about my part? Who'll play that?'

'Gemma Hartigan can double. You're not in any scenes together.'

Nora thought for a moment. She adored the part of Anna but knowing the lines was very different from giving a performance. She had watched carefully as Tim had choreographed the actors' movements and she felt familiar enough with the character to give it her best shot.

'All right,' she said, with a weak smile.

Tim took her in his arms and kissed her.

'Nora, how can I ever thank you? I just hope

this turns out to be your big break.'

'You'd better announce it,' said Nora. 'And I'd better go and change into Anna's clothes.'

The next few minutes were a whirlwind of activity. As Nora dressed for the part, she heard the announcement to the audience that Deirdre Breslin was ill and that the role of Anna would be played by Nora Davis. The curtain would go up in five minutes.

As if in a dream, she found herself waiting backstage while the two actors who opened the play went on. She hadn't had time for nerves while getting ready, but now, as she stood in the wings listening to the familiar opening lines, she felt sick with apprehension.

'The roar of the greasepaint, the smell of the crowd,' Tim appeared behind her and put his arms around her. 'You'll be fine, Nora. I'd have given you this part, if it had been up to me. That's how confident I am in you.'

Nora heard her cue.

'I'm on,' she said, pulling away from him.

'Break a leg!' said Tim, and the next minute she was on. There was applause as she entered. The audience was aware that she had taken over at the last minute and were giving her a vote of encouragement.

Beyond the lights, Nora could dimly discern a sea of faces. Somewhere in that sea, Frances, Aisling, her father and Madge would be sitting – willing her to do well. She would not let them down. 'So this is Anna, of whom I've heard so much,' said Harold Walsh, the male lead.

Nora paused momentarily and for a horrible moment, she thought she had forgotten her first line. But it was there, locked in her brain with all the rest of the lines she would deliver that night.

'And you are the poet I most admire,' she said. 'Wouldn't it be fun if I could be your muse?'

The first half of the play was over and Nora was relaxing in the green room with Tim and the other actors. The audience had responded enthusiastically enough at the curtain but the real drama happened in the second act and Nora knew she still had a lot of work to do.

'Will you run some lines with me, Harold?' she asked the male lead, who was known to be somewhat difficult.

'No point,' Harold told her, with a condescending smile. 'If you don't know them now, you never will.'

Nora had to fight back an urge to slap his face. She knew he was an arrogant man who probably disliked being on stage with an unknown like her but if she lost her temper with him he might make things difficult for her on stage, so she sat quietly reading her lines until the call came for the second act to begin.

In this act, Anna had to turn her back on her erstwhile lover and begin to establish herself as a writer. Unable to cope with her growing success, her ex-lover seeks to destroy her, first with words and finally with a bullet. As she lies dying, Anna confronts him with his treachery and wonders whether her success was worth the loss of love. It was a hugely demanding role both physically and emotionally and Nora had seen how drained Deirdre Breslin was at the end of rehearsals. With its post-feminist theme and its examination of the role of relationships, *Fallen Idol* had received great acclaim wherever it was performed. Nora hoped that she could do it justice.

'You have them in the palm of your hand,' Tim told her as she prepared to go on stage. 'Oh, and the stage manager just gave me this note for you.'

Nora opened the note which was written on a scrap of paper that had been pulled from a filofax.

'Excuse the paper, Nora,' it read, 'but we had to tell you how delighted we are to see you where you should be – playing the lead. You're a star! Love, Fran and Ash.'

Nora felt tears well in her eyes. How typical of her sisters to make sure she knew she had their support in this, the biggest moment of her life.

'And they're right, you know,' said Tim, who was reading the note over her shoulder. 'You are a star, Nora. You'll get offered all the best roles, after this.'

'Let's hope the critics share your opinion,' said Nora, but the note and Tim's words gave her confidence and the second act of the play went like a dream. Despite her fears of drying, Nora was word-perfect. Indeed, it was Harold who momentarily lost the thread of what he was saying in his final speech. A prompt came from offstage but Harold didn't hear it and seeing that he was flustered, Nora rescued him by supplying an improvised line of her own which allowed him to recall this thoughts. As the curtain fell to huge applause, Harold murmured, 'Thanks,' and Nora knew that any reservations he had had about playing opposite her were gone.

The curtain fell and rose again and the five actors took another bow. As Nora raised her head, she saw that several people at the front of the audience had risen to their feet. In a moment, they were joined by others, until – like a Mexican wave that moved gradually to the back of the theatre – the entire audience was giving them a standing ovation. She felt a lump in her throat. Irish audiences rarely afforded this honour to a group of players and to receive it now, when she was only standing in for a better-known actress, was praise indeed. The curtain fell and rose again for a third and final time and at last the six actors left the stage. Tim was waiting for her in the wings, and she fell into his arms, exhausted, but happy.

'What can I say?' he gave her a big hug. 'You stole the show. Even Fergal Hughes looked pleased.'

Fergal Hughes was a reviewer with one of the Sunday papers and was renowned for his scathing comments.

'Well, if he's pleased, then so am I,' Nora said, reaching up and kissing Tim on the lips. 'You know it's funny, Tim,' she told him as they made their way to the green room, 'I've never been happier in my life and yet I felt able to relate to all the tragedy in this play. So much for method acting!'

Tim looked at her seriously.

'Happy or miserable, you'd be a great actress,

Nora. You just needed a chance to prove yourself and now you've got it. I can't wait for another chance to direct you.'

They stood outside the green room and kissed again. Then Tim opened the door and followed her in.

TWENTY-NINE

Some time later Frances and Aisling fought their way through the admiring group of actors, stagehands and visitors, who were gathered around Nora in the green room.

'Nora, you were fantastic!' Frances flung her arms around her sister. 'We're so proud of you.'

'Even the baby was giving you a round of applause.' Aisling joked. 'I feel bruised all over!'

'I'm still in a state of shock,' Nora confessed. 'I haven't even changed yet. I'm far too excited.'

Tim, who was standing close by Nora, greeted Frances and Aisling, whom he had met on several occasions when he was leaving their sister home. He handed them two glasses, full to the brim of champagne.

'I'd better not.' Aisling handed her glass to Nora. As she looked around for somewhere to sit, Tim pulled a chair forward for her and she sat down gratefully.

'I'll get you a coffee instead, if you like,' he volunteered.

'A Ballygowan would be fine.'

'Sure you're OK, Ash?' Frances' voice was concerned.

'Just a bit tired.' She took the glass of water from Tim. In truth, she had been feeling uncomfortable for the past few minutes. Perhaps it had been that over-enthusiastic standing ovation for Nora. A wave of pain swept across her and she bit her lip but at that moment, John and Madge arrived and in the commotion of kisses and congratulations, nobody noticed her distress.

'I never knew you were so talented.' John looked at his youngest child in amazement. 'I nearly burst with pride.'

'You were terrific, dear.' Madge's eyes were bright with reflected glory. She was looking forward to telling everyone about her step-daughter's success.

Mr Davis glanced at his watch. 'Unfortunately, we can't stay for some of that bubbly, because we've a table booked at Roly's for ten minutes ago. So we'll run on. But we'll all celebrate together next week – that's a promise, Nora.'

We may be celebrating more than the play, Aisling thought, as the Davises left. Another pain had swept across her body and she was seriously worried that something was happening. Bonzo wasn't due for another two weeks and while it would be unusual for a first baby to arrive early, it wasn't impossible. Maybe she should whisper something to Frances but she didn't want to steal Nora's glory by creating a drama. Glancing around the room at the chattering crowd, she wondered how long the party would go on. With a sigh she noticed more people coming in the door. Then she did a double-take; one of them was David. She was sure that Frances had no idea that he would be at the theatre tonight, let alone backstage afterwards.

Now her mind was made up; she would keep quiet about the pains she was having, because she was not going to do anything to hinder a meeting between him and her sister.

He walked directly up to Nora and shook her hand. Frances threw Aisling a panic-stricken look and her sister gave her a warm smile of reassurance. 'You were wonderful, Nora.' David said quietly. 'I didn't even know you were in the play, so you can imagine how surprised I was when you turned out to be the star!' He gestured to his companion. 'This is Vincent Keogh, whom you've probably heard of. He's the theatre critic for the *Sunday Clarion*.'

Nora began to chat vivaciously to Vincent and Aisling noticed David taking the opportunity to approach Frances.

'How are you, Frances?' David's voice was just about audible to Aisling over the buzz of general conversation. She said a silent prayer that her sister would not spoil things by being cold and distant.

'It's nice to see you, David, I heard you were home. I'm fine,' she continued in a deceptively casual voice. 'We're all thrilled about Nora.'

'She was terrific.' He leaned closer to her, 'It was a stroke of luck that Vincent was invited backstage afterwards. It's lovely to see you all.'

Aisling saw Frances smiling up at him and heard her murmur, 'It's nice to see you too, David.'

'It's been a long time, Frances,' David reminded her, 'lots of water under the bridge.'

'Maybe we can get together some time. I'd love

to hear about Africa.' She paused and Aisling saw her take a deep breath. 'There are things I need to explain.'

'I'll call you.'

Aisling was pleased that David didn't seem bitter about the past. Perhaps he and Frances would work things out. Suddenly, a wave of extreme pain swept across her and she gave an involuntary moan.

Nora and Frances were at her side immediately.

'What's the matter, Ash?'

'Is it the baby?'

'I think so,' she said between clenched lips.

David began to ask cool, professional questions about when she had got the first pain and whether the waters had broken.

'It may be a false alarm, Aisling,' he said, ' but I think you should head for the hospital. It's better to err on the safe side. I'll ring to let them know you're on the way. Where are you booked into?

'The Coombe. Dr Phillips is my gynae.'

'Come on, Frances, we'll get the car. Keys, please, Aisling.' Nora, still high on adrenalin from her spectacular success, had turned into a natural leader. Her coat slung over her shoulder, she held out her hand to Aisling, who fished the keys out of her bag and obediently handed them over.

'David and Tim,' she instructed, 'you bring Aisling out to the entrance. We'll be as quick as we can.'

They picked up the car in Harry Street, drove at breakneck speed around the Green and pulled up in front of the entrance to the Gaiety. Frances was so concerned about Aisling that she hardly noticed that Nora put the two wheels of the GTI up on the pavement.

David and Tim helped a pale-faced Aisling into the car.

'Are you sure you don't want one of us to come with you?' David asked.

Nora looked slightly aggrieved. 'We can manage. Tim, give Da a ring in Roly's restaurant. He'd want to know.' With a roar of the engine, she took off.

It was at this point that Aisling recalled that she had never seen Nora drive before.

'When did you learn to drive?' she asked curiously and with a certain amount of trepidation.

'I've driven a bit in London.' Nora replied airily. 'I've got an English provisional licence. Couldn't see much point in doing the test here, since I'd no dosh for a car.'

'I hope the police don't stop us,' Frances said in a worried voice.

'This is an emergency run. Nobody will dare to stop me.'

Despite her increasing pain, Aisling smiled to herself. Nora was so obviously enjoying the drama of the race to the hospital. Then the car swept far too quickly around a corner and hit the kerb, wiping the smile from Aisling's face. The baby's head was pressing strongly down by now and she felt certain that this was no false alarm.

'Sorry,' Nora put a protective hand over Aisling's stomach but continued to keep her foot on the accelerator.

With an earsplitting screech of brakes, the Volkswagen jerked to a halt in front of the glass entrance of the Coombe. Leaving the car door wide open, Nora ran into the reception area.

Frances leaned over the front seat and touched Aisling's shoulder sympathetically, as she noticed her wince in pain at the force of another contraction. 'It'll be OK now, Ash. They'll give you an epidural.'

'I don't think the baby is going to wait for that,' Aisling said in between deep breaths.

She looked out the window and saw a middle-aged nurse with an ample bosom heavily decorated with status symbols, waddling slowly out to the car, flanked by an agitated Nora.

The nurse opened the door gently and put a calm and reassuring hand on Aisling.

'You'll be all right now, dear. Let me have a quick look at you.'

After a brief examination it was decided that Aisling was very near delivery, so she was taken away on a mobile bed. Nora and Frances stood beside the car, watching her being wheeled away and feeling superfluous.

'Go and park the car, girls,' the nurse shouted back at them. 'Then come in. We may have a baby for you by then.'

'Oh yeah,' said Nora when she was gone. 'Poor Ash will probably be struggling all night.'

But the nurse was right. Within twenty minutes the baby was born. Ten minutes later, Frances and Nora were being ushered by the nurse into one of the private rooms. Dr Phillips, who had arrived barely in time to see the baby make its appearance, smiled at them as he left the room.

'Five past twelve,' he said. 'Could be the first Valentine's baby.'

In the bed in the corner an exhausted Aisling lay back on the pillows. Tendrils of damp hair clung to her forehead and her face was streaked with make-up but her eyes were bright with joy. In her arms was a small bundle.

'It's a girl,' she said. 'I can't believe it. I was certain that Bonzo was a boy. All that kicking! But I'm thrilled that it's a girl. Come here and see her.'

They moved over and stood on either side of the bed.

Wrapped in the pink blanket a perfect little girl lay sleeping. Her hair was thick and black and her features were small and delicate.

'She's a dote.' Frances leaned down and touched her tiny fingers. 'What are you going to call her?'

'Remember the litany of names we went through? Well, they all went out of my head. As soon as they put her in my arms, I knew this was Lucy.' She looked up at them, anxious for their reaction.

'Lucy!' Nora was incredulous. 'The only Lucy I know is that drip that Wordsworth moaned on about – you know, "a violet by a mossy stone". I don't think much of that, Ash, but,' she added hastily, 'she's your baby.'

'I like it,' Frances said. 'I like it very much.'

Aisling looked so pleased that Nora relented.

'I guess I'll get to like it and, anyway,' she brightened up, 'this Lucy won't be a dull, boring little violet! I'll see to that. She'll be a wild, exotic passion flower!'

Lucy stirred in her mother's arms and, opening her eyes, gazed through a misty haze into the laughing faces of the three sisters.